Advance Praise

"In her novel *Frieda's Song*, Ellen Prentiss Campbell intriguingly explores the lives of two women—one the real-life psychiatrist Frieda Fromm-Reichmann—as they work among the mentally ill and struggle to find acceptance and love in their own lives. In different decades they inhabit the same cottage, suffer anguishing loss, and fight to understand themselves. The connection between the two characters is moving and unusual, and the book is a small miracle."

> — Jack El-Hai, author of *The Lobotomist* and *The Nazi and the Psychiatrist*

"In *Frieda's Song*, Ellen Prentiss Campbell deftly weaves a fabric of history and chance from the lives of two very different women separated by time and space, both struggling to balance the claims of work and life, both thoroughly acquainted with their own capacity for self-deception, and both dedicated, heart and mind, to the life-affirming profession of healing."

> — Valerie Martin, author of *I Give It to You* and *Mary Reilly*

"Ellen Prentiss Campbell's riveting *Frieda's Song* brings to vivid life the remarkable Frieda Fromm-Reichmann—German psychotherapist, teacher, and ex-wife of Erich Fromm—and her experiences of exile, love, and loss in mid-century America. Counterposing Frieda's life with that of a present-day therapist dealing with a troubled son, this beguiling novel offers a tale at once historical and contemporary, which the reader won't expect—and won't want to finish."

> — Martha Cooley, author of *The Archivist* and *Thirty-Three Swoons*

"In this rich psychological thriller the author's subtle choices make for a compelling read. A book that cannot be put down!"

— Gary Stein, author of *Touring the Shadow Factory*

"Seventy years apart in time, two women's lives form the basis of this provocative novel of parallel narratives. On the eve of the Second World War, Frieda Fromm-Reichmann comes to America in the aftermath of a broken marriage and forges ahead with her passionate commitment to her psychoanalytic practice… Living many decades later in Fromm's cottage we find Eliza Kline, facing her own struggles as a therapist and a single mother determined to protect her vulnerable son. Binding these two forceful women is their resolve to save and hold fast those who give us reasons to live. Like the best therapy, *Frieda's Song* pushes headlong into unraveling the mysteries of the human heart."

— Steven Schwartz, author of *Madagascar: New and Selected Stories* and *A Good Doctor's Son*

"In *Frieda's Song*, Ellen Prentiss Campbell makes the history of Frieda Fromm-Reichmann and psychotherapy relevant politically as well as surprisingly romantic…Frieda says, 'Human nature tends to health like plants to sunlight.' All of Campbell's characters—both past and present—yearn for their own kind of sunlight. A wonderful, compelling read."

— Diana Wagman, author of *Life #6* and *The Care and Feeding of Exotic Pets*

"This beautiful novel glows with wisdom and warmth as Ellen Prentiss Campbell shows us how our common humanity links the mentally ill and the healthy, the dead and the living, and the loved and the lost. Readers will be caught between wanting to eagerly turn the pages to find out what happens to Frieda, Eliza and Nick, or slowly savoring the experience of this rich story."

— Carrie Callaghan, author of *A Light of Her Own and Salt the Snow*

Frieda's Song

Frieda's Song

A Novel

Ellen Prentiss Campbell

Apprentice
House Press
Loyola University Maryland

First Edition

Hardcover ISBN: 978-1-62720-322-7
Paperback ISBN: 978-1-62720-323-4
Ebook ISBN: 978-1-62720-324-1

Printed in the United States of America

Design: Apprentice House Press
Promotion plan: Francesca Paone
Managing editor: Danielle Como

Cover art: "Diamond Quintet" by Marilyn Banner, courtesy of the artist.

Published by Apprentice House Press

Apprentice House Press
Loyola University Maryland
4501 N. Charles Street
Baltimore, MD 21210
410.617.5265
www.ApprenticeHouse.com
info@ApprenticeHouse.com

Also by Ellen Prentiss Campbell

Contents Under Pressure

The Bowl with Gold Seams

Known by Heart

To Judy Karasik and Beth Hess,
for believing in my work.

Try to love the questions themselves.
—Rainer Maria Rilke, *Letters to a Young Poet*

ONE

1935

"The director will meet our train in Washington," Erich says.

"You don't need to come with me," I tell him. Still disconcerted by the reversal, his taking care of me: pulling strings, arranging the funds for my passage, his affidavit to obtain the visa. And now brokering this temporary position at his friend's private sanatorium outside of Washington, D.C. Uncomfortable, being in Erich's debt, dependent—always before the other way around.

Perhaps I should have stayed in Palestine, or London. We have been separated for five years, almost half of our marriage. And there is no question of reconciliation. I knew that long before setting foot on the *SS Berengaria*, bound for America. I knew that when we separated when he left for the sanatorium in Davos. Necessary, temporary parting to treat his tuberculosis while I continued my work at my own hospital, my *Therapeuticum* in Heidelberg. Just till he was well, we'd both agreed, both knowing it was over—how could we not know? Both adept at reading signs and secrets as analysts must. Myself born with the gift of the third ear, the second sight—essential and sharpened as oldest child of a father and mother growing deaf. And hadn't I trained him? Trained Erich, my student and my patient, in the practice of analysis, the craft, the art? Taught him to divine and discern.

And he taught me the nighttime arts—born with his own gifts, sensory genius, master of the selfish, selfless arts of loving. I knew

1

the nights with him were over, but I remembered in the deep cabin darkness crossing the Atlantic, suspended in transit between past and future, the ship's groan masking mine as I touched myself the way he had taught me.

Remembering the light filtered through long sheer curtains on the balcony windows. The mirror he'd held between my legs.

Look, he said.

I don't need to, I said, closing my eyes. *I delivered forty babies, Erich, I know.*

Look.

Ten years younger, wise as a child in the ways of instinct, he taught me the art of loving my body, and his body, as I had taught him the art of listening to himself, listening to patients. Listening to psyche and soul in pain.

Tried to teach him.

I never should have loved him. We never should have married. I'd known that even as I shivered in the *mikvah,* futile attempt to wash myself, wish myself pure again on the eve of my wedding. But I, ever the good daughter, ever the good doctor, ever the good teacher, the good Jew, was ashamed. What I'd done. Broken the rules, broken the analytic frame. And I was thirty-five, already despoiled by that other secret defiling: the assault on the dark street corner, long before Erich. The seal broken, the stain only my mother knew, and blamed me for. If I had been married, safe, not out doctoring, coming home late alone, it would not have happened.

Eight years after our marriage, I knew it was over. I lay on the surgeon's table to have the tumor cut out of me, growing for the nine months Erich had been gone in the sanatorium. A tumor growing where a child, our child, should have grown. The child I was too old to bear, the child I knew I would never have even before the surgeon took my womb as well.

Alone on those long nights crossing the Atlantic, I imagined the ocean parting for me like the Red Sea for Moses. Letting me Passover, thanks to Erich's intervention, unlikely *deus ex machina*. I had left it almost too late. I had left Germany almost fatally too late. Leaving behind my mother Klara, my sisters Grete and Anna— mother refusing to come, sisters refusing to leave her. Mother refusing to listen. How convenient she found it at times to be deaf.

I couldn't think of them without that constriction in my chest, the clench of the muscle that is all, after all, the heart is. Just a muscle, just a pump.

Oh, the heart is so much simpler than the brain, I'd told my students—Erich as well. Remembering the young soldiers' shattered brains I'd seen in the neurology unit, just finished my psychiatric training in 1914. Hopeful, naïve, beginning my real apprenticeship treating those young soldiers—what was left of them. Cardiology is carpentry, compared to neurology, to psychiatry, I later told my students. A mind is indeed a terrible thing to lose, a terrible thing to have blown apart.

I sensed Erich was the student I should not accept for analysis, though no protocol forbade it. I knew with him I must keep the desk between us, this time only be teacher, not confidante.

And yet I said yes.

At his first session, I waited as I always did for the patient to stretch out on the chaise, to settle into stillness, before asking my ritual question.

How can I be of help?

I'll show you.

I froze in my chair.

I'll show you, he'd said, crossing the room.

On that lonely ocean I remembered everything but with no illusions about the future. My mother Klara had enough illusions for all of us.

Go, go, she'd urged—not because of the hoped-for job, though we were desperate for money, all our assets frozen. My Therapeuticum in Heidelberg stood empty and shuttered, my very own, my hard-won hospital. Everyone had said it was impossible, a woman running a psychiatric sanatorium. But I'd done it for the decade since my father Adolf died (as my mother would have it) or since he killed himself. Work is my balm. Grieving, I opened my hospital. Grieving, I taught Erich. Though grief is no excuse.

No, I had no illusions about reconciliation, but I dreamed on those rocking ocean nights and awoke moist with longing and let my fingers stray. He'd taught me that; I'd practiced the lessons (Erich watching, coaching, admiring, exhorting: *Love yourself, Friedl, it is the beginning of everything else*). Always the dutiful student, I practiced the finger work the way I'd practiced scales and chords learning piano. I played myself on those dark ocean nights, and afterward, in my mind, played Mendelssohn's *Songs without Words*, especially my favorite "Lost Happiness." The recordings traveled in the hold—heavy silent discs riding the waves while I took myself riding on those nights suspended between the old life and the new. And I was not seasick, though others retched at table, leaned over the railing on deck. Instead, I indulged that secret, selfish appetite he'd unlocked, that inner physical hunger that feeds itself without satiation.

The days were peaceful on the ship, the illusory peace of transit between before and after, remembered and imagined. With Gertrud Jacob (friend, my former student, fellow analyst) I walked the third-class deck; read beneath rough plaid wool blankets. Not talking—if we tried the wind whipped the words away. Silence was relief; we'd talked enough the two of us, over the months of deciding. Visited Palestine together, ruled it out together, needing money.

Now, serendipitous shipmates, we sailed toward America, a different promised land.

Gertrud set up her easel by the porthole in her cabin. *Sit for me, Friedl.*

No. A little afraid, if I'm honest, of what she would see and represent. I know the quality of her work, the accuracy of her brushstroke. When she paints it is as though the subject is her living cadaver, cut open, exposed. The scent of paint and turpentine reminds me of the laboratory scents of formaldehyde and alcohol.

Please.

I could not refuse the entreaty in those eyes—so deep and soft and eloquent.

I didn't recognize myself in the portrait. Oh, I'm not vain, know I am no beauty with my forehead too high and broad, my nose too heavy. But that ravaged woman with the deep purple crease down her brow like a scar, green shadows like bruises beneath her eyes? Not me! Rather, surely, certainly, it was Gertrud projecting her own fatigue and psyche onto me, in some painterly act of countertransference. Yes, surely, unconsciously, it was herself Gertrud represented.

I tried to think that and yet I knew. The series of portraits she painted of her psychiatric patients in Hamburg were staggering and true. It is unique, the way she combines artistic talent and training with her doctor's wisdom, her analyst's training, to synthesize inner state and outer countenance. But if she accurately portrayed me—I look as ancient and careworn as her portrait of a senile.

Sun, water, air. The crossing was the rest cure I might have prescribed for a fragile patient, never for myself. The ugly portrait Gertrud insisted I keep (and I, tuning fork with perfect pitch for the feelings of others, could not refuse) was surely not an accurate likeness after the restorative days and nights at sea.

5

Erich meets us, after the indignity of Ellis Island. Gertrud's cough did not (despite my fear) strand her in the island hospital or (worse fear) send her back. She goes to the hotel arranged by the Psychiatric Institute. Erich takes me to his borrowed flat.

After we eat, after the sharp red wine, he removes his gold-rimmed spectacles (always the cue) and leans across the small table. I push my chair back; my wine glass trembles and almost spills. I stand, knowing what my training, my intuition, warned me ten years earlier, though I did not listen then, wanting so much.

But now I know. The limitless depth, the yearning in his naked eyes is authentic—but not specific. The gaze is brilliant but shallow, like a light with a mirror behind to amplify the brightness. He wants, yes. Loves, yes. With inexhaustible but indiscriminate appetite.

No, I say, standing up from the table. The wine spills. I remember the wedding goblet wrapped in the stained white linen napkin, crushed beneath his foot.

But Friedl, I love you.

I love you as well. But that is over.

Later, in his bathroom, I read the clues, study the evidence of blond strands mixed among dark in his hairbrush. I'd given him that silver-backed brush, comb and yes, a hand-mirror: wedding gifts for my bridegroom. Engraved with his initials *EF.* I had not added mine, nor twined our letters together.

I finally allow myself to recognize what I've always known and denied, marrying him. Loving Erich means sharing Erich. I am a generous woman. But not that generous.

Going forward, work will be my chosen one—as I'd intended, expected, before he appeared, uninvited, unexpected prince from the Grimm's fairy tales read as a girl. I will love and take care of my mother and my sisters, to the extent Mother Klara permits. I will love and take care of my patients.

I will never love anyone, ever again, the way I'd loved Erich. No one ever again like that, I tell myself. Believing it true.

That first night in New York I know it has been a mistake to accept his invitation to the flat rather than going with Gertrud to stay at the hotel with the other refugee analysts brought over by the Institute. A mistake? There are no mistakes. Accepting was an act of self-sabotage. I have let myself be deaf to what I heard in my inner ear.

Rebuffed, he sleeps in the living room of the borrowed flat (how close a friend is the lease holder, a woman or a man?). I lie in his bed, consigning him to the high-backed horsehair sofa, knowing it will scratch and blotch his sensitive skin. On his pillow I scent sex and perfume—my sense of smell already hyper-acute, in compensatory preparation for the inevitable future when I, like father, like mother, will be deaf.

He sleeps, and I weep. Quietly, careful not to seem to invite him in from the adjoining room to comfort me. Though didn't I desire that? Why else, Dr. Frieda Fromm-Reichmann, brilliant renowned analyst, did you come here, to him? Behind the fear is the wish. As I taught him, and he taught me.

Erich pulls his strings and works his charms and secures my position as *locum tenens* at a private hospital in Maryland, the Chestnut Lodge. It sounds like a hunting retreat, not a sanatorium, but it is just for the nonce, just an opening wedge to a permanent position somewhere better, somewhere well-known. McLean perhaps, or Menninger, Sheppard Pratt. For the summer, I'll substitute, fill in. I'm homesick for my Therapeuticum, homesick for my shuttered, abandoned hospital as though it were my child. Homesick for my hospital as though I were the lost child and it my sheltering mother. The keen grief of homesickness a child believes will kill her (and perhaps she's right) that's what I feel for my hospital in the Villa

Cornelia in Neuenheim, loveliest neighborhood in Heidelberg—or so it was, when I said goodbye.

That painful catch of longing again in my heart, silly muscle. Never mind. Beggars can't be choosers. Refugees can't be refusers.

I leave for Maryland with my suitcase, my box of records, Gertrud's painting wrapped in a blanket. He carries just his familiar leather rucksack; the book bag he slung across his slender shoulders as a student in my class now holds the few items he needs for the weekend. He will soon be free again.

At Penn Station, Erich hails a Negro porter. A red cap, he calls him. Gertrud would love the reflective skin, the iridescent white of the man's eyes. I recall the Rembrandt in the Rijksmuseum, shadowy portrait of an African man. The porter catches me staring and I look away. He trundles my suitcase and box down the platform. I carry Gertrud's painting. *My god, she has you to the life*, Erich exclaimed when I showed him, not telling him it was meant as my likeness. So that's how I look to him, *une belle laide*. So that's how I look.

We board. The conductor says something unintelligible. My mind tires of wrapping itself around English (that's the problem, not my hearing). Erich reaches into his breast pocket for the leather travel wallet. Embossed *EF*, my gift when he left for the clean healing air of the cure in Switzerland, with his ticket to leave me, the train ticket I'd paid for, slipped into the soft leather pocket.

He returned cured, of the TB, and of me.

Breathing is so simple. All you need is a pump and a bellows. When pumps and bellows go bad, some can be repaired. Not so easy with the switchboard of intellect, instinct, and emotion, nerves and impulses. Patching up the detritus of the trenches after the Somme, I did my best with damaged brains. I could never eat calves' brains again.

What haunted me, after any possible patching and mending was done, was the damage to the intangible mind. What could be done for the tangle of memory, thoughts, and dreams? What is the cure for fear, for despair, for anger? What is the cure for a broken heart that is really a broken mind? That challenge has become my life's work.

Rocking south along the rails. Beyond the window it grows dark. Erich sleeps, his head heavy on my shoulder like the weight of a sleeping child, my niece's head on my shoulder on other train rides, in that other, older world.

The director, Dr. Dexter Bullard, and his wife meet us at Union Station. Drive us past the fountain. *Christopher Columbus,* she says. Drive us in their enormous car past buildings like temples. *The Capitol,* she says. *The Supreme Court, just completed...The Lincoln Memorial...And the memorial to Jefferson will be there, they've just started.*

Strange seeing the foundation for the new memorial, like a ruin in reverse, going up instead of down. Strange new world, white marble, wide avenues and vistas—aspiring, imitative Acropolis. It's like a huge stage set, so different from the gray buildings and narrow streets at home.

She and I sit in the back, the men in the front. Erich, animated, almost manic, chats in a stream of rapid English. I don't try to follow, feeling small as a tired child on the back seat, my feet not quite reaching the floor. The scale of this American car is wrong for someone less than five feet tall. The car purrs through the night. Air rushes in the windows, velvet soft and humid. *Too much breeze for you?* Mrs. Bullard asks. Bad air for Erich's sensitive lungs but I breathe deep, greedy for warmth after the chill in Strasbourg, the smut in the German air. And the chill cast by that other Adolf—spoiling my father's name, sharing and staining my birth year, 1889. I breathe

the moist air as though inhaling the healing steam of the spa at Baden-Baden, in other days.

Always I will remember my first glimpse of the Lodge: tall, elegant building looming in the dark beneath its mansard roof, long windows alight—reminding me of my Therapeuticum. Inside, a grand piano in the parlor. My fingers itch to touch the keys. The wood floors gleam and like a child I want to take off my shoes and skate in stocking feet across the surface.

It feels more like a hotel than a hospital, I say.

Keen diagnosis, laughs Dr. Bullard. *It was a hotel when my father bought it. Rockville was a summer resort.*

He's younger than I expected, late thirties I'd wager and I'm as good at divining age as all other information not spoken. Young to be director of a hospital, as I had been. Though I created mine; he inherited four years ago when his father died of a heart attack. We share that, too, the sudden loss of a father.

And our patients are our guests, in a sense, she says. *We're like a family here.*

The director's family lives next to the hospital, in what she calls the little lodge.

A menagerie, with our children, the dogs. More chaotic than the sanatorium, she smiles. *So you'll be in a guest room we keep in the hospital for family visiting patients.*

A room? Does she think we share a room, a bed? Has Erich explained?

We're walking down the corridor. What to say?

Dr. Fromm-Reichmann, you'll be here. The bath is shared with a nurse who lives in. Erich, you're in your usual room down the hall.

Later when I know about his affair with Karen (let myself know) I will wonder if he'd brought her here. She would have been interested in their methods; they would have been interested in her. Did Dexter Bullard want to hire the well-known, well-established Karen Horney? Did she refuse to leave New York—her work is there, and Erich? Did Bullard settle for me? But that first night, exhausted, I don't suspect any of this. All I feel is relief for two separate rooms. Whatever he'd said, he'd prepared them.

Please, call me Frieda, I say to her.

I'm Anne. She is gracious, kind eyes. *We're informal here. The patients will mostly call you Frieda. And Dexter says we're the only hospital where the director sleeps with his bookkeeper.* She laughs, a musical laugh. *We'll go over the paperwork tomorrow.*

Lying in the bed, a wooden bedstead, lying beneath heavy cotton sheets and a thick coverlet of tufted chenille, I listen—the way I always listen, everywhere to everything, trained to listen by growing up the oldest child, my parents' ears and go-between. I've never heard insects before like these in Maryland! Almost tropical: chirring, whirring. I must get a nature guide, learn my new habitat, flora and fauna. I will write Anna, the baby of we three sisters, nine years my junior—a mother herself now. She loved to trap crickets, as a child. Come! I'll say, tempting her with the bugs, your little one will love it here. *My family must come,* I've told Erich. *Difficult,* he's said. The waiting lists, the quotas. *And they do not have anything to offer, like you.*

Nothing to offer? Why must we prove our worth, to earn safety? But of course, first, my dear ones must have the hunger to come, to fuel the effort that will be required to obtain the papers, the stamps, the certificates. I must earn enough to pay but they must jump the hoops. I worked to get here, as did Gertrud, but Erich and the Institute opened the door. Just in time, as the restrictions and dangers increase in Germany—and the resentment grows here, as well.

I clench with fear and yearning. Restless, I kick the covers off and turn onto my side.

Sudden silence! The insect noise gone!

I roll onto my other side again. *Chirr, chirr, chirr.* The chorus returns.

Onto my back: the buzzing insect choir continues.

Onto my right side again.

Utter silence.

I lie still, afraid to run the experiment again but force myself to roll back and forth, collecting the data.

Finished, I lie rigid staring into the dark. The family curse of deafness is stalking me and catching up.

If Erich were beside me, I'd wake him. Tap his shoulder, whisper the dread news.

He would hold me, comfort me.

We never lose that primitive longing, to be held as our mothers held us.

I wonder sometimes, did Klara hold me? How early did our complicated dance begin, magnetic poles attracting, repelling? Later it often fell to me to hold Grete, and little Anna, mother to my sisters.

I ache with missing them. It is possible, surely to die of homesickness.

If Erich were here.

Tap, tap.

Friedl? Friedl?

The power of my covert wish has summoned him. That mysterious tie still runs from heart to heart, or loin to loin—or other cruder words he'd use, arousing me.

Behind the fear is the wish. I must take care of our over-due divorce, if it can be done here, by an alien visitor.

Tap, tap. Friedl? Lieber?

I lie still, will myself not to move, not to answer.

He retreats down the hall.

Every goodbye, like terminating with a patient, is a rehearsal, a practice, a confusion with the final irrevocable parting of death.

I see Klara, Grete, Anna, on a distant shore. Receding out of the reach of my protection. The clench of fear and longing will break my heart, that silly muscle.

I rise to check the door and find no lock. I am in a hospital again.

I am home.

TWO

Eliza slammed the brakes. She'd almost hit him, pulling out of the carport too fast, sightlines blocked by overgrown forsythia. Had she checked her mirrors? She jumped out of the car.

"Sorry! I didn't see you."

The man's head retracted into the parka's hood like a turtle hiding. He reached in his pocket.

Stupid risk, confronting him—frightening him, provoking him.

He pulled out a cigarette, not a gun, not a knife.

Eliza breathed. She usually said hello to these forsaken residents from the halfway house across the street, though they did not even see her as they walked the grounds of the empty psychiatric hospital. Inpatient lifers, they'd been discharged to so-called community care when Chestnut Lodge closed. Castaways stranded by the defunct mother ship. The Lodge was a hard place to leave. Hadn't she been drawn back too after almost twenty years, renting the cottage, living on the grounds of the hospital where she'd been a social work student intern and then stayed on for her first job?

They're more afraid of you than you are of them, she'd reassured Nick last summer when they moved here. *But don't cut across their yard,* she'd added, trying to warn without scaring him.

The man zipped his parka though it was already eighty humid degrees. Psychosis screws with your thermostat, makes it easier to live under a bridge or in an inadequate halfway house.

He shambled off, talking aloud, probably on his way to the library where he shelved books. Prince Valiant, she called him, for the shaggy bowl cut that always needed trimming. His weight was up, maybe he was taking his meds. The outfit who managed the halfway house had a reputation for low bids and lax care.

Checking her mirrors, Eliza backed out. The forsythia had to go; Nick would be driving soon. She'd cut back the bushes without waiting for permission from the historic society.

She took the local road, not the highway. Part of her wanted to be there already, part of her was afraid to arrive. Usually driving to pick Nick up at camp she was eager after the summer separation. But it had only been two weeks.

Eliza drove out of town, passing the Victorians and bungalows, then through suburban developments and office parks, and into the remaining fields and orchards.

No line at White's Ferry this early on a Saturday. The man waved her down the steep bank and onto the flat chunk of floating metal—more like a section of bridge than a boat. Oldest operating ferry on the Potomac, *The Jubal Early* was named for the Confederate general who crossed here on his way to raid Rockville, she'd told Nick the first summer he went to camp. *There were battles in Rockville?* he'd asked, agleam with excitement. That fall they'd visited Antietam, Harper's Ferry, Gettysburg, and the Civil War Medicine Museum in Frederick. She'd thought an eight-year-old was too young for such sad history, but he'd worn his navy blue Union cap to bed, and read every easy-reader Civil War history in the library. Walking the battlefields, she hoped he'd never be on one in earnest.

The ferry began its slow progress, tethered to an underwater cable, winched across by a motor. The only other passengers, a young couple in matching spandex tanks and shorts, leaned with their bicycles against the rail, kissing.

"Round trip?" The man had cured leather skin, deep wrinkles. *That's the job for me,* Nick had said, the first time they rode the ferry. *You could run the store Ma and we'd live upstairs.* She'd hugged him, enjoying his fantasy of a Mom-and-Boy business. And what a welcome fantasy it had been, that tense summer of 2002. Just nine months earlier the hijackers had forced the plane along the river, aiming for the Pentagon.

She stared into the water, red brown like the clay banks. A tangle of sticks floated by. A heron dropped for a fish. Eliza would like to ride back and forth all day, float suspended in the timeless zone of transit. Postpone arriving at camp.

But Nick needed her. She wished suddenly she could fly and drop into Hopewell from the sky, like that heron. Magic mama to the rescue. But she had no super-power to rescue him.

The ferry man unhooked the chain, waved her off.

It's different on the Virginia side, Nick said.

Southern, she thought as she drove through Leesburg and into the Shenandoah Valley. The azure mountains startled every time. *No wonder they call them the Blue Ridge, Ma.*

Today Hopewell's one stoplight flashed green.

Almost there! Even two weeks earlier he'd said it, forgetting to be almost-sixteen-cool. She passed the gas station, the post office, the fieldstone Friends Meeting, the Dairy Cupboard. He was always too excited to stop for a cone on the way to camp; it was ritual consolation for leaving.

Three curving miles to the sign.

HOPEWELL CAMP NUCLEAR FREE ZONE.

The faded rainbow needed re-painting. He could have done that.

Eliza parked in the field, her dusty green Forester the only car. Arrival and pick-up days the field was jammed with mini-vans and

Volvo wagons plastered with bumper stickers. *Visualize Whirled Peas. Hate is not a Family Value. I'd Rather be Weaving.*

A grasshopper landed in her hair, trapped and buzzing in the thick curls. She batted it away, found a plastic clip in the glove compartment and pulled the heavy tangle off her neck. Eliza left the car open. *You don't lock here, Ma. No one takes stuff.*

Crossing the plank bridge over the stream she sat in the white plastic chair (arrival day lice-check station) and shook a pebble out of her sandals. She would have worn sneakers, if she'd been thinking. If she'd had time to think. If she'd expected the call.

She climbed the hill. A hot breeze carried a whiff of wood-smoke.

"May everyone 'neath vine and fig tree live in peace and unafraid." Kids were singing as they set tables in the dining shed—the song Nick taught her on the ride home after his first summer. *But it's supposed to be a round. We need more people in this family.* He'd taught it to her parents at the Thanksgiving table. Her father let him use the pitch pipe. *We're okay,* she'd thought, exchanging a glance with her mother. It had been their holiday grace ever since, until this year—her father too ill, her mother too sad, Nick frightened and angry to be losing his grandfather.

"Can I help you?" The counselor had a thicket of brown curls, a lump of amber on a leather cord, Haverford T-shirt, a butterfly tattoo hovering by her wrist bone. Nick had been asking for a tattoo.

"I'm here to see Cole."

"Try his office." Sympathy in her soft eyes. Nick would have been old enough to be a junior counselor next summer, a junior hanger-on angling to sit next to a girl like her at the fire circle or in the kitchen after lights out for campers.

The singing hushed. "His mom," a whisper buzzed.

"Water glasses," the young woman said. "Who wants to ring the bell?"

The director's office was a prefab garden shed, dark and smelling of mulch. Cole sat in a webbed aluminum lawn chair at a card table. The fad for shaved head and light beard worked on him. Forty, give or take. *If I were ten years younger,* she'd said to Dee. *You always have some excuse,* her friend said. He looked like a gentle pirate with the small gold hoop in his ear. Nick wanted a pierced ear. She'd said no. *He may do it himself,* Dee said, *we did.* Eliza rubbed the knot on her earlobe, souvenir of that over-night with Dee: ice cube and singed needle, sweet smell of blood on gauze, the sting and scent of rubbing alcohol.

A scruffy three-legged dog, bandanna around its neck, yipped and sniffed her ankles.

Cole scooped the dog up. "Thanks for coming."

As if it had been a choice. What if she hadn't showed up? Passive resistance, civil disobedience. Wasn't that what Quakers were all about?

She perched in the too-low plastic Adirondack chair at the familiar strategic disadvantage of an elementary school parent in a little chair. Called in, called out, for Nick's behavior. His success and his shortcomings rested on her alone. No one to share the joy, no one to share the blame. *Which was your choice,* Dee said, blunt and close as she came to a sister.

"What exactly happened?" He'd told her on the phone, but maybe the story could be different. Maybe she could lobby for a different ending, or a different reading of the facts. Therapists know how much depends on who's telling. *As reported by,* Eliza wrote in her case notes. Not that she'd play the therapist card. She was just a mom here, though it was impossible to tease apart her mother self and her work self; she brought both parts of herself to therapy and mothering. But here, she was just asking for help.

"Nick's bunk is building a sweat lodge with me. Wood and daub, bark. Our theme this year is respecting the indigenous."

She and Dee had done beadwork the summer they met. It was just called Indian beadwork, no lesson about history or politics or exploitation.

"Last night, after lights out, counselors smelled smoke. We evacuated the kids to the stream. Got it out."

"Who was with him?" She sounded defensive. Hadn't she learned anything since another two-year-old bit Nick in daycare? Mama bear on the alert, she'd stormed the office, forgetting everything she knew about child development. Next day, Nick bit.

Still, she hoped for a ringleader here, or at least a co-conspirator.

"No one," Cole said, gentle and firm like a good parent. She'd almost called him last winter when Nick's grades fell. He taught at a Friends school, the kind of place she'd send Nick, if she had the money, the kind of school she'd taught in during that brief other life right out of college.

Cole led past the bathhouse—the concrete bunker reeked of urine even from the path. The only masonry building on the dry forest hilltop, she realized, seeing the rustic structures with new eyes. Everything was flimsy kindling; the whole camp was a fire trap. Passing the drama shed she noticed a tangle of extension cords. Nick had planned to play his Theremin in the talent show, proud of building it from the kit, the instrument's fingernail on blackboard strange electronic voice. *The only instrument you can play without touching. Cole will love it,* he'd said, packing it into the padded gig bag that had cost almost as much as the instrument. Money she didn't have but money well-spent.

Eliza followed Cole through the warren of bunkhouses packed close as matches in a box and past the fire circle. The air grew thick. Smoke stuck to her throat like when she used to torch tar onto wooden cross-country skis.

20

He stopped at a jumble of charred logs. "This is it," he said. "Or was."

How could it be? She wanted to explain, wanted this man to understand. Nick loved building with Lincoln Logs at her parents. He'd cried the first time she lit candles on his cake. After 9/11 when he was in third grade, he'd had nightmares, slept on the yoga pad by her bed. Then here at camp the next summer, his first time, he began to master the fear of flames. He'd proudly showed her his place at the fire circle and later that year, in Scouts, began to learn to light wooden matches—quoting the troop rules like a protective mantra. *Beware of oily rags.*

"He's always been scared of fire. Can't even light paper matches."

The smoky breeze carried laughter and guitar. Her eyes stung. Nick was losing Eden. "Could you suspend him? Till next session? I'll find him some community service?"

"Sorry, Eliza. Has to be zero tolerance on fire. We were lucky. He could have been burned. And everyone else."

Eliza flashed on the image of the man who'd immolated himself, protesting Vietnam. His photograph had been reprinted on the fortieth anniversary, with an article about him. *Mom,* Nick said, looking up from the paper. *This is awful. He was a Quaker.*

"I'm so sorry. And—I'm so worried about him. This isn't like him. You know Nick." She brushed sudden tears; the back of her hand came away smudged with soot.

"He's seemed down."

"Tough year. We moved. Better school, but he says the kids are snobs."

"Thought about therapy?"

"Says if I make him, he won't talk. Guess if your mom's a therapist, that's one way to rebel."

"I'm sure you know plenty of people—but someone I used to teach with years ago is a therapist now—near you in Rockville, I think. If you'd like his name…"

She struggled a moment, with her pride. This was her field, after all.

But she was a mom here, and Nick—if he would listen to anyone, it might be Cole.

"Thanks," she said. "Never hurts to have another good referral in the rolodex." She had one, a mark of age. Cole nodded, wrote on a piece of paper, handed it to her.

"Let's go get your guy," he said.

The bunkhouse was stuffy with heat and boy funk. He lay curled on a bottom bunk, face to the wall, hood of his sweatshirt pulled up.

She sat down on the edge of the bunk, putting her hand on his shoulder, as she used to when he called out in the night. The curve of his shoulder felt good, solid.

He didn't move. She pushed back his hood and leaned into his wiry blond curls, smelling sweat and smoke; remembering scooping him up from his daycare cot and inhaling the scent of pee and apple juice as she carried him—gritty with sand—to the car.

"Need you on the footlocker, Nick," said Cole, his voice firm as a good father setting limits. Tag team parenting would be different.

Nick rolled over, pushing away her hand, and stood. How tall he was. The recent growth spurt still surprised her.

She hugged him, rigid man-sized block of wood. "Come on, honey," she whispered. "Time to go."

Eliza followed Nick and Cole, yoked together by the footlocker like a father and son. She carried the Theremin and his duffel.

"Hold on," said Cole at the dining shed.

The pretty counselor came out.

"Sweet potato biscuits for Nick for the road," Cole said. Knowing his favorite, like a dad.

The woman was back in a moment, paper bag in hand. "Take care, Nick."

He didn't look up from tracing a pattern in the dust with the toe of his sneaker.

Thank her! Eliza bit her lip. Wait.

"Thanks," she said, finally, taking the bag, grease spots shining on the brown paper.

She popped open the hatch for the footlocker.

Nick slammed it closed, the way he knew not to.

Eliza sat watching in the rearview mirror. Cole rested his hand on Nick's shoulder, Nick kept his head down.

Look at him. Say you're sorry. Ask for a chance.

Nick pulled away and climbed in beside her.

Cole leaned at her window—what a nice mouth.

"Safe travels. Stay in touch, Nick."

"Thanks," she said, covering his silence again, turning the key in the ignition too fast, hearing it rasp.

Usually the message on the exit sign amused her. Not today.

CAUTION RE-ENTERING THE REAL WORLD.

She pulled in at the Dairy Cupboard. "Bet you flavor of the week is strawberry."

"I'm vegan."

Eliza sat at the blue painted picnic table—the blue repels wasps, Nick had once explained, an expert on country lore. She chipped through the chocolate shell on the dip-top, let her mouth fill with the tooth-aching sweet cold. She ate it all, even the wisp of paper napkin stuck to the soggy bottom of the cake-cone.

Back on the road hot air rushed through the open windows.

"When are you fixing the AC?"

Anger flared over the ache of sadness. "You just sent a thousand dollars from Gran up in smoke. And believe me, she doesn't have money to burn right now either."

Silence. He'd pulled his hood up, put on his sunglasses—like a misbehaving toddler making himself invisible. Another time, she would have laughed, teased him.

"What were you thinking? You could have killed people."

A truck appeared out of her blind spot. The driver blasted his horn.

"Careful, Ma. You could kill people."

Silent miles later she tried again. "Was it like an experiment that got out of control?" Leading the witness, she knew better.

No response.

He stayed in the car on the ferry.

The Maryland shore approached. Red canoes lined up on the bank. They'd always meant to rent one. What about now? *Hey, Nick. Let's go paddling.* Maybe he'd talk.

Driving beneath the arch of trees, light and shadow flickered like a flip book of past trips—without the usual soundtrack of songs and talk. She turned on the radio. A talk show interview. *Tell me about finding out the doctor was using his own sperm. How devastating.* She switched it off and drove through silence thick as smoke until she couldn't bear it. Now, while he's a captive audience. Now. One reason kids got better in therapy was the time they spent in the car with the parent, back and forth to the sessions. Protected private time together.

"Honey, I'm worried. It would help to talk to someone."

"So talk to someone."

"I mean it would help you."

"One of your shrink friends?"

"No one I work with. Someone I don't know."

Stone silence.

24

She'd find a good referral, out of network if necessary. There were so few people doing really good therapy these days, what with the insurance companies' demands for short-term treatment and pitiful reimbursement. Maybe someone in private practice with a sliding scale. Good enough, brave enough, to do that. Maybe someone who'd cut her a break, professional courtesy. Maybe Cole's person did that, though she'd want to check him out first. She would love to be in private practice, able to be flexible, able to call the shots. To have the freedom to do real therapy. Her two best friends at the clinic were leaving, setting up shop, done with jumping through management's hoops. They'd invited her to join them.

But she couldn't afford the risk of giving up a paycheck, however small, and benefits. She never asked her parents for money and wouldn't now with the expense of moving her dad to the nursing home, their house still on the market.

She'd sign up for shifts on the clinic's after-hours beeper to pay for Nick's therapy. She'd already been told there would be no cost of living increase this year, and it was looking bad for getting the promotion to department head. She wasn't even likely to get the smallest merit raise—dinged by the quality review system for errors with the computerized charting. *I'm concerned and disappointed. You're resisting adapting to this, Eliza*, the clinic director had said. Ironic, to talk about quality review when the templated system was just checklists for symptoms and interventions, canned multiple-choice phrases for progress. And although it was superficial, it was cumbersome. So many cases, so little time—sounded like a bumper sticker. She was trying to catch up, going in early, staying late. She'd have to find a way to do it, even with Nick home. Rumors were going around about lay-offs. Insurance reimbursement and county grants were drying up. Some people predicted the clinic was moving toward cutting the psychotherapy service altogether.

Well, what she needed to worry about right now, what she could do something about right now, was find a therapist for Nick. A good therapist would connect with Nick. She'd seen it happen. Done it herself when luck and need and chemistry were right.

She'd seen it fail, too, and failed herself. But she couldn't think that now. Therapy would work and she'd find the money. "No negative thoughts," she told herself, the new boss's simplistic rubric. She preferred what she told overwhelmed clients: "Break it down." Figure out the first small thing you can do, what's within your power. She needed to remember that.

Eliza passed through the stone bollards marking the driveway, beneath the garish new billboard. *Chestnut Acres. Luxury Homes! Coming Soon Deluxe Condos.*

A truck was parked beside her carport. A man in purple shorts and a matching polo shirt rolled a round table-top across the lawn.

"What?" Nick took off his sunglasses.

"The historic society's having a party here tomorrow."

"On our front lawn?"

They'd been the only residents on the Lodge grounds almost the entire year. A family had recently moved into the first of the new houses.

"A fund raiser. Part of our rent deal with the historic society." A condition of her below market rent was opening the cottage for occasional events and tours. This would be the first.

"Your deal. I never asked to live in a shrink museum."

"They wanted to do it in May. I asked them to postpone till camp."

"No worries. I won't be here."

He stomped up the steps, shouting over his shoulder, "Left the door unlocked again. Invite the psychos across the street in why not?"

Eliza put her head down on the steering wheel. The horn bleated.

"Need help ma'am?" The purple uniform made him look like a delivery man dipped in Easter egg dye.

Oh my, yes, she needed help.

"Could you get the footlocker onto the screen porch around back?"

"No problem. Dan!"

She carried the Theremin inside, took some singles from the lunch money drawer in the kitchen.

The assistant frowned when his boss waved the tip away. "What's the nightmare on Elm over there?" the younger man asked.

Eliza bristled as though he'd criticized family. But the Lodge—first floor windows covered with plywood, crumbling brickwork, peeling paint and unkempt shrubbery—did look haunted.

"A psych hospital. They're turning it into condos."

"Whoa, couldn't pay me to live in a loony bin. But wouldn't say no to that," the man said, gesturing at the new house behind the cottage: fake Victorian, three stories of teal and apricot vinyl siding, complete with turret. It was the only one occupied and the first completed, except for the model, but two dozen more were staked out on muddy cul-de-sacs. The Lodge school, the recreation center, patient dorms, and open rolling fields, all had been bulldozed away.

"If you've a spare million, they're building more," Eliza said.

The side door slammed. Nick careened down the driveway on his skateboard. No helmet, no wrist guards, her vulnerable Achilles soared past the stone bollards onto the street. Eliza didn't know who she prayed to, but she prayed.

She left the door to the screen porch open, and the front door, letting light and air sweep through the house. Standing on the front steps she gazed across the broad expanse of lawn stretching to West Montgomery Avenue. Despite everything, just standing here in the airy entry way, made her feel better. "I love your house, Frieda," she said aloud.

The legendary Frieda Fromm-Reichmann had already been dead for more than thirty years when Eliza came to the Lodge as a student intern, now she'd been gone for fifty. When Eliza worked at the Lodge the cottage had been shabby and rundown, used for offices and storage. Last summer she'd seen a post on the list-serve of former Lodge staff. Frieda's Cottage was for rent. She'd come, out of curiosity, drawn back to the Lodge like a homesick kid.

The historic society had restored it. Wood floors, white wood-work, natural light in every room, views of the green trees, the old Lodge—she'd been smitten. It wasn't big, but spacious compared to their cramped apartment. And Nick would be in the best high school, her commute to work would be shorter. On impulse, she'd signed the lease, afraid to let it get away.

It had been a miscalculation—taking him away from friends, living here on the deserted grounds. Although she couldn't quite regret it or imagine giving up the privacy and quiet for an ordinary apartment, the lease was up for renewal in August and she'd have to decide what to do.

Eliza opened the crammed fridge. She had to admit the vintage replica appliances were small, and the kitchen. According to Frieda-lore at the Lodge, she never cooked. And she certainly had never lived with a teenager!

Eliza ate on the screen porch: arugula straight from the plastic tub, one of Nick's sweet potato biscuits, a glass of wine box Chardonnay.

A few straggling nasturtiums marked the remnant of what had been a flower bed behind the cottage. Her new neighbors were grilling. The woman wore the toddler on her hip like an accessory. The family could model for the developer's brochure.

Stop it, she chastised herself. "Hi, folks," she called.

"Hi!" said the woman, waving the baby's hand. "Say hi to Miss Eliza!"

Oh, she remembered, what it was like, the physical closeness. Thinking you knew exactly what he needed, exactly what he wanted, could speak for him.

She always made her mother's baked ziti for his first night home from camp. They should be sitting here together, talking and eating and laughing and catching up. Eliza gave up on dinner and retreated to her study.

She texted him, looking at Frieda's photograph hanging above her desk, as required by the historic society. The famous doctor looked tiny in a big leather chair. She wore a cardigan draped over her shoulders, a string of pearls, and held a black spaniel on her lap. Nick said it was weird, but Eliza liked having her there: quiet, non-judgmental—the perfect analyst, the non-anxious presence Eliza aspired to be. Frieda's eyes gleamed with intelligence and warmth, and she had a faint all-knowing, Mona Lisa smile. It was the classic analyst face: neutral, kind, the expression that opened you up.

"I'm scared, Frieda," she said. It did help, as Eliza told her clients, putting it into words. And though Nick would tease her if he knew, it did help having the wise woman smiling down from the frame on the wall, listening. Too early to call Dee, and her mother had too much to cope with already.

Eliza pulled her diagnostic manual from the shelf and found it: *The essential feature of Pyromania is the presence of multiple episodes of deliberate and purposeful fire setting.*

"It was just one fire," she said to Frieda. "One impulsive, pointless fire."

No response.

She texted Nick again.

Eliza remembered the slip of paper from Cole, found it in her purse, googled the man. His office was in Rockville. He'd been in practice six years, gone to social work school at Smith. She'd prefer someone she knew. Though maybe, Nick being Nick, a total stranger would be better.

Call someone, she almost heard Frieda say. *Now.*

Eliza called the therapist known for being the best with adolescents in the D.C. area. She'd sent Dee to him, when one of the twins was having a rough time.

She left a message. "This is Eliza Kline. We've met a couple of times at the Family Networker conference. I'm looking for a therapist." She took a deep breath. "For my son."

The first call for help was always the hardest, she told clients.

"I did it," she said to the photograph and re-shelved the diagnostic manual. Eliza picked up her well-thumbed copy of Frieda's *Principles of Psychotherapy.* She'd first read it in graduate school and had been re-reading it since moving here. Frieda's commonsense wisdom validated everything she believed about therapy. She would like, she would really like, to go out on her own. To run a practice that did things the slow, thorough, old-fashioned way. Of course, she'd refer for medication, but she'd take the necessary time to really develop a therapeutic relationship.

Eliza went outside onto the porch, settled onto the glider to read, picking up where she'd left off. *Every human being has an innate tendency toward health.*

Nick had been skinny and a picky eater. Eliza had worried, but her mother and Dee and the pediatrician had been right. He ate what he needed.

The new family was still outside. Eliza watched the toddler stagger back and forth between his parents, practicing separation and reunion, learning object constancy between the two beacons of his world.

Well, Nick had certainly learned to separate. Where was he? She felt the familiar ache she'd felt the first time she'd left him at day care. And the fear.

Eliza drove to the skateboard park by the pool. Not there, not in the parking lot by the closed grocery store, not hanging out in the square by the fountain.

And still not at home when she returned.

The phone rang. Nick! She snatched it up.

"Eliza, nice to hear from you. Sorry, but I've got a waiting list. There's some other good people, but everyone's running full—or on vacation."

"I know how it is," she said, ashamed of the quaver in her voice. "If you could put us on your list—and who else would you suggest? He may be—a little hard to engage."

He suggested two therapists she knew of. The third name was Cole's referral, Brent Richards.

Eliza called all three. The first two weren't taking new referrals, according to their messages, but she left her name anyway.

Brent Richards's message said he would be on vacation for the next week, gave his answering service for emergencies. At least he didn't rule out new clients. She said Cole had referred them, the connection might help. "It's not an emergency—but I'd like him to see someone as soon as possible."

Hanging up, Eliza stared at Frieda. "I wish you could see Nick," she whispered.

It was hard and exhausting, asking for help. Good to be reminded what it was like on the other side.

Eliza sat down on the glider with Frieda's book.

A psychiatrist who is lonely must see that his own need for physical comfort does not interfere with his coming to the correct conclusions about the patient's needs.

Loneliness had seemed almost a luxury, during those juggling years when he was small, dependent, and the job at the clinic was new. Now though, Nick was changing. He needed her, but not so hands on. He needed her and pushed her away. Always when you figure out one stage of parenting, it changes. So-called work life balance was such a moving target.

She scribbled a note for Nick. "Gone to Ben and Phil's. Call."

Locking the doors, she made sure his hide-a-key was in its hiding place under the metal gutter and walked through the building sites toward Rose Hill. The director's family had lived there when she came to the Lodge as a student. Their fieldstone house and the barn had been the first parcel sold, when it still seemed possible to save the Lodge. She'd already had to jump ship by then. One thing to take a chance if it was just you, another altogether with a toddler.

She rounded the corner of the weathered barn—Phil's studio now, and the garage for Ben's car. The lavender beside the flagstone path brushed her bare ankles, releasing the sharp scent that always reminded her of her mother's cologne. She'd love to be able to really talk to her mother tonight, but she couldn't burden her. Ben and Phil would do.

"Juleps," called Phil from the patio, lifting a glass. He lay on a chaise in jeans and T-shirt, teacher on vacation. "Training for tomorrow."

"Here you go," said Ben, pouring from a silver pitcher filmed with frost. He looked every inch the corporate attorney, still in tie and button down, eyes puffy with fatigue after his day downtown, the drive home. *I was late figuring myself out,* he'd said once. Knowing the men only since moving here she couldn't imagine either without the other.

"To our first dip," said Phil. "Pool guy comes this week."

The bourbon did its work. Eliza nibbled the stalk of mint and listened to Phil's plan for garden rooms and a swimming pool.

Western sunlight slanted across the slate patio, the satin surface of the koi pool.

A phone rang inside. "It'll be Ruth," Ben said, as he left.

"Ben's not just Ruth's treasurer for the historic society, he's her fixer," Phil said.

"Come see your proofs in the studio." *I'm fifty-six,* she'd objected, when Phil and Ben and Dee gave her the online dating membership for her birthday. *Just my age when I met Phil five years ago,* Ben said. The quick glance the two men exchanged stirred her with yearning. *Well, okay….Nick will be away all summer,* she'd said.

"I can't do it, Phil. Sorry for the trouble."

"Why not?"

"Work stuff. Nick's home."

Phil sat up, swung his long legs off the chaise and leaned forward to listen. What a good teacher he must be.

Ben called from the doorway. "Did the caterers set up the tents?"

"Tables," Eliza said. "No tents yet."

Ben disappeared indoors.

"What happened?" Phil asked.

"Kicked out. Lit a fire."

"Kids," he groaned.

"Don't tell Ben."

"He'd get it. His parents sent him to military school. To straighten him out." Phil never talked about his own estranged family—Mennonites. But now, on Ben's behalf, he sounded bitter.

"I should head home. He left angry."

"He'll be back. Look at your pictures, on the way."

Phil unlocked the barn and threw on the light switch. Ben's car gleamed, aqua and white fins, polished chrome. Phil slid open the massive door to the silo. He'd transformed the space this winter, scraping off bat guano, whitewashing the curved walls.

"Here you are," he said, unclipping the photographs from the clothesline.

He'd caught the woman Eliza saw on good days in the mirror. Her face was growing angular, with a faint cross-stitch of lines etching her mouth and eyes, like her mother's. But here, she was smiling. She'd put her thick hair up in a French braid and somehow the few gray streaks looked like highlights in the photo.

"Nice! I was dreading—yearbook."

"It's the Leica," he said. "The camera teaches the eye to see, Dorothea Lange says. Besides, you're easy on the eye."

"Sorry to waste your effort."

"Keep them. Things will change, they always do." Phil meditated every morning, here in the silo studio in bad weather, on the patio if it was nice.

"For now, Nick's the priority."

"Of course. But good for both of you if you don't lose sight of your own life."

"He's my life," she said, surprised to blurt it out, surprised to be crying.

Phil handed her a handkerchief. "It's clean."

"My dad used to carry these," she said, dabbing her eyes.

"What's plan B?"

"Theremin lessons, if you'll take him back. Driver ed if it's not too late. And therapy, if I can find someone and convince Nick."

"There's this guy everyone likes at school—" Phil began.

"I'm on his waiting list."

"We'll hire Nick. To help me."

"No. You deal with problem kids all year." Phil's small school downtown was known for second and third chances.

"Kids have problems. Don't we all. Nick's a good guy and I need help on the landscaping. Send him over tomorrow."

He walked her home. The cottage was still dark.

"Want me to go out looking? Or wait with you? Kill him for you when he shows?"

"I'm more scared than mad, honestly. But I'll get there."

"He's going to be okay," he said.

"I hope you're right."

She texted him again. Sat down at the piano, playing random scales and triads. It was like meditating—forced her to focus on the moment. She hadn't had a piano since high school, but Frieda's had been in the house, and the historic society had found a volunteer conservator to tune it. Eliza opened the bench the first night and found a trove of yellowed sheet music. Playing the piano came back to her like speaking a language she'd once known. There was something intimate, about sharing the keyboard, the music which had been Frieda's. As though Frieda were her teacher. *Play, my dear,* she imagined a kind voice with a faint German accent saying to her now, *it will help.*

At midnight she went upstairs. Watched pots don't boil, better not to keep vigil.

Eliza sat on the edge of the tub, swirling the bath salts as the water flowed. Her room adjoined the full bathroom. The plumbing in the half-bath in Nick's room didn't work yet, to his irritation. Her father used to quote someone who said the world needed plumbers as well as philosophers. Well, the historic society could use a pro bono plumber. She got up to light the candle, a ritual she'd started when bathing in Frieda's tub bothered her a bit, at first. Now the tub was hers, but she still enjoyed the soft light of candles. Eliza opened the medicine cabinet for her lighter. Gone.

The blank blue stare of Nick's computer monitor revealed an underbrush of shoes, clothes, magazines. The camp duffel bag was still full, untouched. The desk littered with wadded tissues, candy wrappers. She wouldn't dig through the trash looking for the lighter. Eliza closed the door, nostalgic for the old days, the old mess: cedar chip smell from the gerbil cage, the neon orange dust of cheese puffs over the sharp plastic building blocks. Well, she didn't miss the way those blocks used to bite into her bare feet when she trespassed.

She bathed in the dark, crawled into bed, and called Dee.

Her friend picked up on the first ring.

"What's up?"

How many hours had she and Dee logged like this in the forty-five years since that first night at camp when Eliza heard Dee crying in the bunk below and climbed down?

"Nick got kicked out."

THREE

Night skating was the best. Wind in his face, in his hair. Like the zip line at camp once he got up his nerve. "Do it. Just do it," Cole said. "Only way to kick fear's ass."

High-fived him when he did.

Screw camp. Screw Cole.

One good thing the frigging developer did was the smooth-as-glass new asphalt on the driveway for the suckers coming in to see the model house. He'd gone in it with her. Wine cellar. Home theater with stadium seating and cup holders. Fake homework station set up for little kids in the tower. Screw homework but it would be a cool place for a computer or an awesome music studio for the Theremin.

Not like the dump cottage with the slowest wi-fi on the east coast, no cable, old flat screen TV from his grandparents because the big one Nick finally convinced her to buy got busted when they moved because she was too cheap to hire real movers. At least when he cat-sat for Ben and Phil he could watch their television. Maybe they'd go away somewhere far for a long trip but not likely with his luck.

He hit the last speed bump and got great air, zooming. He was that silver owl they saw in the woods last week, a horned owl, Cole said. Horny owl, they'd cracked up. But falling asleep in his bunk he kept seeing it and now he felt like he was the owl. Big, pale, flying like a ghost, flying like one of those shape-changers in the Iroquois legends.

The good asphalt ended and he was on the street. Pushing off, bump and grind like Boomer said. A car honked by and he felt the hot exhaust and his heart did that skip. Flipped the driver the bird.

Flew down the street, inhaling the smell of curry when he cruised past the Bombay Bistro. Their samosas and chai were about the only things from here he missed when he was at camp. If he had money, he'd stop. He should have taken the sweet potato biscuits. He was starving.

No one hanging at the fountain in the Square. The bike cop must still be hassling them. Where would Boomer and the rest be? Skating at the old grocery parking lot? Crap asphalt, lumps and splits and grass growing in cracks but it beat the city skate park with its lights and fence and lame plywood runs.

The cemetery? Yeah, the cemetery over past the civic center.

He morphed into a bat now, a bat out of hell. The traffic light clicked to green as he came to the Pike. He surfed across the six lanes on two kicks, personal best. Always skated best mad and when no one could see him. Maybe anger was like doing speed. Speed would mess him up, like weed. Boomer called him goody good.

Blasted down Baltimore Road, catching good air over the speed bumps. She nixed snowboarding. *How about the ski club?* No way. All the kids in the ski club were from the IB. International Baccalaureate stood for Idiot Buttfucks, Boomer said. He snowboarded out west because his dad had a guilt complex about the divorce and Boomer was making him pay through the nose. Boomer said east coast skiing was pathetic.

Red light at Route 28. A guy got killed crossing here, drunk old geezer heading out from the liquor store. Still Nick waited for the light.

He'd been so messed up over getting canned. So what? This was better than sitting around eating granola in the woods.

He had to walk up the hill to the park around the civic center, stayed in the shadows on the driveway. Theater dark, and no lights at the mansion. No show, no party tonight. Kid from scouts had his bar mitzvah there. Which must have cost. Next life he was most definitely going to be Jewish.

At fire circle Cole always talked about his next life, karma, all that hippy dippy shit—reincarnation, the whole nine yards. Well, who knows?

She made him go to the bar mitzvah, even the synagogue part, though he and the kid weren't friends by then or even still in scouts. Nick still had the action figures, the old good ones he'd taken back when he spent the night when they were like eight. The kid had so much stuff he never noticed. Where were those figures anyway? Everything got fucked up and lost when she packed his stuff last summer while he was at camp and then put the boxes in the cesspool of a basement and the built-ins upstairs.

"You'll be in school with your old friends from scouts," she said, springing the move to the freak-a-zoid shrink museum on him, driving home from camp last year. "If you do well, you can get into the IB when you're a junior." Even though you bombed the test, she didn't say, but he knew what she was thinking. It used to be neat that feeling they could read each other's minds. They'd lock eyes and smile, a secret club. One for all and all for one, they said, if they were by themselves.

As if he even wanted to be IB. He took the test using a miniature golf pencil instead of a #2, by accident on purpose. Not that he would have been smart enough whatever pencil. Who cared? The IB kids were socio-economic snobs, Cole would say.

He grabbed up his board and ran down the hill, past the playground, through the parking lot behind the theater, up the sledding hill. Jumped the low stone wall to the graveyard. Blocking the idea of ghosts grabbing him. Like trying to forget about sharks and jellyfish while diving into a wave at the beach when they used to go with Steve and Dee and the prepped-out twins to their ginormous house.

The cops found a naked kid here. Tied up to a stone. It was on the radio, in the paper, though he didn't hear till he got to school. She always tried to disappear the news when there was bad shit. Like when the guy who'd been a camp counselor got beheaded in Iraq. He was the most non-violent person you could imagine. Super Quaker they called him. Which didn't faze him. Nothing made him mad.

He didn't like to think about that.

The pine needles were soft underfoot. Iroquois could definitely sneak up on someone here. Boomer and the others would be at the crypt choosing up teams for capture the flag. Or sardines. Last time, squeezed on top of someone in the dark, he got a hard on. Faggot, the kid whispered.

He smelled weed and burst into the clearing before anyone could jump him.

They must all be hiding.

His heart was doing the skipping thing. He'd checked it out online. Arrythmia, pretty sure. Which didn't necessarily mean he was going to have a heart attack but it wasn't good. The first time was when he had that laser tag birthday party and it was so dark and smoky and there were all the light sabers and he thought he was going to die and couldn't breathe and they had to leave. Pretty lame at your own party. He had to go to the doctor and get all hooked up to electrodes and stuff and you could die from an electric shock if they accidentally amped up. No, he wasn't telling her again.

"Boomer?"

"Shit man, a little louder why not, for the cops." Boomer peeled off the crypt wall like a shadow, holding out a joint.

Nick shook his head. No way was he going to get stoned in the graveyard. Talk about asking for trouble.

Boomer lay on the long marble thing like a bathtub with a lid. It had bones inside, or dust.

The last year he did scouts, sixth grade, a kid died in a car accident and got buried here, the one who'd won the soap box derby. Well, his dad the engineer won. After the derby, back home, Nick ripped the wheels off his lame loser car.

Don't be a bad sport, she said. You won the cake walk.

As if that mattered. He was the only one in the whole fucking pack without a father to cheat for him. When that kid died, she made him go to the funeral with the troop. All in their fascist uniforms, a parade of cars across town. The grave was somewhere near here but he wasn't sure where. Not that he wanted to find it, but he thought about the kid sometimes. She couldn't make him go back to scouts after that.

Something almost hit his head. An aerosol can landed at his feet.

"Safety orange," croaked Boomer, holding his breath for the buzz. He was standing on the marble bathtub shaking another aerosol.

Boomer blended in with the dark, all in black, but the orange spray made a neon tic-tac-toe board on the wall of the mausoleum. If they got caught they'd be in serious trouble.

Boomer won. He sprayed the next side of the tomb and won again. They covered all four walls.

He didn't want to do it but it was kind of fun once you got going. "If my family were buried here, I'd be pissed."

"Well, they're not."

Car lights! The guard driving through on the road to the nature center.

Nick stuffed the paint canister in his pocket. You had to love cargo pants. Grabbed his board and ran down through the woods. Splashed through the stream she made him clean up with the other scouts on Earth Day. Boomer was crashing behind. Didn't know diddly about orienteering or walking softly on the earth.

At the edge of the woods they watched cars go by on Route 28.

"You should come over. Dad came through with *Assassin's Creed.*" He lived near in a crap little house. Said his dad had a mansion out in the outer burbs with the trophy and the brats. Maybe it was better not to have a father than have one like that.

"Not tonight."

A break came in the traffic. Nick made it to the median strip and sprinted across into Lincoln Park, the Black neighborhood. Streetlights busted. A dog hurled and snarled against a chain link fence. Cole said not to show you were afraid. Never turn your back. Never run from a bear. Make yourself look big as possible. Shit, he'd like to be able to shrink and disappear right now.

A door opened with a blast of music. "Who's that?"

Nick ran down the center of the dark street. A car was heading straight at him! He ducked into a side street, and turned again, and again.

Where the fuck was he? He couldn't go up to one of these houses and ask.

He ran until the stitch in his side was definitely a heart attack waiting to happen.

Oh! This was the warehouse and autobody strip, where she rented the U-Haul last summer. And there was the giant brick church where the scouts brought canned food Thanksgiving. Okay. He knew where he was. Stopping to catch his breath helped his heart. He wasn't going to die. At least not this time.

Board down, he kicked off.

The sign for the pedestrian bridge across the train tracks was all lit up. The Peace Bridge, winner of the naming contest at school. The girl who thought it up stood near him in chorus. Pale but pretty. Jenn. In a way she was right, crossing over from East to West Rockville was kind of like going over the Berlin Wall or the Rio Grande. One night his mom was driving him to basketball practice in the community center over here and a cop stopped her. He was too little back then to know why. The cop thought she was shopping for crack. That would be the day, her shopping for crack.

The bridge had a cage of wire, but someone with an assault rifle could do serious damage from up here. Like the sniper when he was in fourth grade, cruising around in an old green car shooting people at gas stations, even a kid in a school parking lot. She drove him to school till they caught the man. She made him wear his seat belt and sit on the seat even though a bullet could come right in and he would have been safer hiding on the floor. Turned out the sniper had a kid with him locked in the trunk who did some of the shooting. He was in jail now too, for life. The guy wasn't his father.

The bridge steps had no backs, like the cellar stairs at his grand-parents' house—their old house now. The kind of stairs you could slip through. Don't believe everything you think, Ma told him. But look at the people who got their feet trapped by shoelaces on Metro and had to have their legs amputated. Things happen.

He made it across. Down the stairs—easier.

Solid ground. West Rockville. Right by the futon store and the pho shop, closed now. Boomer said he went all the way with the Vietnamese girl who worked there, in the stairwell at school between classes. He said everything was tiny and tight. Maybe he did, maybe not.

A police car pulled into the parking lot! Nick dodged into the gas station and ran. His heart was about to explode. He might be stroking out.

Ran till he got to the post office. Someone was smoking on the loading dock. People worked all night there. Sort of good, though he wouldn't want anyone to see him.

He jumped on his board and zoomed to the parking lot by the pool and on into the woods and the skate park. He almost crashed into a busted grocery cart left on the foot bridge.

Back out onto West Montgomery Avenue. Home stretch. The funeral home was all lit up by the spotlight on the lawn. Lights were on in the building in back too, where they drained the blood out and shot the bodies full of preservative. Probably embalming someone right now.

He wouldn't think about it.

Almost to the Lodge.

He had to stop to catch his breath beneath the sign for the con-dos. *Chestnut Acres.*

Nick pulled the aerosol out of his pocket. He breathed better with every shot of spray. The can rattled empty. He threw it deep into the bushes and walked up the drive.

She'd hear him if he rode the board unless she'd been hitting the wine.

No lights. No lights in the new house behind them where the Perfects had moved in with baby Perfect. Across the street one of the psychos was smoking on the porch like always.

She'd locked the front door and the kitchen door and the porch door. Maybe she was listening to him when he said it was danger-ous to leave it open with those crazies across the way in the halfway house or maybe she just didn't want him coming home.

The hide-a-key was in its box.

He was home. He didn't bother to sneak. Made a racket. Chugged milk in the kitchen. Went to the front room she called his studio. More like his walk-in closet with the recycled desk from her clinic, the crap TV, the Theremin stand.

Got the Theremin out of the gig bag and plugged it in. Screw using the earphones.

Shit, just a week without practice and he was losing the hang of it. Right hand for pitch, left for volume. Careful. Better.

Nothing like the magic feeling when his hands made it sing and the sound just flowed through him like current. Really did flow since his body was the connection and his hands the grounded plates. He could have gone for one of the cheap ready-mades with a volume knob. No way. This was real. He still couldn't believe it was his, something he'd wanted ever since he played *Kill All the Humans* and heard the spacey soundtrack.

Shit! How long had she been standing there?

He dropped his hands and the Theremin stopped singing.

"Where have you been? I was scared."

"Out of your way, so I don't mess up your summer."

"We can wait till we're both rested but tomorrow we have to talk."

"Okay. Okay." He started upstairs.

"Hungry? Noodles and cheese?"

Caught him off base, her not reaming him out. And he was starving, practically drooling just thinking about it. He wanted to be grating cheese while she whisked sauce.

It was a trick to make him talk. She never got tired of talking. Talking things over. Her theme song. Do you want to talk about it? You should talk to someone. Like talk ever changed anything.

"Please, let's talk, have something to eat."

"You know what I want to talk about? How my loser father whoever he was gave me his stupid genes and I'm doing stupid shit. That's what I want to talk about."

She looked awful. Like that one and only time when he'd done something stupid (what he couldn't even remember) and she slapped him. Not hard but shocker-roo. She looked bad now, and he was the one slapping her down. He could say he changed his mind. They could cook, play the old midnight kitchen game, radio on, dancing around. But there wasn't room to dance in the kitchen here.

"He wasn't stupid," she said.

"Checked out his IQ on the registry?"

He ran upstairs. The cat came and lay on his stomach, purring. He couldn't sleep. He could go over to the computer, put on his headphones, get back to *Doom*, see what the online people had done while he was gone.

But he was too tired to move.

The bunk was on the first night of the Appalachian trail hike. Cole always let him light the campfire. Who was helping Cole tonight?

The school directory was under his bed. He'd looked Jenn up so often it would open to the right page. If he called, she might answer. He'd never actually called. It would be nice to hear her voice. They might have caller ID. He'd hit *67.

Lame. Perverted.

He turned over and reached under the pillow, really careful. The razor blade was there in its paper sleeve. And the lighter, and the box of matches.

Knowing the stuff was there was good enough for now.

He heard her come upstairs. Stand by his door.

He pictured holding a wooden match. Letting it burn all the way down to his fingertips.

Later, much later, he went downstairs. Went into her study. Took the credit card from her purse. Shrink lady on the wall watched while he dialed and ordered the game. He was supposed to get *Ghost Shooter* for passing Spanish and then she did her typical bait and switch and said a D wasn't passing.

He started upstairs.

46

She was standing there, like some kind of ghost herself in that white nightgown. "I can't sleep either. I'll come down. It would help to talk.

"No!"

He slammed his door. Lay in bed staring at the ceiling. Like talking changed anything. What he wanted was a re-do. Like the backwards party the girl had back in third grade. Her dad videoing everything at the party and then running the tape backwards so the end happened first. Goodbyes before cake before presents.

The girl disappeared almost right after. Turned out her dad was FBI or something and had known some top-secret important thing before 9/11 that could have saved everyone and blew it and didn't tell. They had to go and get new identities, the works.

He wouldn't mind a new identity. A new family. Somewhere else.

But not a father like that girl had.

He studied the weird thing in the ceiling. It looked like a boob. One in every room. She said it had been a bell system to connect the house to the hospital when shrink lady lived here. Maybe. Maybe it was some surveillance device from back in the Cold War.

He took the razor out from under the pillow. He slipped the blade out. Held it on the pale skin with the map of blue veins right under his wrist. If you cut vertically you bleed out. You have to slice on the horizontal.

One cut and the sting and the beads of red. The tiny sound, he could swear he could hear it like air from a balloon as the sting and the pain came out.

He blew a breath out the way Cole said, a mind trick to deal with pain.

Though he didn't mean this. Imagined how Cole would look at him and the scar at the edge of his mouth disappearing the way it did when he frowned.

47

One more slice. Just one more and he could sleep.

FOUR

She slept with one ear open, as she had since he was a newborn. Perhaps it was too intense, the tie between them, the invisible tug. Dee had cut the umbilical cord after Nick was born, the first in the long chain of necessary separations. But she couldn't imagine living without the connection. Though it happened all the time, as she knew from her clients—estrangement, worse. Sometimes sessions seemed like lessons her clients were teaching her in how to live if the worst happens, sometimes previews of coming attractions. Often her clients' strength and persistence awed her, helped her manage her own easier life.

It had helped, talking to Dee. Eliza would track down a good therapist. Jeff, with all his cronies, he would have gotten Nick bumped to the top of the list, right in for a consult. She rarely thought about him. And when she did? Over the past fifteen years she'd been glad he wasn't around, complicating things.

But now? His influence might have been handy. Well, that ship had sailed. And she'd given it a push.

Nick's feet thumped up the stairs and into the bathroom, then a geyser of peeing.

Sounds only a mother could love. Eliza nestled into her pillow. He was home. He was safe. They were both too tired to talk tonight. Tomorrow would be better.

Relief made her bones heavy as sleep paralysis crept over her. She lingered on the border between waking and sleeping, present and past. Succumbed and slipped into the forbidden zone.

1992

The eggnog was homemade, real cream and bourbon. She'd never been in Rose Hill before, but the director had invited all the staff and the social work interns, too. The wood paneled room glowed with candles, firelight, the sparkle of silver and crystal. Earlier there had been carols around the grand piano, with her supervisor Jeff Wilson at the keyboard, a Santa hat on his blond curls. He'd encouraged all the interns to come at their last group supervision before vacation. *The Bullards really know how to throw a party,* he'd said, *consider it your last assignment of the semester.*

After he'd left the interns began to gossip. *My friend was here last year. She says Jeff's the one who really knows how to party.* Someone else chimed in, *Did you hear he's left his wife?* The woman who'd spoken first laughed, a snarky laugh. *Or she's left him. My friend said that it goes on all the time.*

There was often gossip about teachers. It made Eliza, daughter of two teachers, uncomfortable. Jeff was such a good teacher, and like a magician with the kids in the group she co-facilitated with him. She knew from experience that sometimes—well, students got the wrong idea, made things up, had these crushes. Her parents were a tight couple but occasionally she and her mother had even had to help her father fend off a star-struck student's late-night phone calls.

And she had to admit tonight, playing the piano, laughing, Jeff was awfully attractive. *Stop it, Eliza!* Must be the camouflage booze in the eggnog catching up with her. Voices sounded too loud; she had a headache coming on. Eliza made her way to the samovar of coffee on the long buffet and burnt her tongue gulping the bitter antidote.

Photographs lined the wall on the broad stairwell to the upstairs bedroom where the coats were. That serious little boy in shorts and suspenders—he must be the director. There was a picture of the main Lodge building rising out of deep snow like a Christmas card. The smiling woman with a cow beside the barn? She might be the director's mother, presiding downstairs tonight in a deep armchair.

A mountain of coats covered the bed. Eliza dug until she found Dee's borrowed curly lamb, recognizing the fleece by touch. She struggled, the lining had a rip and the sleeve tangled.

"Let me help." Jeff held the coat. Her arms slipped in. Eliza hesitated to turn around. She could smell booze. She wasn't the only one who'd had too much. *Jeff knows how to party.*

He was just her height. She looked straight into his eyes, very dark brown with a darker line around the iris.

"You clean up nice, Lizzie," he said, and kissed her. Just as she'd feared. No, as she'd hoped. Like he said in class, behind the fear is the hope.

Just a holiday kiss, just a friendly boozy kiss, but it lasted a moment too long. Supervising doctors don't kiss social work students. A good student wouldn't have kissed back.

Eliza heard footsteps or that kiss might have lasted longer. She pulled away, started toward the door, almost bumping into Roberta.

The head nurse had been on the wards and on the staff longer than anyone. Jeff told the students, *when in doubt, ask Roberta. She knows everything.*

"Can I help you find your coat?" Jeff asked Roberta.

"That would be very sweet of you."

"Good night, happy holidays!" Eliza said, hurrying out of the room.

It was snowing, deep enough already to sift inside her pumps. She followed the path from Rose Hill past the barn back to campus.

Only a few lights in the dorm, most of the kids in Jeff's adolescent unit had gone home for the holiday. *We're strengthening them for real life, not keeping them from it,* he'd said. *And we need a break, too. Enjoy yourselves.*

She pushed the thought of him away. What was worse? The kiss, that foolish, long, unsettling kiss or Roberta catching them?

The windows in Main were dark tonight. No one catching up on notes and process recordings. And there were no lights in the little house people still called Frieda's Cottage where some of the senior doctors had offices.

Eliza trudged through the snow onto the street. Her feet were wet, the shoes would be ruined. She'd have to hurry or miss the last train. The subway system here kept such ridiculous hours.

She managed to reach the Metro station before midnight but it was dark and locked. *Closed due to Ice,* said the sign posted by the turnstiles. No one in Chicago would believe this.

No cabs, no buses. The snowflakes stung as she walked back through town to the Lodge.

Main loomed up like a dark mirage. She found her key, walked through the echoing lobby and up the stairs.

Her third-floor office was tiny, but luxury compared to the bullpen at her first-year student placement in the county social services department. She moved the waste basket, the desk chair, and made room to stretch out. Eliza shrugged off the heavy coat and laid it fleece down on the floor. She pulled her baggy work sweater over the velvet party dress she'd borrowed from Dee, wishing to be home in her apartment, wishing for slippers, wishing for her mother's sleep potion of hot milk with vanilla.

Sitting on her desk she gazed out the window. Snow sifted down, covering all the edges. If only it had blizzarded before the party and she hadn't come. If only snow could make tonight's mistake disappear.

As she walked down the hall to the bathroom, Jeff came up the stairs.

"Eliza! What are you doing here?"

"Metro's closed. What—what about you?"

"I've been staying in my office. Domestic difficulties, shall we say."

So it was true. But no one had mentioned he was staying here.

"Apologies, about what happened back there. Sloppy drunk. The boss's eggnog packs a punch."

"It's okay." It wasn't okay—he'd just recommended her for a staff job here. And it really wasn't okay that she wanted to kiss him again. "But—Roberta."

"Don't fret. She sees all, knows all, tells nothing. Talk about confidentiality, she's the high priestess of secrets. Been a lot of water under the dam here, Eliza. Our little moment? Safe with her."

That smarted. He dismissed it so lightly. It was no big deal to him, routine. What they said must be true. He was a party-boy, a flirt.

"I was just about to have a nightcap." He paused by his office door. "Join me?"

She glimpsed a bottle on the low table in front of his shabby black leather sofa.

"Why not?" she said. Knowing exactly why not.

He poured bourbon into glass tumblers, lit a fire in the fire-place, and sat on the floor. The room felt smaller by firelight, not at all like the same room where he held the student supervision sessions.

"I didn't know the fireplaces worked," she said.

"We not supposed to use them. Chimney cleaning's not in the budget. But, hey, Lizzie, I always say rules are made to be broken."

No one had ever called her Lizzie except her ex-husband. Snowflakes hissed against the windows; smoke tickled her throat.

She couldn't keep her eyes off Jeff's face. His mouth, to be exact. Such a soft, generous mouth. *Stop it!*

"I'm sorry about you and your wife."

"Breaking up is sort of a chronic disease with us. Camping out here, from time to time, is our version of me sleeping on the couch. Well, I do sleep on my couch here." He poured himself another drink, held the bottle up toward her.

She'd had enough already, way too much, but Eliza let him fill her glass.

His wife Xandy attended the welcome picnic. Taller than he was, glamorous. People said before med school she'd been a dancer. Now she was head of a lab at the National Institute of Mental Health.

Jeff walked to the window, spoke with his back to her. "She says I've put the work with the kids first. Shortchanged us. Not that we ever wanted kids of our own. She's at her lab all the time. Classic case of the pot calling the kettle black."

But the glib tone was gone. Poor man, likely the partying, flirting, was covering up pain. There was something poignant about a strong person showing his vulnerability.

She held her last sip of bourbon, listening to him, their usual roles switched. He listened so intently to the kids in the group. *Listen,* he'd told her and the other social work students. *Really listen. Sometimes it's all we have to offer, and it's always the most important. Always. Read Frieda Fromm-Reichmann. She got it right.*

He put on another log and stirred the fire with iron tongs. "We fight, we make up. We fight, we make up. It's a drag."

Long silence.

She broke it, even though he'd taught them to respect silence, not try too hard to fill it. "What about—counseling?"

He laughed. "Found someone in Philly, too small a world here. Got her to go, only once. Doesn't believe therapy helps. Doesn't believe in what I do. She's the real deal, hot shot research scientist."

Silence again.

"Ever been married, Lizzie?"

She should tell him to stop calling her that.

He turned to face her with his listening face on, the kind eyes, the slight angle of the head. She'd seen it work with the kids. How could you refuse that invitation?

Remember, he's drunk and so are you. Remember what they say about him. Remember, who he is and who you are. A question is just an invitation. You don't have to answer.

"Long time ago. Right after college."

"Not that long," he chuckled. "What are you—thirty?"

"Almost forty." People always said she looked younger. She used to hate it. Even though she knew he was flattering her, she was pleased. And, god help her, she kept looking at that mouth.

"So, older and wiser, been around the block. No wonder you're so smart and good with the kids. Age and life experience count in our field."

Ridiculous how thrilled she felt at the praise. And worse than ridiculous, how she kept looking at those soft lips and eyes—such striking eyes, dark brown with a darker rim around the iris. And worse than ridiculous, the sensation she was feeling was moving south. *He's drunk and so are you.*

"Tell me about you and your husband, Lizzie."

"Taught at a boarding school. Mr. and Mrs. Chips. Practicing for our own kids."

"So how many kids do you have?"

"None. He fell in love. We split up."

Enough! More than enough. She wouldn't say another thing. Talk about sloppy drunk! At least she'd held back from telling him

55

about the pelvic infection from the IUD blowing out her tubes. Ironic, it was called "The Shield," and that she'd chosen it out of caution during her lonely post-divorce season of rebound. Instead of protecting her, the shield almost killed her.

"Poor Lizzie. How could anyone leave you? Then what?"

"I changed schools. Went into therapy. Burned out on teaching, decided to go to social work school. Like my therapist. How trite is that?"

"Why not med school?"

Always that superior thing psychiatrists did. "Way too late for med school. Too old and too liberal artsy."

"Well, you've got the makings of a great therapist with your experience, your smarts, your instincts. This is good work—but don't let it be your whole life."

The seductive thing was the way he listened and he praised. The kids in the therapy group said talking to him was like taking truth serum. She'd better ask the questions instead of answering. "You and your wife didn't want kids?"

"We're really not parent material. I hate to think what we'd put a kid through. She says I'm a kid, which is why I understand them so well. And she's not crazy about people, especially not kids. That's why she's so good at research. After med school she said her goal was never to touch another patient."

How could you be married to him and not want to touch him? She wanted him to be quiet. She wanted to put her fingers on that mouth and shut him up. She wanted to kiss him.

She looked down at the floor, studied the woven rug's geometric pattern.

"Navajo rug, from our indentured servitude on the reservation. Med school payback. Top off your glass?"

"I've had enough. Time for bed." She felt a flush of embarrassment as she said the word "bed." Just like a teenager with a crush on her teacher.

He stepped toward her. She sat as though waiting.

Get up! Get out of here!

He came closer, leaned over—just to lift the cushion beside her. "Take these cushions, you'll be more comfortable."

He walked her down the hall, arranged the cushions on the floor of her office.

"There you go, Lizzie, my dear. Unless you're the princess and the pea, you'll sleep okay." He rocked back on his haunches, looking up at her with those dark eyes.

Fish on a line, she felt the pull, felt the manipulation enough to make her mad. Just enough to keep her from being even stupider.

"Thanks," she said, stepping away as he stood.

"Sleep tight," he said, and left.

That was that.

A good thing, too. They'd had a little flirt, had a little stupid, risky fun, and talked through the danger, the way you swim through a riptide, relaxing into it.

Despite the cushions, she didn't sleep well. The light changed from black to gray, the gauze of a snow morning.

He knocked, shaved, smiling, but dark circles under his eyes. "Radio says Metro's running. Walk you to the diner, for breakfast."

The snow was almost untouched, except for tracery of rabbit tracks. The street had just been plowed but there was no traffic; they walked down the center. It was as though the two of them were all that remained in a world of snow.

The diner was open. A waitress with short gray hair served them: weak coffee, limp white toast with grape jelly, eggs sunny side up.

"This place is old school," Jeff said.

"Isn't that what they say about the Lodge?"

"No," he said, fierce. "Sometimes you have to slow down to speed up. Sometimes it's radical, to be old-fashioned. I was here during that lawsuit. No guarantees in medicine, especially not this game."

He was lecturing her. The intimacy of last night was gone, and a good thing, too. Still, she resented his tone. "Does the Lodge keep up better now, with psycho-pharm?"

"We do. We always have. Hey, Eliza, we're on break."

She let him pick up the check. After all, it was a very cheap diner, and he was the doctor.

Home in her apartment, Eliza fought the urge to climb into bed and hibernate. She wanted the pillows over her head, comforter up to her chin. She needed to pack, wrap presents, get to the train station. Her mother's early Christmas gift had been the roomette. Eliza loved trains. She would sleep all the way to Chicago, make up some of the semester's sleep deficit. Much better than a crowded airport, cramped flight.

Union Station swarmed with storm-diverted holiday air travelers. Model trains circled a huge tree in the center of the vaulted lobby. Eliza bought a mystery in the bookstore. She'd ask the conductor to make up her berth early and read. Vacation had begun.

The train left late; pulled out of the station in the early winter dusk and a cloud of more snow. Eliza leaned against the cool window. The first stop was Rockville. Just this morning, she'd been boarding Metro across the tracks. Eliza turned on her reading light and opened the book. She was hungry, soon it would be dinner time.

The train left Harpers Ferry as she entered the dining car. The waiter showed her to an empty table. Good, she'd had some nice conversations with strangers, enjoyed Amtrak's system of shared tables, but tonight she'd brought her book. Eliza was tired, not in the mood for chatting.

She ordered the steak, and wine.

"Wine's not included with the sleeper," the waiter warned her, kindly.

"That's okay." After all, the meal was complimentary with her roomette.

Eliza sipped and read.

"Here you go sir," said the conductor.

"Okay if I join you?" Jeff asked.

She felt the blush rising.

"You all acquainted?" the waiter asked.

"A bit," said Jeff, sliding into the banquette. "Red wine, please."

The waiter handed Jeff the menu. "Here you go, sir. Be back for your order."

"What a coincidence," Eliza said, willing the blush to fade.

"There are no coincidences," Jeff grinned, putting on a fake German accent. "Guess we're fated to have a little more time to chat."

"Looks that way," she agreed. It might be good, to talk casually, away from the Lodge. Put what happened the night before to bed. Talk about Freudian slips. She felt the blush rising again.

His eyes glowed, deep brown, different from last night—that dark line around the iris had disappeared. Maybe it was just the lighting.

The train lurched. His foot touched hers briefly. "Sorry." He gave a fake frown, eyes mischievous behind the menu.

What a terrible flirt. She'd have to be careful.

In the bustling public space of the dining car, shoptalk was off limits. They spoke of childhood, of family, almost as though they'd just met, equals, with the pleasant superficial intimacy of strangers sharing a table, a meal in transit, suspended in time and place.

He was on his way to Pittsburgh to see his father for the holidays. "I always drive," he said. "But the snow." His mother had died a couple of years earlier. He and his father would go to the midnight Mass on Christmas Eve. He'd been an altar boy. His mother had thought he might be a priest. "Maybe," he laughed. "Except for the celibacy. Shrink next best thing. One confessional to another."

"Are you still religious?"

"Lapsed. Very lapsed. But I pray for my patients, sometimes. And when things are really tough with me? I find myself on my knees. How about you?"

Eliza explained growing up a professor's kid in the Chicago suburbs, attending major holiday services at the non-denominational chapel on campus, the habit of praying but not being sure to who.

He invited her to the lounge car for a brandy. The miles slipped by. The chance meeting eased the shame of the night before. It detonated the charge, normalized everything. Maybe flirting a bit, but just for fun. Nothing on the edge of a huge mistake like last night.

Eliza finished her drink. "That's it for me."

"Enjoy your holiday," he said. "I'll be getting off in a couple of hours, think I'll stay here a bit longer."

The sleeper coach was at the end of the train. She went from one carriage to the next through the heavy sliding doors. The air on the connecting platforms was cold and smelled of diesel.

The porter had flipped the seats to bunk position. The reading light shone on an inviting white pillow. The roomette smelled faintly of soap and chemicals from the ingenious washstand commode. Eliza brushed her teeth, put on her pajamas, settled into her berth to read, and discovered she'd left her book behind.

"Eliza?" Jeff called softly down the corridor.

She opened her door. He held out her book, grinning. "Another coincidence?" The fake accent again.

The train jerked and he stumbled into the roomette, into her arms. For just a moment she hesitated before reaching around him to slide the door shut.

Kissing on the narrow, swaying berth Eliza remembered making out with her first boyfriend, rocking in the rope hammock in the secret dark of the backyard. But she and Jeff kissed deeper and slower than teenagers could. Pressed closer and closer together, knowing exactly their destination.

She hadn't done this in a very long time. But the body remembers.

Afterward, she whispered, "I'll have to leave the Lodge."

"What are you talking about?"

"We can't work together after this."

"Oh, Lizzie. Forest rangers set fires, controlled burns, to reduce the chance of fire. Consider this our controlled burn," he said. "Things like this happen, all the time."

"Not to me," she said.

"Well, now it has. What happens on the train, stays on the train. Can be our secret. As for continuing as my student? I promise I can forget this."

"I can't," she said, pulling away as far as she could in the cramped space. She'd been stupid. Incredibly stupid. The placement at the Lodge, the possible job offer—it was as though she'd been given a Ming vase and intentionally dropped it.

"Okay, okay. If you prefer, I can have you transferred to the adult service. There'll be a job opening there, too. You'll be even more valuable to the Lodge, more marketable outside, with some adult experience." And he chuckled, a deep chuckle. How could he think this was funny? "Hanging out so much with

61

adolescents—maybe it rubs off. Maybe you'd like to grow up and join the adult department."

"It's not funny. And I'd have to terminate with the patients on the adolescent unit."

"No therapist is indispensable, my dear. We'll work that through, it'll be a learning experience, for you and the kids. Besides our group you only have two individual cases, right?"

He was cavalier, as though a therapist was just any interchangeable object. How sad and guilty she felt at interrupting the therapies. She was sorry for the kids, and yes, sorry for herself.

"Continue the individual patients, with your new supervisor. I'll get a new co-facilitator for the group. Attachment and separation, it's the name of the game."

It was pat, this neat solution he proposed, even giving it a positive spin. Nothing like a little life experience, he'd said earlier. He'd done this before. What a cliché she was. A crush on your charming, sexy supervisor. A drink, a kiss, a tumble—a mess for your career.

She pulled her pajama jacket closed and started to button it.

"Shutting the barn door after the cows are gone, Lizzie?"

"I want a transfer."

"As you wish," he said. "Just so you know, you're one of the most brilliant students I've ever had." Did he intend the double meaning?

"Get out. This shouldn't have happened. It's not going to happen again."

"Too bad." He dressed and left the roomette.

Eliza lay in the bunk. Yes, Jeff was great with the kids. And pretty good with interns, too. She'd acted like a kid, a stupid kid.

The train ground to a stop. The conductor walked through the corridor, softly announcing Pittsburgh. She raised the blind. In the bilious yellow platform light Jeff walked away in his dark duffle coat, head down as though against a wind. He looked young. Sort of like an over-grown teenager.

She pressed her face against the burning cold window.

The semester and the new adult placement began. She couldn't drop his seminar, but sat at the far side of the circle across from Jeff. His jokes didn't strike her as funny anymore, and his jeans and cowboy boots looked affected.

Her new supervisor, a woman psychiatrist, was aloof, but a good teacher. Eliza sometimes missed the excitement, the unguarded drama of the kids, but there was a rich depth about doing therapy with adults and the change suited her. Her supervisor said Eliza's work was promising and recommended her for the adult staff position.

February flu ripped through the staff and patients. Eliza couldn't get out of bed for ten days. Dee insisted on taking her home, kept her quarantined from the twins, up in what had been an attic maid's room in the big old four-square the couple had bought.

She surrendered, enjoying being marooned, sleeping, and waking. Dee brought trays with applesauce, toast, and ginger ale. They visited while the twins napped. *I've begun writing book reviews,* she told Eliza. *Keeping my hand in. I want to go back, to the paper.* Her oval face had grown softer and fuller since the babies; the hazel eyes sparkled and even pale with fatigue, she was lovely.

Recovered, Eliza went home to her apartment. Her first day back at work a patient brought cookies she'd made, so proud Eliza couldn't refuse. Jeff had talked about accepting gifts from patients. *Sometimes it's necessary.* She hoped her new supervisor would agree.

Roberta found her in the bathroom, kneeling on the cold tile, throwing up in the toilet.

"Come to my office," the nurse said.

Lying on the cot felt like falling ill as a child at school. Here she was, in the nurse's office. Roberta covered her with a cotton blanket, rested a cool hand on her forehead.

"When did your flu begin?"

"About three weeks ago." A wave of nausea hit. Roberta positioned a wastebasket just in time.

"I'm so sorry," Eliza said.

"What's a little vomit? I started in Vietnam."

Eliza closed her eyes.

"When was your last period?"

"Don't have a regular cycle." Her mother had taught her to mark first and last days on her calendar. Eliza had given up keeping track with her periods so intermittent and irrelevant.

"No fever. Any chance you're pregnant?"

"No."

Roberta nodded, her face smooth and inscrutable. *Sees all, knows all, tells nothing.* "Well, head on home now. Get some rest. Maybe you came back too early. Or maybe, it's something else."

Eliza stopped at the drug store as she walked to the apartment from the subway. Did the test.

Sat very still, stunned.

Positive. Pregnant.

She called Dee. "May I come over?"

"Sure. Bring your toothbrush and stay. Steve's working late. The kids will be asleep soon."

The nursery in the big front bedroom smelled of lotion and powder and the cloying rotten fruit scent of dirty diapers. A menagerie of stuffed animals covered the floor.

"Peaceable kingdom," Eliza whispered, picking up a lamb.

"Peaceable mess. And this potty training! Still wearing diapers at night, I'm a failure. Let's have a glass of wine while the going's good." She led the way to the kitchen.

"Herb tea for me."

"Still not feeling well?" Dee said, a motherly worry-crease between her eyebrows.

"I'm pregnant." The room buzzed with a thrum of appliances, refrigerator, static from the baby monitor.

"But—that doctor said…" She'd been bedside, the night Eliza almost died from the pelvic infection. Dee had held Eliza's hand hard when the blunt young doctor said she was lucky not to have died. *You can always adopt. New fertility techniques coming along all the time. You just won't be able to get pregnant the old-fashioned way,* he said.

"He was wrong."

"But—you didn't tell me you were seeing anyone."

Eliza shook her head, looked away from Dee's sparkling eyes, traced a stain on the wooden table. "I'm not."

Dee's voice sharpened. "It's that supervisor. Why you switched placements. Stopped talking about him."

Eliza nodded.

"Isn't he married?"

"Separated."

"Have you told him?" Her gaze was grave.

"No."

"What—what do you want to do?"

"Have the baby." She started to cry.

"You have to tell him."

"No!" She hadn't meant to shout. "It was just one night. And he told me, flat out told me, he's not parent material. That he and his wife are always separating and getting back together. Don't want kids. He's a jerk, Dee. I was stupid."

"The baby's his, too. He'll figure it out."

"I'll tell him—tell him I did fertility treatments."

Dee shook her head. "He'll never believe you. What if he and his wife deep down want to have kids and that's why they keep splitting up? What if he fights you for the baby? Maybe you should see a lawyer."

"He doesn't want kids. And if people know about me and Jeff—I won't get the job."

"So? You'd leave, get a job somewhere else."

"There's nowhere like the Lodge."

"Get used to compromising." Her voice was soft, but stern.

Steve came in, his square-jawed face red from the cold. He kissed Dee, and as he did, one of the twins started crying through the monitor.

"Right on cue," he laughed. "Carry on, I'll check in on him."

"We're supposed to let them cry. Leave the bedroom door closed and let them play when they wake up. But we just can't be consistent, and he hasn't seen them all day," Dee said after he left the room.

His voice murmured from upstairs, broadcast through the monitor.

"That's not a two-way intercom thing is it? Like your parents had?"

"No." Dee laughed. "Remember how scared you were, when my father told us to be quiet and go to sleep? You thought it was the voice of God through the walls!"

"If I tell Jeff and he changes his mind? We'd have to figure out custody. I don't want her to be my baby's step-mother!"

"But you're going to need him. Financially, for one thing. And kids need dads."

Steve was reading, a calm rumble came through the monitor.

"Can you turn that off?" Eliza asked.

"He can't hear us."

"Please." It hurt, listening to Steve's kind voice.

Dee unplugged the monitor.

"If he fought me—he'd get the baby. They're doctors, secure."

"Oh, for heaven's sake, Eliza. No one takes a baby away from its mother."

"Yes, they do. They can."

Dee came around the table, put her arms around Eliza, rocked her. "Tell him, please. You just can't keep something this big a secret."

"I'm not big yet!" Eliza tried to laugh, but she was crying.

"I'll make you an appointment with my OB. About the custody stuff, I'll ask Steve to find someone to help you. He doesn't do family law but he knows people."

"Don't tell him! Don't tell anyone!"

She obsessed over telling Jeff. What if she did, what if she didn't. She almost called him several times. Maybe Dee was right. Maybe it would be best to get it out in the open. She wouldn't have to lie, to him, to the child, to anyone. Get it out now, so it didn't cause trouble later. Except—it would always be causing trouble. She thought of Athena, wasn't it Athena? Springing from Zeus's head. Parthenogenesis. How convenient.

Late one afternoon she encountered Jeff on the muddy path between the art barn and the main campus. There was no one else around. If she was ever going to do it, this was the opportunity.

"Eliza," he said, very serious. "There's something I need to tell you."

She wasn't going to get the job.

Eliza swallowed, bracing herself. Dee was right. There would be other jobs.

"Xandy and I, we're moving back to Boston this summer. Top secret for now. She's been offered a position at Tufts. I'm interviewing, with McLean. Fresh start."

Good, they were back together, and they were leaving.

He sounded so eager to be on his way.

She wanted him to go, wanted him already gone. Once he disappeared, things would be simpler.

But there was still the whole semester to get through. And she would show before long. "I have some news too."

"Don't tell me. Someone's taking you away from us. I told them to hurry up, make the offer. Before you got a better one."

"I'm going to have a baby."

He looked stunned.

"Mine," he said. His dark eyes burned.

So proprietary, the way he said it. *Mine.* Clinched keeping her secret. "No—no. I've been seeing a fertility specialist, trying to have a child before it's too late. I got lucky."

She looked into the dark eyes, didn't look away. He'd taught the students that if the patient looks away, she's hiding something, pain or a lie, or both. He'd had the students play a game, two truths and a lie, practicing holding eye contact.

"They say if you want something badly enough. When is your baby due?" His face was taut, the tone wary.

"End of October," she said, adding a month. He'd be long gone anyway.

"Amazing—well. This is just incredible." He was looking away now, not meeting her gaze. What he'd taught them not to do. He was lying. He didn't believe her. But he wasn't challenging her.

He'd jumped at the out. When he'd said *mine* it wasn't because he wanted the baby. He was scared. Just as he'd told her that night, he wasn't parent material.

She would work twice as hard. Make up to her baby for the absence of a father. Eliza's own mother had said, consoling her after the divorce, "A husband has to be pretty good to be better than none." Well, surely the same went for fathers. Jeff wasn't good enough to be her baby's father.

"He's copping out," Dee said when she called. "And you're letting him. This is wrong. This is a mistake, Eliza."

"It's the way I have to do it."

Silence.

"Are you still there, Dee? Don't hang up."

"You're crazy," said Dee. "And me too, but I'm in."

At ten weeks she spotted briefly and was terrified. The bleeding stopped, the offer for the job came through, and she signed the contract in March.

The same week, Jeff announced to the students he'd taken a position at McLean and would be leaving in June.

The Lodge job offer finalized, Eliza finally told her parents about the baby over the phone. Grateful for the shield of distance and invisibility to protect the lie. *I didn't want to tell you I was trying this, until I knew it worked. You're going to be grandparents.*

She did not tell anyone at the Lodge except Roberta. *You knew before I did. I'd been told it was impossible, I'd been trying fertility treatments. Such a long shot!* The nurse gave an enigmatic smile. *Congratulations.*

Eliza talked to the baby when they were alone. Though she never felt alone now that it was the two of them. She explained how wonderful the world would be, and how much more wonderful her own world already was, knowing the baby would soon be here. She felt the first flicker of movement one afternoon as she sat in session with a patient. She willed herself to listen to the woman while her swimming child sent her coded messages.

Even in Dee's fashionable borrowed maternity wardrobe of loose blouses and elastic waistbands, she began to show. She told her supervisor, who'd had been through it herself. But she didn't tell anyone else, colleagues or patients, unless asked. Except in seminar, she avoided Jeff—or he avoided her.

She graduated like a whale in the black gown, her parents baffled and worried, applauding in the audience.

She went to the goodbye party for Jeff in June, wearing Dee's best maternity party dress. Xandy was there, elegant in tailored slacks, and Eliza felt fat and dowdy and wouldn't have changed places for anything in the world.

She took her licensing exam. Began her job.

Dee went to Lamaze classes as her coach. Told her the teacher was lying when she called it discomfort. "It's pain. But I'll be there."

Her water broke on September 22nd.

Dee met her at the hospital.

And Dee was right. It wasn't discomfort. It was pain—white hot blinding pain. She was splitting into pieces with every wave.

Pain was terror when the doctor called in a neo-natal specialist, saying something about meconium. And then she had to push, couldn't hold back.

The baby was out. The room was silent.

A cry, at last. "The cord was around his neck, but he's fine, he's fine, you have a fine baby boy," said the nurse.

***

2009

Even over the whir of the coffee grinder, even once the fragrant promise of coffee was in the air, she couldn't shake the memory of that endless moment before he cried. The first time she knew what it was like, the melded love and terror. *Grief and worry are the price you pay for love*, her mother said. *Once you have a child you are a hostage to fortune.*

And once you have a child, you are on a new, shared journey. She'd walked with Nick warm and safe in the front-pack, walked and talked to him. Nothing had prepared her for the intensity of the bond, joy as strong as the fear. And now that Nick was a teen? The journey was getting pretty rugged.

Eliza sat on the steps with her coffee. The architect working on the condos at the Lodge jogged by on his morning run. Carter had done the work on Frieda's Cottage pro bono for the historic society. Eliza had talked to him a few times; she looked forward to seeing him every day. Tall, a runner's physique, crewcut. Perhaps he'd been in the military.

Beyond the Lodge, on the far edge of the property, the elderly woman with the wild gray hair was wandering between the trees, pausing to touch each trunk, like a child touching base in some private game. Another discarded Lodge lifer, she always wore a long black raincoat. Nick called her the witch lady, although Eliza told him not to.

Ben trotted past, awkward in flip flops. "Ruth says someone vandalized the sign last night!"

Last night. Last night. When? Where had Nick been last night?

Eliza followed Ben, reaching the defaced sign just as Ruth pulled up in her red Mini. Carter was already there.

Fuck Nut Acres scrawled in orange spray.

"I told Ed not to let the security guard go," Ruth said.

"Me too," said Carter, running a hand through his hair as though his head hurt. "He just made a deal with the city. Police will use the Lodge to train patrol dogs—give us a detail."

"When?" Ruth snapped. "Too little too late. He should see this."

"I texted him a picture," said Ben, putting a consoling arm around her shoulders.

The new neighbor, Mike, arrived pushing the baby in a huge stroller with one hand, towing their retriever on a leash. "Wow, is there like—bad feeling?"

Nick's witch lady drifted closer to them. The dog growled at her and she walked away.

Mike struggled to pull the dog back; the baby wailed. "All these sketchy people—those men across the street, her, it's freaking my wife out."

"Are you and your wife coming to the party this afternoon?" asked Ruth.

"Party?"

"The historic society, right here on the lawn. Come."

"Oh, yes, we got the invitation. Try to." The baby thrashed. "Okay, okay, little guy. We're going. Bye."

Ruth sighed. "Ed better get this place secured, if he wants people to buy the condos."

"Believe me, I've told him the same thing," Carter said. "I'll be back, take down the sign before the party. What an eyesore."

"That's okay," said Ben. "We'll take care of it."

"See you this afternoon," said Ruth. "Talk some sense into that boss."

Carter gave a tight smile. "Doing my best." He jogged away.

Eliza and Ben walked back to the cottage.

Ben sighed. "Bubble burst last fall. There's no market for high end condos. Nothing's selling on spec. We're lucky Ed sold the society the cottage when he was feeling flush. We wouldn't get such a good deal now."

Nick sat on the front steps, in a long-sleeved black T-shirt despite the heat. She'd be glad when he moved on from this Goth look.

"We don't have any milk."

"Aren't you a vegan? Carton on the door of the fridge."

"Empty," he said.

"Wonder who finished it?" Almost adding *last night.* Catching herself, with Ben there, with the vandalized sign. Had Phil told him why Nick was home from camp? That he hadn't been home last night?

"Come borrow," said Ben, casual and friendly. Maybe Phil had kept her confidence.

Nick returned with milk in a glass bottle from the new organic grocery in the rebuilt town square. Eliza missed the shabby former shopping strip, especially the grocery store. Back during her student days at the Lodge some psychiatrists still walked patients into town to practice shopping, dealing with the world. Occupational therapy combined with analysis was a Lodge trademark. Now no one even had time for a fifty-minute hour at Eliza's clinic. You had to keep it to thirty minutes for the insurance companies, get special approval for longer sessions. She longed to take the risk of joining her friends, start a practice. But that would mean giving up the steady salary check and benefits.

Nick ate sprawled on the metal glider that had been on the porch when they moved in. "They need me to help with yard stuff. Ten an hour."

"Good," she said, careful not to be too enthusiastic or he'd balk.

"Where are my work gloves? Phil and I are taking down the sign."

"Was it okay, when you came home?"

He slurped the milk from the bowl. "It was dark, Ma."

"Why didn't you answer your phone?"

"Off. We were playing capture the flag."

"Where?"

"Civic center."

"That's trespassing, after dark. Listen, Nick. Getting kicked out of camp—I'm sorry, but it's like a warning, you know? Chance

73

to re-boot. I'm finding someone for you to talk to. We need to get things back on track."

"I need my work gloves."

"Try the cabinets."

Last summer she'd shoved plastic tubs into the under-the-eaves storage, Nick too angry to help, and Eliza furious with him.

At least now he wanted his work gloves. Working with Phil could be like occupational therapy, and she'd find him a psychotherapist. It was going to be okay. It had to be. Talk therapy and work therapy, just like the old days.

His feet were sticking out of one of the storage cabinets in his room.

"Any luck?" She crouched and peered in.

He squirmed out with a small cardboard box. "This isn't mine," he said, pushing it aside. "Hot as Hades, my stuff all probably melted," he said.

He disappeared and emerged dragging a big rectangular bundle wrapped in a dusty plaid blanket.

"What's this, Ma?" he asked, opening the blanket, revealing a layer of yellowed newspaper wrapping. "Say, like a surprise ball," he said, throwing her a quick grin. He loved the cheap party favors Eliza used to slip under his pillow from the tooth fairy; loved unwinding the crepe paper, uncovering the plastic trinkets as though discovering treasure.

He peeled back the newspaper and revealed a portrait of a woman with dark shadows beneath haunted eyes, a deeply wrinkled brow. She looked familiar. A younger, careworn version of the familiar photograph downstairs.

"I think—it's Dr. Fromm-Reichmann," said Eliza.

"Your shrink lady?" He was unwrapping another painting. His face turned crimson.

The nude had a long slender torso, heavy breasts with magenta nipples. Her hand hovered between her legs. The eyes were challenging and bold.

What a provocative painting. No wonder Nick was blushing.

Nick turned back to the cabinet. "Where the fuck is my stuff?"

"Language! Maybe I put everything in the other cabinet."

For a small house there was a remarkable amount of storage— enough space to lose things in.

He crawled into the other cabinet. "Yes!" he shouted and pulled out a plastic tub. Opened it; rummaged.

"Shit. No gloves."

"Stop swearing. You can borrow theirs."

He was off, feet clomping down the stairs, kitchen door slamming.

Eliza carried the paintings downstairs, leaned them on the mantel in the living room. Despite dust, the colors were vivid. *Jacob* read the bold printed signature on each. The portrait was Frieda. But who was the nude? Why were they hidden here?

The doorbell rang. Ruth's cleaning crew had arrived, vacuums strapped to their backs. Eliza explained Nick's room wasn't to be cleaned.

She went upstairs to close his door and noticed the small cardboard box he'd found. Eliza opened it. The scent of dust on warm paper filled her nostrils, like an old library book. It was full of paper, some pages typed, some handwritten. A manuscript of some sort?

It couldn't be Frieda's. Everyone said her secretary had taken almost all of her personal papers right after she died.

The house was full of the cheerful noise and bustle of the cleaning crew. Eliza needed quiet, and privacy, if she was going to trespass.

She carried the box out onto the porch, settled onto the glider and began to read.

1957

I sense time grows short. Virginia, best of secretaries, you know I trust you with everything. If you find these pages when I am gone and we cannot discuss it, please, these scribbles don't belong in any archive. This is not even exactly a diary, really, just jottings I've written, on and off, over the years.

Long ago, in that other world, the lost world of childhood, I kept a tradi-tional daily diary. Wrote in bed, hid it from Mother. What happened to it? Lost with that whole world. I remember the magic of the process, the alchemy of putting down what I remembered of the day, what I had seen and felt, the best, the worst, on the page. And the way patterns emerged, invisible in the moment, but clearer afterward. I wrote and thus understood myself better, put experience into words, listened to myself. I learned to interpret myself. I learned to believe in the power of words and listening. Later, I shared what I learned, by teaching my patients to speak—to me, to themselves. To put experience into words. How early our destiny finds us.

But I never kept a daily diary after those schoolgirl days. Coming to America, I began these intermittent notes, writing when the experience or cir-cumstances prompted. Writing in English for practice at first and continuing over the years as that language almost became my own. For over twenty years now, one third of my life, English has been the language of my waking hours and working life. Being my second language, it gives me distance on myself, the familiar distance I am accustomed to, listening to my patients. Making it easier to see and understand—myself. Building in the necessary pause, the interrup-tion, between observation and understanding. Over the years I have written and hidden the pages away. Too involved with living and working to look back.

I took these pages with me, on my sabbatical two years ago to California, planning to turn them into something orderly, a memoir. But I procrastinated on every project there. These pages are almost like process recordings on a lifelong session with myself, just rough impressions, an exercise in speaking and listening—to myself. Listening with what a dear friend called the analyst's third ear.

How I need that third ear now, how I must depend on it. It grows more and more difficult to hear, posing the ultimate obstacle to my work—listening. This is the obstacle, the punishment I've feared all my life.

Now, even this odd one-sided listening to myself on the page, how powerful it is. It works.

Much more important unfinished work and writing waits in my desk. This must wait. I am afraid I may not finish all I've meant to, all I've promised.

Please, these are my secrets. Keep them hidden. If I had the energy, perhaps I should burn these pages. But somehow burning memories seems as forbidden as suicide and cremation. Do what you think best if you find this. I am too tired.

For a year, Eliza had been talking to Frieda. Was it her turn to listen now? Or—was this eavesdropping? *Forgive me, Frieda,* she whispered. *I'm a therapist, too. I've been telling you my secrets. I promise, I'll keep yours.*

Her fingers trembled as she turned the page.

FIVE

1935

The first morning at the Lodge is like waking in Eden, a child again on holiday in the Black Forest.

Erich and I breakfast with the family in their "Little Lodge," drink good coffee, rich cream.

How do you like your eggs? Anne asks me, the Negro cook waiting behind her chair. *Sunnyside up, or over easy?*

She likes them sunny side up, Erich answers. I take note of the expression but don't like him speaking for me.

Such eggs! I admire the deep orange yolks, glistening whites.

We've been so fortunate, despite the Depression, she says. *It's farm country all around Rockville, and I'm keeping my own chickens and several cows now, over at Rose Hill.*

Rose Hill is a former farm next door, Dexter explains. They've purchased it, plan to renovate the big house there and move. When there's time, when there's money.

We're bursting at the seams, as you can see, she smiles.

The three children, two boys and a girl, have left the table, followed by a Great Dane.

After breakfast, Dexter, Anne, Erich and I walk the grounds. Light sprinkles down through the high leaf canopy, every shade of green. American Chestnut trees, Dexter says. (We're Dexter and Frieda to each other now). His father named the sanatorium for the trees, believed in their healing properties, made the tree the emblem of his purpose. *My father loved nature. Said it is better for patients to plant roses than make paper flowers.*

We pass a man on a ladder, pruning. *A patient,* Dexter says. *The work is therapeutic.*

And we give him a credit on his bill, adds Anne.

The lawn is green. *Flawless as a tennis court,* I say.

Rockville is mad for tennis, Anne says. *We have a local star, he's winning all the matches on the East Coast.*

A woman walks by, barefoot, followed by a nurse in a white uniform.

She's progressing, Dexter says softly. *You see Frieda, we have no fences here. Close relationships, not bars, keep our patients secure.*

Their children are at play, darting in and out between the tree trunk columns. I feel a pang, a wish. Does Erich feel it too, walking by my side, so quiet for once?

Could it ever have been so, for us? Parents of flesh and blood children and parents of a hospital?

No, never.

Oh, fortunate family, twice blessed Anne and Dexter. The pang I feel? Name it, call it what it is, pull out the sting. Envy.

Birds chirp in a holly tree. Bright feathers flash overhead: blue, vermillion, yellow. Blue jay, cardinal, gold finch, Anne tells me. And promises a bird book, binoculars.

It's like a park, I say. *I can't believe you are so close to Washington.*

Not as close as we used to be, he says, gesturing to a little open shed with a bench at the edge of the road. *The trolley just stopped running into the city.*

There's still the train, says Anne. *And perhaps it's better for us, to be a little more contained.*

I hear church bells. *Is there a synagogue?*

80

Erich puts his hand on my arm. I feel his warning. Don't make an issue of your difference.

In Washington, Dexter says.

And Baltimore, she says. *We'll inquire, make arrangements.*

Frieda doesn't attend services often, says Erich.

True, but I am angry at his papering over who I am.

We're here because we're Jews, Erich, I say.

It's dreadful, she says. *The churches—we all signed a petition, sent it to the State Department. I wish there was something…*Her voice breaks.

I've heard of these petitions, over dinners in New York with analysts from the Institute who'd joined in a rally there, with a Rabbi Wise. Well-named, they said. He's trying to sound the alarm.

The petitions are useless, Erich says. He's angry now, not caring to blend in, not caring to be grateful. *FDR doesn't want to hear.*

He does! And Eleanor does, said Anne. *We're so very glad you're here, safe with us.* She links her arm through mine.

Thank you, I say. *But so many are not.*

And though the morning is warm and bright, the walk is spoiled with the blight of fear and guilt.

Erich leaves. I feel both bereft and free. I walk the grounds and an aide mistakes me for a patient, asking where I am going, do I need help? Perhaps I look as crazed and desperate as I sometimes feel. I am safe, here in this peaceful park, finally able to work again. My family, my dear ones, my people, are in danger. The contrast tortures me.

I go on evening rounds with Dexter, we sit up late and talk. He's respectful. *What do you think, Frieda? What might we approach differently, in this case?* It is good, to focus on patients, on each patient and each problem. The individual, the small human scale, that is something I can do something about.

I fall into bed exhausted and uplifted and sleep like a child. Oversleep, awake, vaguely aware of stirrings in the ward above my room. Turning over onto my good ear, I let the silence take me. Selectively deaf, to the patients above who are not yet quite my children, my life.

But only wait for a moment and then with eagerness, I throw the covers back. Time to Begin!

Besides Dexter, there are two doctors here who will rotate vacations while I fill in. Only twenty-five patients. This hospital must grow.

We have a cottage on the Bay, Anne says. *I'll take the children there, for a little while, later in the summer.*

When I am settled, perhaps Dexter could go too, I suggest.

Perhaps, he says, but he's not ready to trust me. There's a fierce pride there. The Lodge is his.

I understand and feel envy again. Remember my proprietary pride in my Therapeuticum. I must prove myself, make myself indispensable.

Please let me take her, I say to Dexter, insisting on taking on the newest patient, a young woman in spasms of fear and anger: smearing feces, striking out, biting. I withstand her threats and filth, meet her pure need, calm her, subdue her with firm tenderness. Her need calms me too, brings me back to my stronger self. Eases my ache of worry. This work is what I can do, the blows I can strike against darkness. I instruct the aide to swaddle her in a cold pack so the cool wet sheets contain and soothe her. After the sheets have done their work, I release her. We are bonded now. There is the beginning of trust.

Later, after I have bathed and changed, after rounds, Dexter invites me to have what he calls a "nightcap." A glass of whiskey called bourbon from a place called Ken-tuck-y. Sweet and strong as fire, smooth as slivovitz.

"I was worried," he says, eyes a little bloodshot above his glass. "She is quite violent. We don't know her yet."

Worried because I am small, because I am a woman? Or because he worries, carrying the responsibility for all and everything? I know how that is, too. I even miss that.

"Thank you for trusting me. My intuition is good. I'm not afraid of madness, it's only a manifestation of pain. Evil scares me."

"You've seen plenty of that," he says.

I need a long pull on my cigarette, remembering my young soldiers. My young German soldiers. It is so strange to think my countrymen, my soldiers' sons (if any of my broken soldiers lived long and well enough to father children) are now the uniformed menace stalking my people, my familiar streets at home. We talk a long time, about our training, experience, our beliefs and aspirations as psychiatrists.

He believes, as did his father, in the benefit of active engagement in the tasks of living. Occupational therapy, he calls it.

I explain my opposition to any surgical techniques to treat mental distress. Explain what I saw, the blasted, eviscerated brains of my young soldiers, their ravaged souls.

He agrees. There will be no lobotomies here.

I tell him that the talking cure can reach even the deep loneliness of schizophrenia, that it is possible to cure with listening, with relationship.

Ameliorate, you mean, he says, leaning back and blowing a smoke ring.

Cure, I say. Not every time, not every one, but it can be done.

No one is doing that, he says. It's not possible.

I've seen it. Done it. We could do it here.

I have him, at least intrigued. And isn't it why he wanted me, after all? The small Jew, the goose with her golden egg from Germany.

We talk, until Anne in blue robe and slippers appears. She's walked across the lawn from home in the Little Lodge to fetch him.

Bedtime, she says, to both of us. Corking the bottle. Emptying the ashtray.

I like them. There is vast difference between us culturally, and yet deep sympathy. And what a truly wedded couple. There is nothing between me and Dexter of disturbing undercurrent, nothing to threaten our work. We are colleagues, and perhaps something verging on friendship, but no dangerous attraction like with Erich. Dexter and I *recognize* each other in that profound way of shared passion for the work, the struggle, the suffering of our patients. We are true believers in our oath: first do no harm. Comrades in the effort to heal. We walk together on rounds, he slows his long gait, I hasten mine and we fall into step with each other.

Easy in these first busy summer days to forget my position is just temporary. Easy to forget I aspire to a hospital with more stature and renown.

The invitation comes unbidden, unexpected—almost unwanted. Karl Menninger invites me to visit, to interview for a position in Kansas.

Why not tell Dexter I'd rather stay here on staff? I suggest to Erich. Extravagance to call him in New York, and I fear the switchboard ears even speaking in German, but I need to. *This invitation might press him to make me an offer.*

No, no. Play your hand, he says. *Too soon to fold.*

I follow his advice, though it goes against the grain.

"We will be hard pressed while you are gone," Dexter says.

I have never been a flirt, never coy. My desire was to become a doctor, to learn to deliver babies, while the other Orthodox girls in Königsberg were marrying and having babies of their own. Erich was unexpected. Briefly, I was not myself, not in my right mind. Briefly I made passing acquaintance with delusional obsession—an experience that now proves helpful in my work, deepens my understanding, my sympathy, my belief that the so-called sane and so-called mad are not so different. Sanity and insanity? Just a matter of degree.

But now for the first time in my life I am courted, wooed by rivals.

"Just for ten days," I promise Dexter. "Just to see his hospital, his method. And visit my friend Gertrud Jacob. She's working in a hospital in Illinois."

"Where?" he asks, shed of eyebrows raised.

"Peoria."

"I've never known them to have any analysts," he says. I hear a note of competition.

"Karl may be quite persuasive," Dexter says the night before I leave. We are lingering over our nightcap, the drink and conversation have become ritual after rounds.

"We say," he says, raising the eyebrows, dropping his voice so low I must strain to hear (surely just fatigue from speaking English, the long day, the late hour, nervous about the journey). "We say dance with the one who brung you." He's smiling but the eyes are grave. He's slow to anger, but furious when mistakes are made. I'm not quite sure how to read this response—is he threatened, or threatening? He is established, in charge, but that does not rule out insecurity.

"Promise me you won't say yay or nay until you're home and we can talk."

Home. Just the right note to strike, which shrewd Dexter knows. The big bluff man has keen insight, sees to the heart of things. Hides a little behind his disguise: brilliant doctor in a bear suit.

I've booked my ticket to Topeka. Topeka is an American Indian name, Dexter explains. "You're going to the west." There's a Toledo out there too, in this big, strange country with both native place names and derived place names. I'm far from the first homesick immigrant.

There is a layover in Chicago. Gertrud will meet me there.

I could come to you in Peoria, I'd offered, another extravagant phone call, the first time we've spoken since parting in New York. How good to hear her voice's deep music, even frayed thin by wire and distance. How good to speak German—no matter what the switchboard operator may think.

No, don't come here. If the patients weren't crazy when they came here, they'd go mad from dullness. I'm going mad myself, needing a city. Missing you.

Most people find Gertrud aloof, reserved—too watchful. All true, on the surface. But underneath her shy reserve there is warmth and gentle exuberance. Between us is an honesty I've had with no one else. We've both been passing for so long in this man's world of doctoring; we engage on a basic level, woman to woman. With a visit in reach I miss her more, as though my friend were a third sister. I feel that clench of yearning and count the days.

Raymond, the Negro handyman, gardener, driver, takes me to the Rockville station, a brick building. He opens my door.

"I'll find a red cap," I say, practicing the new phrase. I'm working hard to appropriate this language and its idioms. Language—spoken and unspoken—is the coin of my analyst's realm, the tool of my trade. I must live by my ears, my eyes, my tongue and my wits (and eyes, tongue, and wits must be ever sharper to compensate for my faulty ears). I am an immigrant, a wandering Jew peddling my wares. Fortunately, I am a quick study for words and meaning. But

I must hurry to learn, become fluent in speech and understanding, while I can still hear nuance and subtlety.

While I can still hear.

"No red caps here, Dr. Frieda. We're a whistle stop." The patients call me Frieda, as Anne said, the Lodge is a familiar place. But not for the Negros—there is a formality, a caste system in operation. Money is the root of all evil, they say. Well, I believe it is prejudice. Oh, I've seen it, lived it at home—on both sides. It's why I'm here. But he calls me Dr. Frieda and I call him Raymond.

Raymond escorts me to the platform. The conductor helps me up into the carriage, grabs my bags. "I'll take these, boy."

Gray haired Raymond steps back, hiding, eyes down. He bobs his head, transformed in an instant from man to servant. I recognize that blending in. I know it is necessary. The color-coded caste system underlies everything. Rules, open and hidden, exist for light, freckled Raymond of the hazel eyes and his darker wife, Sally. As a Jew, an exile, a refugee, I feel shame at the ease afforded by my white skin. But I see the glances when I speak German, when I'm identified as a woman doctor, and a Jew.

Goodbye, Raymond, I want to call out. Wanting to acknowledge him, refuse to let him render himself invisible. But I must let him blend in; he knows best. I want to touch his shoulder in a gesture of farewell, and apology. Which would be dangerous for him, for both of us. I must blend in as well.

The conductor stows my bags. The private sleeper compartment is compact as a ship's cabin.

"Five o'clock or seven for dinner, ma'am?"

"Seven, please."

I don't tip him. My coward's silent protest for his rudeness to Raymond.

We pull away from the station, the "Whistle Stop." I jot the phrase in the leather-bound notebook in my handbag that Erich gave me.

To record your dreams.

I rarely dream. Rarely recall them. You put too much stock in dreams.

You do dream. You'd remember if you wrote them down. If you were my patient, I'd call you resistant.

I'm neither your patient nor resistant.

No. That was me. Your irresistible patient.

I'm lying. I do dream, and do believe in the importance of certain dreams: the patient's first dream upon entering treatment, recurrent dreams. I do dream recurrent dreams. Dreams that shadow my days. As I fall asleep, I'm falling, falling down the elevator shaft like Papa, falling with Papa. I ask him as we fall: *Did you jump or, as Mama claims, did you stumble?* I awake with shock and stare into the dark. I ponder again the unlikely misstep in the office building he knew as well as our home. Why alone at work, why at work on the Sabbath?

He was alone everywhere by then, cut off by the isolation of deafness. How can a businessman function when he cannot hear his employees, his customers? How can he succeed when deafness makes him appear stupid? I cannot bear to think of it.

There is the other dream I do not tell Erich. He is the doctor cutting me open, a Caesarean, not a hysterectomy. He lifts the tumor out, pulls off the mucus caul and reveals a baby, our baby.

We roll west out of Rockville, into fields and farms, almost at once. Here's the agricultural land that with Anne's good management has buffered the Lodge from the Depression scarcity. Plenty and scarcity are such relative conditions, how rich and safe this country is, compared to home.

Gaithersburg, Point of Rocks, Harpers Ferry.

The stations shrink, the brick buildings in decreasing size could fit inside each other like the Russian dolls I left behind for my niece. We cross a river on a high trestle, ride beside a deep gorge of rushing water. I close my eyes and see the Rhine, see castles for a fleeting heartsick moment. You can love and hate at once. You can, I'm learning, love a country that has betrayed you, that seeks to destroy everything and everyone you hold dear. As you can love a man, against reason, with a flaw that breaks your heart.

The bell for dinner sounds. The conductor opens the door and directs me to the dining car.

At table alone, I run my hand over the heavy white cloth. Cutlery and glasses tremble as we rattle west. Lamplight catches the sparkle of silver and crystal. I think of my dowry left behind in Germany. I'd never known how much I wanted all the domestic stuff of a home until I acquired it so late, and then had to let it go. I close my eyes and see, can almost feel the glossy surface of my Bavarian Rosenthal china, two sets—*fleisch* (blue and gold Greek key) and *milch* (yellow roses). Erich teased me. *A little late to become observant. Remember what we ate, that Passover night?* At the remembered transgressive taste of that bread and *traif*, bile and guilt rise in my throat.

My meal arrives. Alone, only my own reflection floating in the black mirror of the window, I imagine Erich across the table. I would have talked to him, about Raymond, and the statue to the unknown young Confederate soldier by the Rockville courthouse. Less than a hundred years ago brothers warred against each other here, over slavery. A family *owned* Raymond's grandparents. Jews were slaves in Egypt, it is a matter of only one generation here. There is blood on this land of the free, founded on independence and tolerance. And now? Ever stricter quotas for Jews and other "undesirables." I'm here on sufferance, on Erich's coattails, and my merits—I'm lucky. But what mortal being does not have merit? My mother, my sisters, my little niece—even if they wished, could they get in?

Erich and I would have debated, over this table on the train. Are evil and prejudice innate or taught? I miss the heat of our argument, most of all. It was our foreplay and our after-play. We were always minds first, then bodies, then minds again.

Snug in my narrow berth, rocking and drowsy, I anticipate a good sleep like a glutton before chocolate. *Or a long abstinent woman before a good fuck,* I hear him whisper in my ear. I rarely sleep through the night in my downstairs room at the Lodge, keep robe and slippers ready. With a mother's instinct for her babe I sense the tumult above me before the nurse's apologetic knock. *Frieda, we need you.* Out of bed and up the stairs! I'm always weary and always ready to rouse. Instinct kicks in like a mother's (a good, responsive mother— my patients bear witness to the other kind).

My patients need me, gobble me up, drain and fill me, give meaning and purpose to my rootless transplant's life.

Erich says I'm addicted to the drug of being needed; should learn to love myself first and best. I retort that service is my choice, not need, nor dependence. He cannot understand the satisfaction of putting other before self. My brilliant, limited Erich is so convinced that what I truly need is—him. That what a woman needs is—the crude words he whispers, arousing me. Ah, he is so convinced he knows best. I've seen the way women turn to him, to his heat and charm.

Not Gertrud, which challenges and irritates him. One night in New York, I confided my worry about her, that she wasn't strong, might fall ill. Erich laughed and said he knew what would cure her and used the stevedore phrase he used when we were in bed together. The words still, to my shame arouse me when I recall our nights (and our afternoons, and mornings).

I told him off, knowing Gertrud better than anyone does. Knowing absolutely his crowing cock is not what she needs or wants. She is difficult to read, but I have been her teacher, her analyst, and her friend.

You're wrong! I know my friend, I said. Tempted to slap his face, his dirty mouth. But holding back, not risking touch. Anger is close to the fire that feeds desire.

Yes, he said. *Your friend, your bosom friend. I know you and your friends.*

I recall the heat of that argument and, alone in my train berth, the anger works on me, stirs me, makes me miss him. Alone, at rest, at night, I still keenly feel his absence as presence. The void is easier to fill with the activity of daylight.

Swaying west in this private berth, I let my hand stray and assuage the ache with the tricks he taught. There will be no embarrassing interruption tonight, no nurse tapping at my door. The click and rattle of the wheels on rails covers the soft moan I cannot hold back.

"Chicago! Chicago!" I must remember the emphasis falls on the second syllable, note that down in my phrase book.

This station is another temple, not like the gothic iron and glass sheds at home. How Americans worship their rails.

"Frieda!"

Gertrud, all color and energy, the dancer on a Toulouse Lautrec poster brought to kinetic life, is waving and running. No one could call her aloof now, here. Thousands of miles from anyone we know, we can be ourselves.

I wave and dash across the marble floor, almost slipping, my red cap hurrying after with my bags.

Holding each other, my head reaches just to her shoulder. How thin she is, how sharp her bones are. She laughs and the laugh becomes the too-familiar racking cough. Alarm floods me.

She catches her breath and I can breathe again too. It's only excitement she suffers from.

"We're staying just around the corner. Let's drop your bags and go to the Art Institute. Heaven to see you! To be in a real city! I would die happy if I never saw a blade of wheat again!"

Arms linked, we walk into the glare and din of a hot day. Cars honk, a tram runs on an elevated track above, bells clang. I'm out of practice with cacophony. Once I could filter city noise. Surely the noise is worse here, it is not my ears.

The hotel is quiet, dark as a forest. Lobby carpet deep and green as moss blots the sound of our footsteps. Brass fixtures, mirrors, woodwork gleam. Gertrud claims the key at the desk: one key, one room.

"A little economy, sharing," she smiles at me over her shoulder. "Like the old days. I can't waste a minute with you."

We speak English in the elevator. People stare if you speak German. How to explain our language, our mother tongue has done no one harm? It has been misappropriated. How weary I am of representing a country that has disinherited me, disenfranchised me, stolen from me and threatens everyone I've left behind. I refuse to be ashamed of a language that was—is—beautiful.

Our room is quiet and dim: two single beds, a nightstand in between, two armchairs beside a curtained window. Opening the drapes for the view I discover an airshaft.

"Lunch? Museum first? It's free today!" The cough has vanished, the earlier congestion was just excitement and exertion.

Obvious it's the museum first she wants. I'm happy to oblige, my heavy train breakfast of eggs and biscuits somewhere in O-Hi-O still heavy in my gut.

I've forgotten the vicarious thrill of looking at, no, experiencing art with her. She stands so close to the paintings. She's a child, inhaling the oil and pigments, trying to step into the frame. Guards warn her. "Stand back, ma'am."

The Art Institute is grand and well appointed. If there's anything like this in Washington, I've had no time to see it. We wander through the glorious collection, well displayed and better lit than at home. "I had no idea Americans appreciated art to this extent," I say. "You snob!" she laughs. Yes, I'm not immune to prejudice and preconception.

"Have you been painting?" I ask her, my arm around her too-narrow waist.

"No time. It's a factory."

"Apply to Menninger's with me. They're growing he says. Need people."

"He turned me down. Without an interview."

I hear Erich. *Gertrud treating psychotics? Well, perhaps she knows it from the inside. Those paintings of hers, of the patients. Did she just look in the mirror?*

Has he spread rumors, resenting she was my favorite student, after himself?

You fail to make the distinction between artistic sensibility and psychosis, I tell him. *And don't we all have at least some capacity for madness? Isn't that an asset in our work? Weren't you listening when I taught you? Weakness can be converted into strength. Madness to wisdom.*

Of course, he wasn't listening. I have not been able to teach him real listening, that most important tool in our trade, our craft, our art of healing.

Gertrud is almost running now, as though the gallery would close at any moment. As though this were her last chance to soak in the lines, the color.

Is she thinking of her own paintings sold for escape funds or stored for the uncertain duration with a gentile friend, hidden with the work of other "degenerates?" Hitler, failed artist, destroys rather than creates.

Running, she coughs. Exertion, surely just exertion.

Don't rush, I caution.

There is electricity around her—enthusiasm, not illness.

We eat dinner back at the hotel, soft rolls and creamy butter and bloody steak. She laughs and says they call the Midwest the breadbasket, but really it's the stockyard.

I devour my rich and delicious meal. She leaves her steak almost untouched. *I've turned kosher,* she teases, nibbling a long green bean from her fingers, ignoring the disapproving waiter as he sweeps our table with his silver dustpan and brush. Oblivious or taunting him?

I feel giddy, drunk, though we've had nothing but ice-tea, the strange American beverage I've grown fond of, with mint.

The elevator bellboy presses the controls and the metal gate slides closed. I feel fever radiating from her.

"Pooped," she says in English and we laugh at the word and sway down the hall arm in arm like mismatched chorus girls.

"You should be in bed," I scold, mock stern but serious.

"Yes, doctor," tease and challenge in her tone.

She changes in the bathroom into an apricot silk gown and robe.

I feel shy, seeing her hair loose and shining against the sheen of silk; it's been a long time since our travels together. Seeking work and safety in Europe and Palestine, a seeming eternity ago. Wandering Jews, she called us, laughing to cover the pain. I take my turn in the bathroom, tie my yellow cotton robe, study my face in the rust-spotted mirror. The crease between my brows, the line she emphasized in the ugly portrait, is vivid again in the harsh light.

She's nestled in one of the twin armchairs by the window, smoking.

"No," I say, holding out my hand like a school mistress for the cigarette.

She shakes her head and draws deep.

I've craved and abstained all day, for her sake. I fish the battered pack from my pocket (oh the glorious rich smell of unlit tobacco). I light my cigarette from hers.

She's put her flask on the table between our chairs, two hotel tumblers. Pours, raises her glass to me. *"Prost!"*

We toast and sip. She coughs.

I touch her forehead: hot as a stove. "You're ill." Enough pretense, enough denial.

"Every cough is not TB," she says, coughing as she protests.

"You should be in bed."

"Yes, Doctor."

She stubs out her cigarette.

Crossing the narrow room to bed, she unties her robe.

I blow a last ring of smoke. Extinguish my cigarette.

She's slipped between the sheets. I smooth her covers as though she were my baby sister Anna. Rest my hand on her head. Heat pulses through her hair.

Erich in my ear. *What is it that attracts you to the worst cases? Neurotic need to be needed.*

Hush. Be still, I tell him.

I smooth her dark, damp hair. She catches my hand, kisses my fingers.

"Will the light bother you? I'm studying for the boards in Maryland."

"Diligent Frieda."

Across the room I sit in the armchair and sink into the pages, the work. Board certification will make me essential to Dexter. I want another smoke, but not with her compromised lungs close by.

"You look so sad. You must be reviewing obstetrics."

Her uncanny reading of internal moods.

She and I have talked, of the miracles and tragedies of the delivery room. I've told her I never felt more alive. I believed I had discovered my calling. She alone knows the reason I gave it up. Not because I wasn't strong enough, too slight for the punishing standing and pulling. She knows the truth. I could not spend my life day after day bringing children into the world if I could not have my own. The realization came to me long before I knew Erich. I caught myself once too often pitying a tired mother with too many children at home already. Imagined picking up the baby, the weight of it, the blessed heft. Taking it from her, to spare the mother and save the child.

"Just tired," I tell Gertrud now, looking up from the textbook. Which is true. I am not sad to be a psychiatrist rather than an obstetrician. This is my true calling. What Erich calls neurotic attraction to the neediest is my passion and my joy. Helping the lonely ones, the most psychotic. Easing chronic, constant suffering far worse than acute labor pains is the different sort of deliverance I practice. Delivering my lonely ones, helping them find a way to live in the world. Yes, I yearn a bit, watching Anne and Dexter's children. It passes.

"Well, I'm not tired or sick, and you say I am. And you're not sad, and I say you are. Who's projecting here?" She laughs and coughs, coughs and laughs.

I put the text aside, turn out the lamp. Find my bed by the sliver of hall-light beneath our door.

We lie in the dark.

She reaches across the chasm between our beds, touches my cheek. Her fingers are burning. Touches my lips.

"You do have a fever," I say.

"Maybe I need a cold pack," she laughs. And coughs.

I turn over, turn away, lie on my better ear to block the sound.

I must hear her breathe! I turn back and listen to her hoarse breaths.

"When you were my training analyst, Friedl, did you think I was crazy?"

Intuitive Gertrud. She's overheard my silent argument with Erich.

"No."

"And wanting what I want? Is it crazy?" Her voice is low.

Easy to pretend I cannot hear her. But the tone, the frequency of longing carries. My ears may be dull, but an analyst, this analyst listens with her mind and heart as well.

"Come closer. You'll hear me," she says.

There is nowhere closer except her bed. I do not move. Selective deafness has its uses, as I learned from my mother Klara.

"How is your mother?" Intuitive again.

"Fine, she believes. Refuses to leave Germany."

"Erich?"

"Busy."

"With Karen?"

I know all about Karen Horney. But it hurts to think it is an open secret, my personal life a subject of gossip.

"Will you ever finish the divorce?"

"It's just a formality. I must establish residency here. Convincing mother, visas for her and my sisters—there are other priorities."

"You think being Erich's wife will give your affidavits for them more clout?"

"It may not hurt, to have his reputation and bank account."

"She's stubborn like you."

"I'm afraid it will be too late," I whisper.

She hums the Brahms lullaby, comforting me. Our music, our deepest mother tongue, is the most beautiful in the world.

"What do you dream of?" she asks.

This obsession with dreams, Erich, Dexter, Gertrud. Reality holds enough themes and symbols. "I don't. Or don't remember."

"I dream of you."

I breathe softly as I can, pretend to sleep. Something is waiting for me in the dark. I am a child, playing hide and seek. Wanting, and fearing to be found.

Behind the fear is the wish, as I taught all my students.

Karl Menninger looks to be about my age. "Thank you for making the journey."

"I am so interested in your theories about repairing family injury. We agree the mentally ill are not so different from the rest of us."

He laughs. "You will see the basis for my belief when you meet my own family. Father and brother, we're a team. Family-based treatment by a family."

So, if I come here, I will be guest not family, and Karl Menninger will be at the head of the table. He's smart, maybe wise, but not looking for a peer. Dexter need not fear that I won't come home. But I will see the method in practice. And perhaps I can put in a word for Gertrud.

Karl put on a broad straw hat, an affectation, I thought until out in the baking heat. I missed the heavy shade of the Lodge.

"There's your house," he said.

It was brick, with a long white railed porch. Pots of red geraniums marched up the front steps. The house was solid, simple shelter—the house a child might draw in treatment.

And I wanted it, as though I were that child, dreaming, drawing what I needed. Until that moment, I hadn't thought of a house. Hadn't suspected it mattered. But I was smitten—like the blow when I first looked across my quiet consulting room at Erich.

A house like that would shelter mother, sisters, niece. My family would be repaired, reunited. A house like that would be safe harbor. Offering a house like that surely would strengthen my application, my affidavits for my mother and sisters. It would prove I could care for them, shelter them.

The house would persuade Klara to leave Germany. She would come to safety with me under this roof. She would not be able to resist domesticating me. She would stop using her deafness like a child covering her eyes to be invisible. I would get the visas. Erich would help. She would come if I could offer the bait of a home. My home. Our home.

Karl smiled from under the shade of his hat, a shrewd glance, assessing me, divining my longing.

"Would you like to see? One of my residents lives there. Leaving soon."

My resident. Lord of the manor. I would be his too, an indentured servant, or a fostered child.

A maid showed us through. (A maid! Klara would approve. I must have a maid.)

The dining room had built-in china cupboards in each corner. Klara could separate everyday dishes and Passover dishes. I stood in that stuffy room in Karl's Kansas house and smelled a Shabbat dinner: chicken roasting, dripping and sizzling and scorching. I saw Klara lighting candles in my tall silver candlesticks—my family and my lost dowry recovered, restored.

He escorted me across the campus under the prairie sunlight. Trees lined the walkways in stiff rows.

"What are these trees?"

"Dutch elms. All over the Midwest."

They were graceful, branches swept up like ballerinas' arms. But I missed the Lodge's deep green canopy of chestnuts.

We returned to his office and he produced the contract.

Don't fold too early, Erich said.

That house.

You'll be closer to me, poor me stranded here in Peoria, Gertrud said.

"I will need some time to consider."

"You're worth waiting for," he said. "But I need to move ahead. I've got a foundation to grow."

His ambition makes me wary.

But that house!

"I'm committed to the Lodge through the end of the summer."

"Understood. But I will need an answer in two weeks. You will start soon after labor day." How sure of me he was. Had read my greed for the house. I'd showed my hand.

What does he mean start work after labor day? I could have asked Dexter but not this man. I couldn't risk being at even more disadvantage.

I had not expected Dexter himself to pick me up at the station, Anne standing by the car, arms open.

"Everyone's missed you," she said. "Not only the patients. My children keep asking."

"I've missed you too," I said, surprised by the sweetness of reunion. How long it felt, ten days. How quick and fickle is the heart—finding new family to attach to when we've lost our own.

During the brief drive back to the Lodge Anne faced me over the seat.

"We've talked," she said, in her crisp book-keeper voice. "We want you on permanent staff. We can pay a bit more. Two hundred and forty, with room and board included."

Generous! I know the hospital census, can guess their expenses.

I wanted to say yes.

But that house in Kansas. Klara, my silver candlesticks, my Kiddush cup, must have a home.

Time to show my hand.

"Karl Menninger's offered me a position, with a house."

Silence fell as we motored on. Dexter slowed to a stop at the steps to the hospital.

"We'll build you a house," he said.

I expected Anne, keeper of the books, watcher of the—what was her phrase— watcher of the bottom line to speak.

"To your specifications," she said, as though rehearsed.

Don't fold too soon.

I saw the aproned maid opening the door on the porch in Kansas. I thought of our beloved maid at home. I wanted a maid to take care of Klara so Klara could think she was taking care of me. And I could take care of my patients.

Life would be simpler, easier. It surprised me, the greed I felt for the accustomed privilege and comforts. *Learn to love yourself,* Erich said. I must have caught selfishness from him.

"I will need a maid."

"Of course. Raymond's wife Sally."

I feel a pang of uneasiness at the way she speaks for Sally. *My resident,* Karl said and I'd resented the implication of servitude.

I want Sally. To my shame, I want Sally.

Dexter strode a hundred feet across the lawn.

"We'll put it here," he said.

I saw it, as in a waking dream, a benign hallucination. My cottage, white with dark green trim, dormer windows, a porch, a flower garden. The sort of simple shelter a child might draw.

"Unless you'd rather be a little further from Main? Over closer to us?" asked Anne.

"No. I want to be close to the hospital. But it must have an office. It will be therapeutic, for patients to walk to sessions."

"Yes," Dexter said. "Active engagement in the process of healing."

"And bookshelves and china cupboards." There is so much I want, it's like discovering appetite for food again after starving.

"I know the best architect in town. And his carpenter," said Dexter. Easy to forget how powerful he is in Rockville, how well connected.

"And a flower garden."

"I will plan your garden," said Anne. "Raymond will plant it."

Dexter paced off the footprint of my house in the grass. "We'll call it—Frieda's Cottage."

Done. Done. "Thank you," I said, sensing, though afraid to say it, that I will be—happy here.

"I'll call Walter Peter—the architect—tomorrow. Anne will draw up your papers. And you'll tell Karl."

"Yes."

A patient ran toward me. "Frieda! You came back!"

"Of course," I said. She smelled sour; she'd been vomiting again. "Let's go get you cleaned up."

"You came back," she said.

"Yes. I left, and I returned." Teaching her the lesson she should have learned as a child from her mother, the lesson of separation and reunion. There are good mothers, and bad. "I would never leave you," I said, looking back at Dexter and Anne.

SIX

Eliza looked up from the page. Good mothers and bad? *Frieda, you've never been a mother. Don't be so judgmental. There's a child in your house now. We could use your help.*

Tell me, she almost heard Frieda saying.

Frieda had wanted a child. Had been afraid of the strength of that longing. Had stepped away from obstetrics because of it. Eliza understood—that longing, and the fear as well. She'd steeled herself, before her first visit to Dee after her babies were born, afraid of her own yearning for a child. But when she stood by the bed and Dee looked up, hazel eyes bloodshot and brimming with tears, Eliza had felt only joy for her dearest friend, her almost-sister. She held one of the babies, and she and Dee both wept and laughed.

The cleaning crew was gone. How long had she been reading? The house was scented with lemon cleanser, like the smell of the clinic bathrooms at night. Sometimes she stayed after her last client, catching up on charting while the cleaners' little girl crept in to play with Nick's old toys Eliza kept on a low shelf.

She should get ready for the party. She wanted just to go on reading, stay here, listening to Frieda. Listening across time. Listening and learning and not always agreeing, like with any teacher. Frieda didn't understand parenting from the inside but had such wisdom. Eliza wanted to learn, the way she did with a client, often an older client, wise with experience and suffering. That's what she valued most: listening and learning about *being*, the most precious gift from her work.

Eliza marked her place in the pages and slid the box under her bed.

Downstairs the deep porcelain sink in the kitchen had been scoured free of stains. All the windows glistened.

When he was small, Nick loved shining the balcony door at the apartment. He worked indoors, Eliza outside. She'd saved the note he'd written and held up to the glass door. *IT LOOKS LIKE NO THING IS BATWEN US.*

Eliza phoned him, standing at her desk, looking at Frieda's photograph, channeling the woman's calm, trying to establish, re-establish, connection with Nick.

He picked up! She was speechless for a moment with surprise.

"What do you want?" he demanded.

"Just to tell you the cleaners are done."

"Did they touch my stuff?"

"No. The party starts soon."

"Keep my room shut."

"Where are you going to be?"

"Maybe here."

"It's okay with Ben and Phil?"

"Ma, I'm working for them, remember?"

She'd lost her taste for the party, wishing instead it were an ordinary day. She'd stay here, read Frieda. Walk over to Rose Hill, visit with Phil and Ben—and Nick. Maybe it was good, he'd come home from camp. Gave them a chance to reconnect without the pressure of school. Maybe they could be close again instead of adversaries. Good things can come out of bad things, she'd seen it, with clients.

"Healing and growth—natural forces, right, Frieda? Time for me to get ready for your party," she said to the photograph.

Shouts and laughter floated in from outside. Uniformed wait staff were walking in and out of the tents. A circus had come to town and settled on her lawn. Nick would be upset, but it looked festive—like it used to, at the annual symposium. Nice, that the former Lodge staff still in the area had been invited, tickets comped by the developer.

Eliza picked up the invitation. With just a few lines, Phil had drawn a woman in a big hat, high heels, a flaring dress. *Come as you wish you were in 1940!*

Well, she had the dress. Dee spotted it on the crowded rack at their favorite consignment shop in Dupont Circle. Polished cotton, big flowers, full skirt and patent leather belt—a throw-back garden party dress.

"Just what that historic society woman wants. Try it on."

The skirt floated down around her hips.

"Let me see," called Dee.

Eliza twirled.

"Perfect with your long waist."

"Too much, Dee for a used dress I don't need."

While Eliza changed back into her jeans, Dee paid for it.

Now Eliza slipped into the dress, pulled her hair into a French twist. I will have fun, she resolved. I will lighten up and have fun.

The doorbell rang.

Ben stood on the steps, in a seersucker suit, bow tie, Panama hat.

"For you," he said, holding out a bouquet of pink peonies. "The roses are full of aphids, but Phil and your boy will take care of that soon."

"How did he do?"

"Big help. They're wrapping up."

"You look like a real southern gentleman."

"New Orleans born and bred," he said. The rueful smile, the sad, pale blue eyes—how could his parents have sent him off to military school? Now she was being judgmental, like Frieda. He'd been Nick's age, his worried parents implementing the supposed solution of another day and culture. She should understand.

"Ben!" Ruth called from the lawn. "Need you over here."

Three men, one on a step ladder, struggled to suspend a giant gold picture frame from a low branch as Ruth supervised.

"What in the world?" asked Eliza.

"It's for taking pictures—you know, like a photo booth," Ben said.

The frame swung from the bough.

Ruth posed behind it, in a polka dot blouse, a dark pleated skirt, a little hat with a veil. She looked pretty, frivolous. And as though she had just stepped out of the past.

"A ghost in the frame," said Eliza.

"Poetic," said Ben.

"Really, it's what an analyst called past relationships that interfere."

"Ben!" Ruth called again. "Come pose with me!"

"She who must be obeyed," he said, tipping his hat.

Eliza arranged the peonies in the silver pitcher she'd brought back from her childhood home after the spring trip out, the last visit there.

Take what you want now. In Sweden they call this death cleaning, her mother had said.

Nick had looked frightened.

No one's dying, she'd said later, alone with him. *She's just really upset, about selling the house, the move.*

Grandpa is, Nick said.

Eliza had hugged him, and he had let her. Parkinson's was incremental death. Nick and her father had been so close. She'd felt thankful over the years, for the way her father had stepped up, seeming to almost fill the space that should have been a father's.

"Knock, knock? We're here!" Ruth and a small woman with bright, probing eyes stood on the step. "This is Wren, from the city's preservation office. She'll lead the cottage tours."

Wren carried an armload of papers and photographs. "I've brought the original plans for the cottage. Where should I put them?"

"How about the dining table, if it's big enough," said Eliza. She felt uneasy, the cottage, her cottage, was about to be on display.

"Thanks for letting us invade. I lived in the gatehouse for a Frank Lloyd Wright house once. It feels—intrusive, doesn't it?" Wren had a nice, eye-crinkling smile. She understood, at least.

"Well, a bit," Eliza said. "My son's room upstairs is off limits. Teenagers, you know."

"No problem," said Wren. "I had a couple of those."

"I thought Nick was at camp?" said Ruth.

"Oh, change of plans. His room will have to be off limits."

"Well, it's not of particular interest. Let's just do the walk-through," said Ruth, impatient. "It's almost time."

Wren paused in front of the mantelpiece. "Wow! Who loaned you the Gertrud Jacob paintings, Ruth? They're perfect here. I thought her secretary had taken the paintings, along with her papers."

"Eliza?" asked Ruth.

"Found them today, in one of the crawl spaces."

"We'll have to check with the lawyer," Ruth said.

"Frieda, obviously. And that nude is stunning," said Wren.

"Anything else up there?" Ruth asked.

Frieda looked down from the mantel piece, pleading with Eliza.

"Nothing," said Eliza. "These were way in the back."

"May I go upstairs? They will want to see the bathroom," said Wren. "Morbid, but that's the way people are."

"Back when I was a realtor, it was a challenge, selling houses where there's been a death like that. But packs them in for open houses," Ruth said.

Eliza cringed at the thought of people crowding into the bathroom, looking at the tub. At least it was spotless. "The cleaners were great, Ruth," she said. "I'm going out to the party now."

"Go! Enjoy yourself!" said Ruth.

Eliza found Phil leaning against a tree, listening to the jazz trio play.

"Not bad Gershwin, for a high school. Talent pool at a big school is different than a little place like mine. Prosecco," he said, offering her a sip.

"The developer's paying for all this?"

"Ben's not crazy about the society being beholden, but it's a nice spread."

"How did Nick do?"

"Fine. Good worker. Who's that in the frame?"

Two elderly women were posing. Roberta was unmistakable, her now snow-white braids in a crown. The former head nurse still lived in the neighborhood. Eliza encountered her from time to time. She never failed to ask after Nick, kindly.

"The one with braids was the head nurse. The other was an analyst here, trained under Frieda Fromm-Reichmann."

Eliza remembered the analyst's keynote at the final symposium here, about the therapeutic effect of the Lodge's natural environment. It was a beautiful talk, almost an elegy, since the Lodge was for sale by then.

Ruth tapped the lectern microphone. Feedback crackled.

"Speech time," said Phil. "Grab seats, I'll make a bubbly run."

Eliza slipped into the back row.

"Here," Phil whispered. "I actually found champagne."

"This is costing a fortune!"

"Yeah, well, developer's dime."

Ruth began. "Delightful to see so many illustrious Lodge staff, and so many supporters of our local history. And our dedicated mayor and council, our senator. It does take a village." The veil on her hat fluttered. "Today we celebrate our special collaboration with Chestnut Acres Properties. Most of you know that after the Lodge closed, the plans for a clinic and later for a school both fell apart. Third time's the charm! Join me in welcoming Ed Johnson."

"Ben says she saved what's left of old Rockville," Phil whispered.

The developer waved away the microphone and walked out from behind the podium, waving at the audience.

"Used car salesman or game show host?" said Phil.

Eliza giggled and almost sputtered wine.

"Greetings, folks. Can you hear me? Sure you can—I'm used to shouting over construction. Well, on this great day, our very first home is occupied. Stand up, Mike." Eliza's new neighbor stood, grinning, seeming to enjoy the limelight. "If you like the look of this guy, come be his neighbor. Check out the model home, open today. And the diorama in our welcome center."

"AKA as the tacky trailer on our back line," said Phil. "Can't wait till it's gone."

"Next up is my righthand man, the guy responsible for bringing you what are going to be gorgeous state of the art condos right over there."

The architect looked dignified in suit and tie, but he hunched over the podium a bit. Shy, Eliza thought, rooting for him. Classroom teaching had burnt out her stage fright, but she remembered.

His voice cracked. "Adaptive re-use of historic buildings, giving them a new life, is my specialty. A hundred years back, this was a resort hotel. People came out of Washington for the cool breezes in Rockville." He seemed more at ease. "Then came the sanatorium, different kind of healing. And now, it's an honor to be working on creating beautiful, energy efficient condominiums."

The developer reclaimed the podium. "Thanks, Carter. A year from now folks, we'll hold Ruth's shindig in the grand foyer. You're all witnesses to the invite. Hold me to it! And now prize time!"

A drum roll sounded as Ruth and the senator stepped to the podium.

"Who's getting the preservation award?" Eliza asked Phil.

"Ben wasn't on the committee. Top secret."

The senator flourished the envelope and slit it open. "The Preservation and Restoration Award for 2009 goes to—Ben Godwin and Phil Wentz for outstanding restoration of Rose Hill, the former home of the founders and directors of the Chestnut Lodge."

Phil's eyes glistened.

"Go!" Eliza ordered, taking his glass. "He wants you up there."

Ben was hoarse. "Thank you all, especially the founding family members here today. The Bullards have been so generous with memories of growing up at Rose Hill, working and living at the Lodge. This award is yours, too. Our home is yours, and our door is open to you."

Perhaps everything for the Lodge patients and staff would have been different if the family had been able to hold onto the hospital, Eliza thought. Perhaps she'd still be working here.

"Now, a last very special guest," Ruth announced.

The boy at the keyboard began to play a familiar melody, one of the pieces she'd been working on from Frieda's music in the piano bench.

A petite woman stepped out of the cottage. She wore a navy blue shirtwaist, a string of pearls, a cardigan draped over her shoulders. Gray hair pushed back from a high forehead. Frieda!

"Thank you," she said, in a low voice with a pronounced German accent. She was so short she had to stretch to reach the microphone. "And thank you, young man, for playing so beautifully. That was my favorite Mendelssohn, his song of lost happiness. I played it so often Dexter called it Frieda's Song."

Eliza felt uncomfortable, possessive. She was good, but play-acting, trivializing Frieda.

After the impersonator's performance, Ruth led the applause and called out, "One more big hand for Frieda, and now, enjoy! Be sure to have your picture taken—Frieda will be over in the frame."

Ghost in the frame indeed, Eliza thought.

She spotted Dee and Steve in the buffet line and started toward them. Someone grabbed her shoulders. She turned, and confronted another ghost.

The shock almost hurt, as though she'd stuck a bobby pin into an electric outlet.

Jeff had grown stout, the blond hair was gray. But the eyes were Nick's. Dark, with that border around the iris.

Once or twice attending a big conference in Washington she'd half expected to run into him. Dressed, did her make up, rehearsed her lines. But they had never crossed paths, moving in the different circles of psychiatrists and social workers. She hadn't expected him to come from Boston today. It was as though thinking about him, remembering, had conjured him up.

"You look just the same," he said. "Absolutely smashing."

The stock compliment was offensive. She didn't look the same and neither did he. He was dressed the same, blazer, jeans, boots— still his idea of radical chic, she supposed. The worn face showed he'd lived hard, partied hard, and it had caught up with him.

"Wasn't that Frieda impersonator incredible? Remember how I made you all read her in the seminar? Perfect! Whole event is a blast from the past!" He was talking very fast.

She searched for signs of Nick in his face. Except for those eyes, she didn't see anything. But it was like trying to imagine a child's face grown old, a milk carton image of an abducted child aged by algorithm.

The paunch made his legs seem shorter. He used to work out on the Lodge paths, skipping rope in shorts, fighting the battle of the bulge, he'd joked. Well, he'd lost that battle. Skinny Nick would never look like this.

"God, it's great to see this place. What a time we had."

He was casual, cheerful. Was what had happened between them so inconsequential he didn't care?

"What are you up to these days?" he asked.

"Still at the clinic where I went from the Lodge. Are you still at McLean?"

"Oh lord no. Solo practitioner. Love the autonomy."

There was something evasive about the quick response. She recalled a rumor on the grapevine. Had he left or been fired?

Jeff, there's a thin line between making independent practice decisions and arrogance, she'd heard another doctor admonish him after an incident on the adolescent ward, a close call. *We do our best, but we're not god,* Jeff had retorted. *Occupational hazards.*

"You must like where you're working, to still be there all these years," he said.

"Used to more. Managed care is no fun."

"Go out on your own."

Didn't he understand a single mother couldn't step away from a paycheck? Even such a master of denial must remember she'd had a child.

"I think about it."

112

A waiter offered a tray of champagne glasses.

"Here you go," Jeff said, handing her one, taking a deep gulp from his. He wore the same silver ring with the lump of turquoise. Still married. "How is—your family?" he asked, looking away. Yes, he remembered.

The bubbles stung her throat. Did he really not even know whether she'd had a son or a daughter? Well, she'd wanted it that way. Still, she almost wanted to toss the wine in his face.

"My son's great but—teens are teens. Nick's having a hard time, actually." Maybe, just maybe, she could ask for his help with a referral. Just a professional favor.

"Certainly worked with my fair share." He was antsy now, scanning the crowd.

"How's Xandy?"

"Says the Lodge is a cult. Home reviewing grant proposals." He drained his glass. "Say, look over there in that frame, with Frieda? That gal was in your class. Don't know what you're all doing to stay the same, but I'd like some of it."

"I don't remember her," Eliza said. She didn't feel like any more reunions.

"Let's go have a snapshot with Dr. Fromm-Reichmann."

"No, thanks," she said. The impersonator was creepy. The set-up was silly. How eager he was, as soon as he heard Nick's name, to break away.

"Here's my card. Give me a call."

She almost crumpled the card, tempted to drop it on the grass; stuffed it into her pocket. Eliza stamped across the lawn to the buffet line, sinking a bit into the grass. Ruth and her historic society weren't going to like the damage done to the lawn by all the high heels. She'd find Dee. No more ghosts.

SEVEN

How long had Phil and Ben been gone? Nick aimed the remote and killed the television. He didn't feel like watching another movie. Anyway, their Siamese cat was weird. Kind of freaking him out with those pale eyes. He'd like to go home. Sneak into the house, up to his room. Play with a normal cat. Play some *Doom*.

Still music over at the party. So much for going home.

He slipped along the stone wall between the development and the Lodge, sneaked behind the trees. Safe on the far side of the building he crept under the bushes by the foundation.

The board was still loose, like he'd left it before going away. He squeezed through. Shit! a splinter! Dropped inside. He reached up and pulled the board across the window. Let his eyes adjust.

Good thing he knew every rotten place on the stairs. Careful not to go too fast and bust through the rot, he climbed to the third floor. Holding back from running but he wanted to be there so bad. His place. His hideout.

Grandpa's binoculars were on the window seat, super heavy but way better than new ones. He'd meant to take them home before going to camp, just in case. Sometimes someone snooped around up here. He hoped not witch lady or one of the halfway house psychos. Maybe it was just an animal. A raccoon, a possum. He didn't care about his magazines and the old sleeping bag, but he was super glad no one messed with the binoculars.

He fiddled with the focus. Even without autofocus and all the bells and whistles, he loved these binoculars. It was like he was looking through his grandfather's eyes. He scanned the branches for birds. His grandfather knew all of them, and what they said. Sometimes his grandfather and grandmother talked in bird calls. Before Grandpa stopped talking.

She was down there talking to some guy. Hitting on her? That would be a miracle though she looked pretty. Boomer said she was hot, for a mom. Boomer didn't have a clue that she was more than fifty.

The window seat was hard. He needed to get a pillow over here. He'd bring her yoga pad maybe. She never used it, though she could use relaxing. Got it for him to sleep on the floor by her bed when he had those bad dreams after 9/11.

Phil, in skinny pants and a white jacket, walked up to her. He was hot too, in a kind of way. You could think about whether guys were hot or not without being gay, though Boomer said no way.

The witch lady was hanging at the edge of the lawn. Ma said not to call her that. Said she wasn't crazy in any dangerous way. That she and the halfway house psychos had been in the Lodge for their whole lives practically and then got released and just couldn't handle it on the outside. Like Elsa the lioness, she said. Crazy and normal were oversimplified concepts, she said. Well, maybe, but they had been locked up for some reason. And lions, even in zoos, kill people—like the kid who fell in the enclosure and got eaten.

People were going into their house. Nobody better go in his room. Poor cat was probably spazzing out. Had he left her hiding cabinet open? Would have brought her up here if he'd thought of it. But the cat would go nuts, with mice and squirrels and raccoons and such. Rats too, maybe, but he hoped not. He'd seen a dead baby possum once which was really gross and it smelled. But when he came back the next time it was gone. Eaten, probably. Cole said nature was a self-cleaning system if you didn't mess with it.

He adjusted the focus. The stuff on the waiters' trays looked good. Scallops in bacon! His stomach rumbled. He was starving. He definitely was going to start eating meat again. Anyway, scallops were fish. But the bacon was the best part.

If he had a decent laptop, maybe he could get wi-fi from the house up here. Live up here like the kid who lived in the hollow tree on the mountain in that book he used to like. He'd charge his Theremin and bring it, too. He'd brought it once, plugged it in, without thinking how of course the electricity and water didn't work. Automatic brain stupidity like during a power failure the way you keep forgetting and flipping the switch. Going to the bathroom though would be an issue. The toilet down the hall was totally gross and no flush. Except for the bathroom issue he could hide out here for days.

He might starve, trapped up here waiting for the party to be over. Dee and Steve were in line for food. She stood out with that red hair. Boomer would say she was hot. Back when he was little he used to worry about what would happen to him if something happened to his mom. She said Dee and Steve were his guardians and they'd take care of him. Back then he sort of wished that something would happen. He'd have two parents and the twins and maybe a TV in his bedroom. But when he thought like that he used to freak and have to go stand by her bed and watch her sleep to make sure she was just sleeping and not dead. If he stared hard enough she usually woke up. Back when he was really little he'd get in bed with her. Before the yoga mat on the floor routine.

He didn't worry so much about her dying anymore. Anyway, at camp they learned the Heimlich and chest compressions and mouth to mouth, practiced on this gross dummy. The thing was not to panic, Cole said. In triathlons the fatalities were mostly during swimming because of panic. Panic is not your friend. Being hungry

117

and tired are not your friends. Right now, he was starving and exhausted. When would this stupid party be over?

Three months and he'd be sixteen. Two years and he'd be eighteen. If something did happen to her, Dee and Steve would be off the hook. He'd be an orphan basically. If you don't count bio-dad loser from some bank of sperm for hire. What kind of guy got paid for jerking off? Probably sold his blood too. Once in a while she put on those sad eyes and said, *if you have any questions, if you want me to tell you what I know.* But he didn't want to know. What was the point? And once or twice, he called her bluff, he pressed it. Said okay, so what do you know? And she got the deer in headlights look. Like how typical last night the one thing she said was that the guy was intelligent. That's what she'd care about. It was like people screwing around with genes to get the kind of kid they wanted. She wanted a smart one. He was a disappointment on that score. And so what if loser dad was a Mensa? That homeless guy at the Metro station with the shopping cart full of his newspaper collection was probably very intelligent. What was the point in hearing about some loser with a high IQ? He had zero interest. Zero.

The band was the jazz group from school. Sounded good, even if they were stuck up IB snobs. Maybe he'd be able to play jazz on the Theremin if he got good enough. Phil said why not, if he was willing to practice. Phil knew all about Leon Theremin and how he invented the ether phone in Russia right after the revolution and how he was a genius and then got screwed out of the rights and everything to what he'd done. Life really wasn't fair. Sometimes it sucked.

His stomach was growling so loud it was amazing people down there didn't hear it and look up. He pulled out the pile of old *PC Gamers.* Something had been gnawing the corners. He flipped through. Too old to really be interesting. He'd bring some newer ones over. He still had the book from school up here too, the one by the girl who was a patient here, saw his mother's shrink lady. He'd kept the book at the end of the year, sort of by accident what with turning in the book report late, with her breathing down his neck. She kept suggesting he tell the teacher where he lived. Said if the teacher wanted the class could come over, like a field trip. Right. Just what he needed, people knowing he lived next to the old psych hospital in the house where the shrink in the book lived.

He pictured the girl in the book sort of looked like that girl Jenn from chorus with the super short almost white hair. Boomer said she was a tad andro, one of those gay-straight alliance types. Well, maybe. And so what? Boomer was a tad Neanderthal. A redneck.

Sitting behind Jenn in chorus, catching the shampoo smell from her hair was the thing, about the only thing, he missed about school. Her hair smelled so good. Like petrichor, the word of the day once in English. *Petri* for stone and *chor* for the fluid in the veins of the gods, the teacher said. It means how the ground smells after it rains after a dry spell. Killer Scrabble word if you had infinite good letters. If he and his mom still played. He'd said no so much she quit asking. He used petrichor in a sentence for extra credit on the final. Maybe it was that word on the final that brought his D up to a C.

He lay on the window seat listening to the jazz, thinking about Jenn, getting horny, taking care of it.

When he woke up, it was quiet. Everyone was gone down there.

A woman was coming out of the door of their house. He trained the binox on her.

Jesus Christ! It was the shrink lady from the picture by his mom's desk! His hands shook. She was gone by the time he got the focus back.

Disappeared into thin air.

Holy shit, he'd just seen a ghost. He was freezing cold like maybe her ectoplasm was floating by.

Or was he hallucinating? Going crazy. Maybe he'd caught crazy germs, living over there in the cottage, hanging out up here. When you think about it, the whole place could be a toxic waste dump of craziness.

EIGHT

Eliza filled a plate with leftovers for Nick—quiche, crab dip, petit fours. And lots of scallops in bacon, he loved those. He'd been drinking milk—the vegan vegetarian phase was over.

"We're going now," Dee said. "Meeting Steve at the car."

The few remaining cars were parked on Thomas Street. Eliza walked with her.

"So?" Dee asked.

"Said I looked just the same. What a crock. Split as soon as I mentioned Nick."

"Want me to stay?"

"I'm okay."

Steve had put the top down; the Mercedes was what he called his mid-life crisis car. He didn't let Dee or the twins drive it.

"When are you coming to the beach? The boys are going to be down over the Fourth," he asked before pulling away.

Eliza hadn't told Dee that Nick had declared the twins preppy snobs.

Strings of lanterns still hung between the trees, in the tents, illuminating the waiters cleaning up. The Lodge loomed like a backdrop for outdoor theater.

The front door to the cottage had been locked. She went around back for the hide-a-key.

"Nick?"

His bedroom door was closed. She knocked. Opened the door.

The indignant cat darted out of the empty room.

She called him. Left a message.

The doorbell rang.

Carter had slung his jacket over his shoulder. "Excuse me," he said. "You're probably not up for a visitor—but I didn't have a chance to see the photographs."

"Come in. There's plans, too, from the architect."

"Those I know. I used them, doing the work."

He stepped in, glancing into the front room she'd turned over to Nick, for homework. Not that he ever studied.

"Frieda's waiting room," he said. "She had a dollhouse I played with when we visited my mom."

"Your mother—was her patient?" No wonder there was a whiff of sadness about this man.

He nodded. "I don't remember a lot. I was little when we moved here to be closer to her. She came home on weekends sometimes. Frieda came to dinner. I thought she was my grandmother."

She'd heard about socializing, drinking. Some doctors even vacationed at patients' beach houses. The boundaries were so porous then, one ethics violation after another by today's standards. How confusing, for children, for everyone.

He lingered a moment in the foyer. "Her secretary sat right here. See the ghost?"

"Ghost?" Was he joking, remembering the secretary?

He pointed. "That faint crack in the ceiling? Where the wall was. We call them ghosts."

"I thought you meant—the secretary's ghost," she said. "After seeing that impersonator."

"How'd you like her?"

"Not much. I'm possessive. Working at the Lodge, living here now. I love this place. Didn't like her pretending to be Frieda. It seemed cheap somehow."

He grinned, the first time she'd seen him smile. It softened the gaunt face.

What would he think of the portrait? "Let me show you something I found."

Carter stood at the mantelpiece and gave a soft exhalation. "It's her. Where was it?"

"One of the cabinets under the eaves."

He looked chagrined. "I thought we got everything out of those crawl spaces."

"Only my kid looking for his stuff would crawl all the way in."

In the dining room, Carter leaned over the table, shuffling through the loose photographs. "This is nice, of Frieda with the dog. Muni was her shadow."

Serious man grown from a serious child. The whole family suffers when a parent is as ill as his mother must have been. Children most of all.

Someone banged on the porch door. A shrill voice called, "Time for my appointment! Time for my appointment!"

Waiting, face pressed to the screen, was the woman Nick called a witch.

"She missed my last appointment."

"I'm sorry, she's not here." Eliza wouldn't challenge her. She was pretty loosely put together, and seeing the impersonator had been a trauma.

"I saw her!"

"She's not here," Eliza repeated, managing to stay calm and firm. So much for Jeff thinking it didn't matter, losing a therapist, so long as you got a new one. This woman must have been barely in her twenties when Frieda died, and she still missed her.

Muttering, the woman walked away, disappearing behind the Lodge.

"Poor thing," said Carter.

"Life is confusing enough for her," Eliza agreed. The phone was ringing in the study. "Excuse me."

"Did they mess with my room?"

It was good to hear Nick's accusatory voice. "Just as messy as you left it," she said, trying to laugh, trying to make him laugh. "I saved you some yummy leftovers. Where are you?"

"Skating," he said, hanging up.

Carter looked up from the photographs. "Everything okay?"

Oh yes, he was sensitive to mood. No wonder. "My son. Not too happy about the visitors. Possessive about this place, like me."

Carter nodded. "Me too. I loved working on this cottage. Took the job at the Lodge against my better judgment. Afraid of someone mucking it up. Now, I'm the one in charge of the muck up." He sounded angry.

"What do you mean?"

"Ed's going broke. Wants to cut corners, do things fast and cheap."

He tidied the pictures into a neat pile. "Going to Rose Hill for the volunteers' wind down?"

She could leave Nick a note; wouldn't stay long. A watched pot never boils. He'd come home if she went out.

It was awkward at first, being at Rose Hill for another party, so soon after dreaming of that holiday night, and seeing Jeff today. Eliza and Carter filled glasses and plates, they sat on the patio by the fishpond. This space hadn't even existed, back then. Relaxing over food and wine, he described a big project he'd been involved in, converting a girls' school into condos. She liked the way he talked about buildings—it reminded her of the way she felt about clients.

Later, they wandered into the kitchen, found Phil cleaning up.

"Can we help?" she asked.

"Absolutely. Ben used the crystal. Can't go in the dishwasher."

Eliza began washing glasses at the sink.

"Get an apron over that frock. In that drawer," Ben said, coming in with another full tray.

Her hands were wet and soapy.

"Let me." Carter pulled out a white waiter's apron and dropped the loop over her head, tied the waist strings, deft fingers touched her for only a moment but it felt—lovely.

"Benj, what did Ed say to do about the left-over booze? Is he keeping it or giving it to the society?" Phil asked.

"He left before the caterers did," said Ben in a clipped voice. He looked spent. "We're keeping it. I paid."

"You mean the society paid?"

Ben didn't answer.

"He skipped out? You picked up the tab? He better be good for it."

"We can write it off."

Eliza and Carter exchanged a glance. Time to leave.

"Between us, Ed's been late with my checks," Carter said as they walked past the barn. "I should quit but it feels like abandoning the Lodge."

"Sounds familiar. I had to leave the Lodge when my paychecks started bouncing."

They walked on. She told him how taking the clinic job had felt like settling for the steady check, benefits, the daycare next door. It had worked out, a good job, good colleagues. "I still miss the Lodge—total immersion. But mothering is immersive enough."

"I don't have kids," he said. "But I get it."

The security light at the new people's house clicked on as they passed.

"I tried to get Ed to install motions lights and cameras over there. For now, it's low tech."

"What do you mean?"

"Me. I'm the security system. I go in. Check things out, every morning, every night. Not that it prevents anything."

So that's where he went, running past. Maybe buildings filled the place of children for him. No ring, no mention of a spouse. A self-sufficient loner.

Nick's windows were still dark. She felt the twinge of fear.

"I enjoyed tonight," said Carter. "Mostly I'm a bit of a recluse."

"Me too," she said.

"Time for my rounds."

He walked away toward the Lodge, a tall shadow against the dark hulk of Main. That developer was getting his money's worth— especially if he wasn't paying.

Eliza called and texted Nick. No answer.

She shouldn't stalk him, but she drove to the Square, the old grocery store parking lot, finally the city skate park by the pool. No skaters. No Nick.

Still no lights in his room when she pulled into the carport.

Eliza changed into pajamas and retrieved the box of Frieda's journal from under her bed. Propped against pillows she prepared for vigil, with Frieda as companion and guide. "I saw his dad today. Bit like your Erich."

NINE

1936

Working with Walter Peter, the architect designing my house, reminds me of analysis, but I am on the other side, the analysand. He listens to me, discerns, gives shape and clarity to my yearnings. He takes in my words and transforms them to blueprints, maps of my dreams (yes, I do dream). It is so seductive to be listened to and deeply understood. It's almost like being analyzed again. I experience the mechanism and alchemy of the talking cure as he listens to me. It is so rare for me to tell someone what I want, what I deeply want. Has anyone ever listened to me like this? Have I ever articulated what I want?

Yes, he says. *I know. You must have light in your study, you will be there most of every day.*

Yes, he says. *Space for a piano. Will a spinet do?*

Yes, windows on either side of the parlor fireplace so you can see Main.

Yes, an electrical bell system to Main. You will be just steps away.

Yes, there will be a room for my mother. And closets and cabinets to store all the belongings a refugee has lost and now reacquires, as though through objects life can be healed and duplicated. Ample dry storage, hidden, capacious as an attic. There will be a deep closet under the stairs, a linen closet on the landing, closets in both bedrooms, long cupboards under the bedroom eaves, big enough to hide in if storm troopers came.

He understands I do not want to waste space on a large kitchen. Unnecessary with the Main dining room steps away. Better to save space for the two china cabinets in my dining room, and the vestibule in the entry for my secretary (I am to have one!), the waiting room for my patients. And in the back of the house: my study, big and quiet, with a view to what will be my flower garden. I will live and write and listen to patients in that room.

As the architect listens, I see how a patient can fixate on the listener, idealize, imagine herself beloved. Not that this happens, between me and the architect. But I experience a kind of transference, infatuation, with this man so dedicated to sheltering me.

I am caught up in anticipation and planning for my home, this new life. I celebrate passing the boards. I grow ever more secure even as my dear ones become ever more vulnerable.

Sally brings my soft-boiled egg and toast, my coffee. I smoke my breakfast cigarette in guilt and safety and read each day's bitter news: civil war in Spain, Roosevelt avoiding "entanglements."

But aren't all mortals entangled? My eyes burn at the photographs in the paper: a woman in California with hungry children, a sign posted on a street corner at home—*NO JUDEN.*

The architect has completed his plan. Dexter clears his broad desk of files and papers for the occasion. Walter Peter unrolls the final blueprint. No document has been so moving to me since Erich and I signed our *Ketubah.*

Mr. Peter's fingers walk through the outlines of the rooms, inhabiting my dreams. For oh yes, I do dream. I have dreamed of this house. This *is* my dream house. I have dreamed it into being.

Here are your double-insulated doors for the study. He traces the double line. For patient privacy, I told him, but really an extra shield from distracting noise.

There will be light and air through the core of the house—even a window on the landing, here. Perfect cross-ventilation, too, front door to screen porch door.

You'll love the porch, says Anne. *You'll live there. We're giving you a glider.*

Dexter and Anne make a ceremony of the "Ground Breaking." I think of the earth opening as in myths, as for a seed to sprout. Anne trims a spade with green and white ribbons—the colors of spring and hope. I shovel up a mound of red Maryland soil, happy as the day I first opened the door of my Therapeuticum.

Yet even as I shovel, I hear the thud of dirt hitting my father's coffin. I think of my mother and sisters. I pray and turn the soil. I pray for everyone, known and unknown, left behind. Guilt struggles with joy.

Anne suggested inviting Erich to the groundbreaking. I did not. He would tease me for my double china closets, taunt me for being more Jewish, more domestic, than I had known. But now of all times, it is important to identify, affiliate—so hard to do here. Erich says I am overidentified with this cottage, invested in it as if it were my child. He is jealous of Dexter and Walter Peter—surrogate fathers for my cottage child. What's the harm of loving the creation of this home? Creating and nurturing, nesting, are maternal acts and arts. I am good at these. I give care. Didn't he tell me to love myself? This house is my gift to myself.

I dote on this embryonic house in progress. Evenings, after the workmen are gone for the day, I change out of the cotton shirtwaist I've adopted as my ward uniform. (Easier to remain calm without worrying about a patient's vomit or feces on my dress. With some of our lonely, frightened ones I swear I need a raincoat!)

Evenings, I walk through the skeleton of my house, with Dexter and Anne, or the architect, or alone. Most happily alone, communing, one on one, in a private session with my home.

The cottage grows, and the Lodge grows, the census grows, our Lodge name grows. Dexter and I must hire new doctors, more staff. Over our nightcap we draw up blueprints of another kind: the map of our treatment philosophy, our regime for patients, our curriculum for our staff.

I'm convincing Dexter that loneliness is truly the great general malady, although its presentation varies. He nods when I say the paranoid, the schizophrenic, differ from the rest of us only in degree of fear, desperation, isolation. We agreed to disagree (his genial American phrase, disagreement isn't fatal here) on some matters. Such as the relevance of dream interpretation. I've become a waking dreamer with this house project, and I believe the waking state, especially of the very ill, is dream-like enough. But I cede this point; the staff will be trained in dream work. We agree that to support our staff in their work we must continually educate them. Staff analysis, debate, discussion, seminars—these will be pillars of our program. These will draw applicants to us! We have already begun a Wednesday colloquium for clinical staff, open to all without hierarchy. And every treating clinician will be analyzed in compensation for what we cannot pay them.

This treatment model is costly, Anne says, with a worried frown.

It's an investment. In our patients, and our staff. It will bear fruit, he says.

Victory! He believes and begins to see it happen.

We take care of each other, he and I and Anne. Our success means Anne can begin renovations to the stone house, Rose Hill, beside the barn. She's happy to finally have ample space for their family, the children, the dogs—and staff seminars. *And parties!* Anne says. *We need some parties.*

Celebration in dark times? At first, I do not think I can find the heart for it but I think of the candles of Chanukah. Yes, we need defiant celebration, too.

They build my house. I offered to pay for it, wanted to purchase it. Embarrassed, Dexter explained, pouring another drink.

There are covenants. Jews may not buy homes here. I'm so sorry, Frieda.

No Juden. No Juden. It is hidden but it is true, even here in Rockville. I've come so far for safety, to escape evil and prejudice. And it is here.

My house is finished! How fast it grew! Balloon framing, the architect explains. Wooden houses go up so quickly. They have such a wealth of forest here.

I look for kosher salt in town, find it at Grossman's. Sally's dark eyes gleam with interest as I explain the custom. She carries the loaf and salt across my threshold—my friend at that moment, not my maid, both of us members of tribes enslaved. We enact the ritual of blessing my new home. It will be my sanctuary.

I walk from room to room, admire the play of light on the glossy floors. Heart pine, the carpenter called the wood. Air flows freely throughout carrying the scent of fresh-cut grass. The footprint is compact, no wasted space, but gracious. It is just the right size for me. Fits me, suits me. The china cabinets nestle in the dining room corners. The carpenter's staircase rises to a graceful turn, white trim on the carved risers like waves—this little house is snug and tidy as a ship. If trouble comes, I can sail away.

Main is close enough to touch. I see the building from my kitchen, my parlor. Sally can fetch my lunch from the dining room there in an instant if I choose to stay at home between my last morning session and my first afternoon patient.

The first night, I try out each of the pair of oversize leather armchairs Erich sent for my study. I test my bed and Klara's across the hall—like Goldilocks. And on the back porch, I smoke a sweet cigarette as the western sky turns red, gold, gray.

Sally, Anne, and I prepare the party—a "housewarming." I buy a new dress for the occasion. I will celebrate my very own home with oysters and champagne, delicious forbidden *traif* from the Eastern Shore. Erich would taunt me for my inconsistency but I love the gleaming oysters on the open shells, the sensual tang of sea and salt. I invite everyone: the architect and his wife, the carpenter, the Lodge staff. Patients wander by and I include them too. The festive moment absorbs me in the here and now, the present.

I do not miss my mother, my sisters, Erich—until the guests are gone. I close my doors. I watch the lights of Main, comforted by its proximity, comforted by the bell in each room here connecting me to the hospital. (Each room, I insisted, not just the hallway, without explaining otherwise I might not hear if they need me.) I put Mendelssohn on the expensive record player I've purchased downtown in Washington (love yourself, Erich says). I turn the volume high—no one to disturb, no pretense, no explanation needed. I will hear every note!

I lower the arm, place the needle onto the disc and listen to Mendelssohn, "Lost Happiness." Yes, my old happiness is lost. But I will make a new one. I will have happiness. It is my resolution, my promise, my defiance of Hitler.

I sit in one of Erich's too-big chairs (his size, not mine) and sip a last glass of champagne. The recording spins to buzzing silence. I slip the record in its jacket and lift my glass to the portrait Gertrud painted. I will not remain that haunted wretch. I stand at the window facing Main to toast Dexter and Anne, the Lodge itself.

L'chaim!

Back on the porch, after rounds, I smoke my last cigarette of this joyful, this defiant day. The stars shine. Tomorrow morning Raymond will plant the flower garden. *L'chaim* indeed, in spite of all.

You should get a puppy, Anne says, watching me play with her children and their comical Great Danes.

"I can't fit a dog in my cottage!"

"Not like ours. A small dog. A spaniel, we know just the breeder, in Virginia."

Raymond has been teaching me to drive—on my very own car (extravagance, love yourself). I crave the independence, the control. He's rigged a block on the brake and accelerator pedals to make up for my short legs. The architect had designed a built-in garage, but I needed the space for my waiting room so he is adding what he calls a "carport."

Anne won't hear of my driving to Virginia for a puppy. Raymond drives, Sally comes along.

We cross the Potomac on a ferry. I smoke by the rail, invite them to join me. They shake their heads, declining. They sit in the car together, eyes fixed ahead. I've forgotten the rules again, off the Lodge property. And the rules hold even there, too, just differently, subtly. I smoke and watch the shore of Virginia approach. At the Olympics in Berlin the fastest man in the world is an American Negro—member of what Hitler calls an alien race.

The litter is just eight weeks old. I want all of them! At last I choose the runt, or he chooses me. Sleek as a black seal he licks my fingers with red sandpaper tongue. Sits in my lap for the ride home, warm as a just baked loaf.

"What will you call him, Dr. Frieda?" asks Sally. In private, she and I are almost friends, Raymond's pretty wife, my maid and occasional cook—though it's easiest most often to walk across the lawn to Main to eat or send Sally for a tray.

The morsel of dog looks up with liquid eyes. I rub his ears, admire the pink lining, veined and delicate as an orchid. He doesn't fuss at this separation from his mother and siblings—both of us have lost our littermates. He is mild, calm. I must emulate him, stop my nighttime weeping for mother and sisters.

"Muni," I say. "I will call him Muni."

"What?" Sally glances over the seat, curious. She's very dark but her nose is long and straighter than mine. No such thing as racial purity, Herr Hitler.

"Hindu. A Sanskrit word for wise one, silent one."

"Like you, Dr. Frieda," smiles Raymond, catching my eye in the rearview mirror. Safe to joke here, be familiar, in the privacy of my car.

"Hardly silent or wise," I say.

"Oh, you are wise, Dr. Frieda," says Sally. "Wisest woman I've come across. And you don't say more than's necessary."

Maybe so. Maybe because I spend so much time listening in session, I listen more than speak outside of my office too. The habit of listening more than speaking is automatic. Perhaps I weary, speaking English. Or perhaps I mistrust my hearing and hesitate. Or all of these are true.

The puppy scrubs my fingers and suddenly my skirt is damp. "Well, I'm not wise enough to know I shouldn't be holding this baby without newspaper on my lap."

We chuckle. Muni rests his sculpted head on his paws and naps all the way home.

I borrow cream from the kitchen in Main, carry it home in a deep saucer. He buries his tiny snout in the cream. I sit on the porch floor, smoking as he laps, both of us contented animals.

The phone rings. Scooping Muni up, I answer

Gertrud rasps, voice thick with phlegm. "I have to leave."

Some problem with immigration? No! "You can't. You can't go back there now." The dangers, what is happening—it is worse all the time.

"Menninger's. I have to leave."

134

But she's barely started the job. I interceded, convinced Karl to take her in my place. *Meet her. She's brilliant, an intuitive genius.* What has gone wrong?

She coughs and spits the words out. Not dismissed; resigned. Quitting because she's too ill to work.

My familiar enemy: tuberculosis. I knew it, even when she evaded the chalk mark on her lapel at Ellis Island. I knew it that night in Chicago.

"Come here," I say. It's the wrong climate, the wrong air. She'll disturb my routine.

She'll fill the emptiness.

My mother continues to defy reason, refuse to even apply to come. Grete remains with her in Germany, frightened but afraid to leave her. Anna at least is in France, though nowhere in Europe is safe. Stubborn Mother Klara turns her deaf ears to the danger she is in, puts all of them in.

My cottage, meant to be shared, is ready. Gertrud will have Klara's room. And if by some miracle Klara agrees to come, and by another miracle we can get them all in? Too much to hope for, but if it comes, we'll deal with that wonderful overflow somehow.

"Come here, Gertrud. We will feed you with fresh food from the farm. You'll rest and get fat and well. You'll paint. This is a sanatorium, after all."

"Tante Gertrud is coming," I tell the puppy, making him a nest of towels by my bed, tucking in a hot water bottle and a ticking clock. Anne says the bottle and the clock will be like a decoy mother, keep him cozy on this first night alone.

He sleeps. I am the one comforted by the ticking clock. I lie and imagine Gertrud asleep across the hall. Remind myself that Erich survived TB; that's not how I lost him.

Just as I fall asleep the bell above my bed rings. It's Main, a patient crisis. Carrying Muni, I rush across the lawn in slippers and my yellow robe.

"Hold the puppy," I instruct the terrified, hallucinating patient. Whether it is my firm presence or the puppy in her arms, she calms.

The healing balm of taking care of something, someone in need—how well I know it. Dexter and I will talk about tonight's serendipitous experiment. I will extend his father's principle. If it's better to plant roses than make paper flowers, how good it will be for patients to care for animals. Surely there's therapy to tap there. Animals are not such dumb beasts after all.

Walking home beneath the stars, the puppy in my arms, Gertrud coming—I feel content.

"Good work, little wise one," I whisper. We sit in Erich's leather armchair, I stroke the puppy asleep, rehearsing what I will say to Dexter at rounds the next day.

"Gertrud Jacob is coming," I will tell him—an announcement, not a request.

I must talk to Erich. Hating the cost, hating the cumbersome procedure of connecting through the operator and the possibility of being overheard by the switchboard (reality, not paranoia, though we all have touches of paranoia). I hate dependence, but I still must talk to Erich. At moments of urgency, I must talk. And I cannot talk to Gertrud, so it must be Erich.

He says Karl has surely sacked her, finding her crazier than his patients.

You of all people know TB, I say.

I do. And she has it. And psychosis, too. You would recognize it if you weren't blinded by—affection.

And I know what narcissism looks like! I retort. *And jealousy, dog in the manger.*

136

No one else makes me so angry. I can imagine his condescending smile, the lips stretched thin. *Always to the rescue, Friedl.*

Must you disrespect her and me? Were you listening in my class? Do you recall that the line between sanity and madness is a continuum?

I heard you. I hear you, Lieber professor.

If you had her sensitivity your prose might sing a bit.

I have no desire to sing. I am writing and publishing. Let her paint but keep her out of the consulting room. I must go.

Has Karen come into his room? I slam down the receiver. Foolish to call, to pay to be hurt. Muni whines, distress is contagious. I cradle the puppy in my lap, he cocks his head to one side, listening—the way I do, favoring my better ear. The little rascal is imprinted on me.

Muni, stupid Erich thinks health means ordinary, conventional social adjustment. As if homogeneity is the goal! How can he think that? A German Jew!

Muni blinks, agreeing.

Erich cannot understand friendship, so driven by id and appetite.

Muni yawns. I must laugh, at puppy and myself.

I picture Gertrud's first impression of the cottage. Raymond brings flowers from Anne's garden for bouquets in every room. I display the portrait, my ugly portrait, on the mantel. I accept the likeness, let go of vanity. My painted face of that moment reflects the anguish of these times. She is brilliant, painter and analyst both, a soul reader.

Raymond and I meet the train. She limps along the platform, leaning on me. I settle her in the back seat, hold her hand as we motor back to the Lodge.

Too tired to eat, she starts to climb the stairs to the bedroom Sally and I have prepared.

"Just let me catch my breath." She sways. Raymond and I catch her and help her to the porch, onto the metal gliding swing Anne and Dexter gave me. I lift her feet, elevate her head, ease her breathing.

She lies still, eyes on the bright scene outdoors. The children are at play, shouting and laughing.

Sally brings tea. She sits up and sips.

The sky turns red with sunset.

"No wonder you love it here."

I retrieve the satchel Klara gave me when I graduated medical school. The leather is dry and battered.

"Mother says I'm not a real doctor," I say, warming the stethoscope in my hands.

Gertrud laughs and coughs.

I unbutton her blouse and place the scope on the tissue of veined skin just above her breast. She's lost more weight, her breast would fit in my cupped hand.

"Breathe, easy breaths." Coaching myself too.

The rapid heartbeat, the occluded stutter is nothing like the hoof beats of a healthy baby in the womb, the steady ticking of Muni's decoy clock. Her lungs are thick.

"I have medicine," she says. "Erich has been sending it to me."

"Erich?" I am torn between jealousy and relief to know they have some bond.

"I didn't want Karl Menninger to know. Didn't want to worry you."

"Well, I'm prescribing for you now."

I send Raymond to Vinson's pharmacy to fill my prescription and bring ice cream. Sally loads a tray with medicine, a bowl of ice cream.

"Thank you both," I say. "You must go home." They live in the Negro neighborhood, Haiti it's called, not far away but I've never seen it, never visited their ghetto, to my shame.

"We're staying till you're home from rounds with Dr. Dexter," Sally says. "Bring me a mask from the infirmary when you get back." Sally withdraws to the kitchen.

Gertrud dozes on the glider. The untouched ice cream melts into a puddle in her bowl. I let Muni lap it up.

I wash as though scrubbing in for surgery before going to Main. I must protect the patients. Dexter knows she's ill, that the workload at Menninger's was too much for her. What more might Erich have told him? I cannot let him know how ill she is or he might insist on quarantine. Such dire measures are not called for. I will take all due precaution, I will stabilize her, I must keep her secret. I will cure her. TB is simpler than the psychosis we cure here, after all.

"Anne invites you and Dr. Jacob to tea tomorrow," Dexter says over our nightcap.

"She's tired, from the journey."

The shed of eyebrows goes up, he studies me with his deep diagnostic gaze. He's caught me keeping a secret, he will be angry. He's slow to anger but I've seen it and do not want to be on the wrong side.

"We can't risk our patients," he says. "Or our good name. My connections, Frieda."

Reminding me, it is not only me, the German doctor with a whiff of Freud by association that accounts for our success.

"I will keep her quite separate in the cottage. Rest is what she needs. I will take all necessary precautions."

"I am uneasy, Frieda."

Anger and fear are so close, so primitive. I feel the flare of both. "She is like a sister. If she goes, I must, too."

"Be careful," he says. "We have a lot at stake."

Raymond and Sally managed to get her up to bed. Muni lies at the threshold to her room, on guard. Gertrud breathes more easily, asleep.

Muni follows me.

I lie in bed, door open, strain to hear her across the landing. I cannot.

"Sleep with her," I tell Muni. Picking him up, placing him at her feet. My little wise one will rouse me if she needs me.

Later, I do hear her, calling out. I hate to hear it but am relieved I can.

"I dreamed I was suffocating," she says.

A fever dream, I reassure her, and pull the sewing rocker bedside, sit stroking her forehead until she falls asleep. Just as I did with my sisters.

And I am asleep in the chair by her bed when coffee's rich aroma rouses me.

Sally is scrambling eggs. There's just room in the kitchen for me to enter and pour a cup of coffee, lean against the icebox, and take in the sweetness of her caring presence, her care for me and Gertrud.

"You mother me," I say, grateful.

She deftly slides the eggs from skillet to my flowered plate—my dairy dishes. She listens and remembers.

"Dining room, please, Dr. Frieda," she gestures. "Raymond and I weren't blessed with children. I just take care of everyone who comes my way."

Ah, so we are kin in that way, too.

No children. I should have asked before, not taken her for granted. I should have sought to know her as a person. I'm aware again, ashamed again, of my own prejudice, the separation between us. It's the old habits in a new place, not fully knowing the person who serves us. My sister writes that our loyal gentile maid still stays on with Klara, despite the danger.

"Well everyone who comes your way is lucky."

"Our neighbor children need more than me. Just put our house up as collateral for the school case," she adds, a frown crossing her face.

"What case?"

"Our teachers don't get even half what the white ones do. It's going to court."

I should have known, shame on me. "May I help you with the cost?"

She leans on the chair opposite me. "Eat up," she says, ignoring my offer. "You'll need your strength, sitting up all night."

After the rich, buttery eggs, the sharp coffee, I crave my first cigarette of the day. I go outside to smoke, thinking of Gertrud asleep upstairs, careful not to pollute the air inside. I sit on the porch in my yellow robe, so comfortable it's like a second skin. It's almost time to leave her for morning rounds. Usually I am so eager but today I hate to go.

"Time you were dressed and over there," Sally says. "I'm here."

I dress in my cotton shirtwaist uniform and spray the rose water the pharmacy mixes for me, to cover the smoke scent.

She is still sleeping. Muni thumps his stubby tail.

"You and Sally are in charge," I say, and walk across the lawn to Main.

***

1937

I believe in the power of healing relationship, with psychological and physical illness. Gertrud's progress is daily evidence. She comes downstairs for breakfast, we eat in the dining room, passing the paper back and forth. Easier to bear the news sharing it. There is another enormous "peace rally" in April, but it is not peace they rally for, rather it's an ugly demonstration calling for greater isolation. I blame the President for setting the tone, she defends FDR, says it's larger than one man.

The Hindenburg explodes and the terror of it, the pain for the victims, is appalling but I'm almost angry at how much attention one disaster gets when the huge, insidious distant evil in Europe is brushed under the carpet. Acute disaster is easier to focus on, to mobilize around, than gradually increasing threat. You know what they say about boiling frogs, she says. Put them in the water and raise the heat gradually and they won't realize until it's too late. She could be speaking of some of my colleagues here. She could be referring to my stubborn mother.

We talk, we argue, we agree and disagree. Terrible to say, but I am grateful she fell ill and needed me. She reads Rilke aloud. The phrase, "protect each other's solitude" stays with me like a rabbi's blessing.

Gertrud sets up her easel on the porch and paints in the afternoons, bundled in layers of sweaters. Sally cuts the fingers out of knitted gloves and creates "painting mitts."

The pungent pine forest scent of oil and turpentine seeps inside. My walls, our shared walls, are hung with what she calls her "rogues gallery." Some faces she paints from memory—I recognize Erich, eyes gleaming with brilliance, and self-satisfaction. She selects the telling detail. Her Dexter looks out from beneath those eyebrows.

She makes quick sketched impressions of patients, glimpsed and committed to memory on her walks about the grounds. She is adding these to the portfolio she brought of her images of psychosis. Erich is partly correct. She does understand these troubled states of mind from the inside, but it is her imagination, her artistry, which permits her to slip inside the other's skin, inhabit the experience. One of my favorites she calls "Delusions." Two silhouettes, two women, float in a fantastical scene of arching trees that could almost be a version of our chestnuts. And the women might almost be us, here in our illusion of peace and security.

After my last patient I emerge from my office; she puts down her brush and we walk to town—slowly. We pick up packages at the post office. I mail my letters to Mother, Anna, Grete, doubtful they will arrive, but a necessary gesture of faith to cast out the lifeline of words on paper. We sit and rest over ice cream at the pharmacy's marble counter before the walk back.

She is gaining weight and strength: living breathing testimony to the efficacy of curative atmosphere. I'll put the Lodge TB cure up against the sanatorium in Davos! She is calmer too. Creativity is the best outlet for disequilibrium. Painting for her is like cultivating roses; Dexter's father would approve. And Dexter does approve, of her return to health, of my keeping my promise to protect our patients.

Sometimes in the evening she and I go into town to the movie in the grand new Milo theater, six hundred seats. Sally and Gertrud both are fans of Clark Gable. Gertrud invited her to join us for the latest opening, *Saratoga*.

Sally declined, explaining about the Colored balcony.

No Juden, No Juden.

Gertrud's cheeks flamed with indignation. It is another sign of strength that her capacity for outrage has returned. "We will no longer patronize the movie theater," she announces. I am relieved. I cannot bear the newsreels. The images, huge and vivid, are my waking nightmare: scenes of fighting in the streets of Spain, *brother killing brother*, the narrator says and music swells as though it is drama, story, not reality. The worst was the scene of daily life in Berlin. A café. My mouth watered for the coffee and pastries— and then Mussolini and Hitler filled the screen and Nazi soldiers marched and saluted, and the Star of David was branded across shop windows.

She is studying for the boards. Competitive, teases me that she'll pass on her first try, as I did. I hope so. I will convince Dexter to hire her.

She grows stronger; the Lodge does too. Our patient waiting list is longer every week. Prospective staff send resumes and we have our pick. Anne and Dexter have completed the renovations at Rose Hill and moved in. Gertrud and I were among the four hundred guests at their housewarming party: people from town, people from the analytic community here, in Baltimore, even New York, and the children's friends. More people than I know in all of America! Perhaps more than I know in all the world now, so many are lost.

I awake in the middle of the night after that party, although I am not on call. Our staff is large enough now to rotate the responsibility—I almost miss it. I awake with a headache and a heavy conscience. It was too easy to celebrate in the bright sunlight among Anne's roses. Too easy to forget the world beyond us here, even for me. Not waking Gertrud across the landing, I tiptoe downstairs, Muni my shadow. I make cambric tea, heavy with milk and cream, my mother's remedy—and lace it with bourbon, my own American addition.

The holidays come, the holy days. I miss my father.

"I'll go to synagogue downtown in Washington with you, if you'd like," says Gertrud before Kol Nidre. "Or to Baltimore." She's joined me on the porch, watching the sun set. She offers to join me in my fast, but I insist she eat the dinner Sally brings her from Main.

We do not go to services. The long, dark day, saddest day of the year, would be too much for her. I fast and rest from labor. I do not

144

see any patients. I withdraw from this beloved community and sit quiet, trying to pray.

Feeling such dread, I cannot pray. Wondering whose names, how many, will be inscribed in the book of life this year, how many in the book of death.

Gertrud and I spend the entire day together in seclusion. We speak German. Protecting each other's solitude. Or are we the two deluded women of her painting withdrawing from the terrible world?

Although studying for the boards is work, although it is the holiday, she studies. Soon she throws down the textbook.

"How insufferably dull psychiatry on the page is. How is that possible? People are infinitely interesting! Every other specialty has illustrated text. We should have an illustrated psychiatric textbook. It could be a study tool and also a diagnostic one—like your birder's book. Students could see what melancholia looks like. Mania."

Muni yips, picking up the excitement in her voice. I stroke him calm. Her eyes glitter and her cheeks flush with creative energy, not TB, not mania.

"No one would want their photograph in such a text. Though it is a good idea," I say.

"Not photographs! You and I will collaborate. I'll use the portraits I brought from the hospital in Heidelberg, and the new ones I've begun. And Friedl—you will write the case descriptions."

No! My desk is piled high. Too often already instead of working at night we talk, play music, read poetry, when I should be at my desk.

But—the project would be good for her.

And might it be good for me? The blank page is never as compelling for me as a living breathing person, or patient. Dexter says I must publish, we must get the word out. She would be muse and spark.

"It's a good idea," I say.

"It's brilliant!" She laughs and doesn't cough.

She turns sketches into paintings, speaking likeness of inner states. After rounds, I sit at my desk, or sit in bed with my lap desk, trying to write the case studies, searching for the words (the English words, one advantage she has over me, painting needs no translation). I concoct vignettes to match the truth of her illustrations. A picture is, as they say, worth a thousand words. I see a hint of Erich in the sketch for grandiosity, and she recognizes him in my description, too. We laugh.

I show Dexter the first chapter. Braced for him to see it as nothing more than an exercise in occupational therapy for Gertrud.

He studies the pages, turning back again to the beginning, the illustration of despair.

"This is unique. This combination—it brings diagnosis to life. We must publish this. It's testament to what we do here. It will put the Lodge on the map."

On his map the Lodge is already the center of the universe. And for me too, there are days like that. Days when the outside world, even the world of Germany, almost does not exist, so intent is my focus, so intense is the work.

I am pleased with his approval. The project ensures Gertrud's welcome. He invites her to be the guest speaker at the next staff colloquium at Rose Hill. Gertrud presents our proposal, shows the first pages. No one would call her shy or aloof. She shines. No one would call her mad. She is clear and direct.

The staff is quiet, then applauds. The portraits spark discussion, almost free association about mental states, about key visual clues. The meeting runs late but Gertrud is energized rather than depleted.

The new psychiatrist is the last to leave. "I wish my wife could see these," he says. "She's an artist herself."

"Well, come to dinner, bring her," I say, carried away by the success of the meeting, and the gleam in Gertrud's eye.

Impulsive, I invite the couple, and Anne and Dexter as well.

Preparing, Gertrud layers paintings on every wall in every room. I arrange flowers from my cutting garden. Sally cooks the entire meal in our tiny kitchen with nothing prepared next door at Main. The rich scent of roast chicken and potatoes carries me back to childhood. I set the table with the cloth, the silver, and the candlesticks from my second dowry, purchased by myself, for myself.

Gertrud disappears upstairs, dressing behind a closed door. She emerges in her black crepe gown with the deep neckline, flushed (excitement not fever), fragrant with her precious Chanel. The hoarded scent evokes Paris. Will we ever see it again?

"You look like a movie star," says Sally as Gertrud glides down the stairs.

"Or a dancing teacher," I tease.

Upstairs I don my gray shantung, my pearls.

Everyone is gathered already in the parlor when I return. I did not hear the bell, the voices. I feel like a tardy guest at my own party.

The doctor's young wife is striking. Her face is pale and rouged, fingers long and manicured—not a working artist's hand. And Chanel! She and Gertrud both wear the same scent, laughing at the coincidence.

Gertrud escorts us from room to room, like the exhibit curator as well as the artist. The husband tags along behind with me.

"All patients?" the woman asks.

"Composites," says Gertrud.

Dexter coughs, uneasy.

"I do not paint patients from life."

"Incredible! I would have thought they had to be life studies—so individual," the woman says.

Gertrud smiles. She's at ease, her best self. I'm happy for Dexter and Anne to see her this way. He must recognize what an asset she will be to our staff when she is stronger.

"Would you paint my wife? If you'd like to do a life study?" the young doctor asks. "I've always wanted her portrait done."

"Now, darling what diagnosis do you think I represent?"

"Perfect health!"

They laugh and kiss.

"Seriously though," he says as they leave at the end of the evening, adjusting his wife's shawl around her shoulders. "I do want her portrait."

"It's getting chilly painting on the porch," Gertrud says to Dexter. "I'll need a studio."

He nods, all seriousness. "Yes, yes. You must have space to finish the plates for the book. We'll find room for you in the art barn."

Her studio is snugged away between the art therapy and the wood working rooms. It's her office, and good for her to dress for work, walk to the barn. Occupational therapy, I tease her, but it is true.

From my study window I watch her stride from cottage to barn, stronger and more vigorous every day. She spends hours painting, often not home yet when I finish my last session.

Muni and I walk over and bring her home. "I reek of turpentine," she says. "I must run up for a bath." I inhale the scent greedily, it's the scent of health on her, mingled with the outdoor air.

"I couldn't get my nails clean," she complains after bathing. She buffs and shapes her nails, polishes. She offers to do mine and I agree, but without any polish. Lacquer only accentuates my ugly nicotine stained fingers.

Most evenings now instead of going to eat in Main, I bring back supper for both of us. Muni sits under the table and begs for the scraps she sneaks him. Afterward we listen to records, or I play the piano while she reads, or she reads Rilke aloud before the fire. It is quiet reunion after the day of work separation, a family evening. My real, interrupted life has begun again. Sometimes later when I return home after my evening rounds and nightcap with Dexter, I find she's gone back to the studio with Muni. I fetch them home. The trees cast long moonlit shadows over our enchanted wood.

One evening Dexter and I have driven to Baltimore for the meeting of the Psychoanalytic Institute. Our reputation flourishes and our Institute begins to rival the one in New York! He's proud, of me, of us.

The cottage is dark. Gertrud must be in her studio.

He drives to the barn. "I'd like to see how her work is coming along."

The strip of windows in her studio glows like a lantern, muslin curtains pulled closed.

Gertrud stands at her easel, back to the door.

The psychiatrist's wife faces her, naked as a goddess. "Hello," the woman says, poised, without fluster.

Gertrud continues working. "Don't tell! It's to surprise him."

Dexter turns brick red and leaves.

"Sorry if I upset him," the woman says, dressing, nonchalant. Leaving with a kiss for Gertrud, a wave for me.

"Oh, Americans," Gertrud laughs, cleaning her brushes. "Puritans."

"But this is patient space, this barn. It's not appropriate."

Hearing the schoolteacher in my voice I know I sound like a prude. But after this? Dexter will not trust her with patients. It's reasonable to be angry.

I leave her cleaning up, walk home counting my paces to calm myself. Muni welcomes me, I carry him upstairs to my room. For the first time I close my door to her.

She taps, calls through the door. Muni whines.

I turn over, onto my better ear. Shut her out. There are times it is useful to be deaf. It would have been better to be blind tonight.

Lying awake I shock myself with jealousy. How can I confuse this with Erich's infidelity? How can this open that wound? Gertrud and I are friends, not lovers. Friends, not spouses. Why so angry? Why does this feel like betrayal? Why do I recall the blond strands in Erich's hairbrush?

I am furious. The line between sanity and madness is not absolute and we're none of us immune. I want retribution. I want the young doctor and his temptress spouse turned out of our Lodge Eden. I want them scurrying down the drive, heads bowed in shame.

I am ashamed of my primitive rage.

Breakfast is silent. I hide behind the paper.

She rips it away. "A live model is no different than a cadaver in medical school."

"Except she is alive. And this is a psychiatric hospital. A patient might see and be traumatized."

Her eyes snap. "Not at that hour! And what would be the trauma? There are patients stripping on the ward, I've even seen them naked on the grounds. Let them work the trauma out in your interminable analysis."

"Dexter trusted you with the studio. You are abusing it."

"What happened to free expression? Are we Fascist here too? I'm a painter, Frieda. Painters paint."

I almost strike her!

I teach my students to be aware of countertransference. Watch out for the way the analyst's own unexpressed desire, submerged longing, memory, may trap and ambush. Beware if any of our own reactions seem out of proportion: a warning of subterranean, sub-conscious danger.

How hard to apply my lessons to my life.

The portrait is apparently not what the young husband expected. He does not pay, refuses it. Gertrud brings the rejected canvas home, dumps it on my bed, like a cat depositing a dead mouse.

I take the portrait she painted of me from the mantel. I look at the two paintings side by side. Stunned by how ugly she renders me, and how beautiful the other. I wrap them, shroud them, shove them deep under the eaves. I would burn the paintings—but she would call me Fascist. I sit at the piano and pound out the notes of "Lost Happiness."

Dexter clears his throat, lights my cigarette as we sit for our nightly review and drink. After we discuss the patient issues he says, "Anne is quite upset." And so is he.

I take a long draught on my cigarette. "What's done is done. Gertrud's not going to continue it. He doesn't want it. We can close this case. Move on."

"A reporter called. Says he heard a doctor is painting naked patients."

Has the young wife planted this story? Laughing at us, hurting us.

"Did you tell him that's ridiculous?"

"Of course. But denying a story never kills it. Frieda, one rea-son for our success is you, my dear. But as you know another is my reputation, my father's, our roots. We cannot afford scandals."

He has never called me my dear. I am not dear to him tonight. He is warning me I may be expendable.

I drink too fast. The liquor burns.

He glowers beneath his brows. "Tell Gertrud not to discuss it if this reporter tracks her down." He looks into his glass. "The husband approached me before this incident. He wants the residential post in Main."

Since Anne and Dexter moved to the Little Lodge, another doctor has been in their former apartment. Now he is leaving. We need a successor, a new live in.

Banish them both, I want to say. Doctor and wife.

Dexter's eyes pouch. The brows droop. "I turned him down today."

Without consulting me.

He sips, I smoke.

"Just as well," I say.

"I knew you would agree." He pours us each another drink. We're colleagues again.

She's waited up, sits in the parlor, listening to the record player—the Mendelssohn.

"It's late," I say, stern. "You should be in bed."

We climb the stairs together, not speaking, Muni at our heels. I claim Muni and close my door.

I lie awake. I get up and open my door, go back to bed and stare at the ceiling. There is no room for pettiness in this life. I am piercingly aware in the lonely clarity of the dark room of my good fortune, the contrast between my safe life and the other, over there. Secure here, with work and beloved friend. Secured by the lucky chance of entry at already almost too late a moment. Now the funnel narrows for the many in need of safety as danger increases. Now the hurdles are even higher than when I gathered up my birth certificate, tax documents, medical clearances, police certificates, listed property down to the contents of my cedar chest and paid tax on it all. Left the required list behind, a map to help the Nazis steal our treasure. Just lost things, it is *lives* that matter and lives I fear for.

The next morning, I apologize. There is no place for trivial quarrels now.

"I was angry. I am sorry." I warn her of what Dexter said, caution her not to jeopardize our places here, his good will.

"I never meant to hurt you, Liebste," she says.

I am her dearest. Love hovers in the air above our breakfast table.

We turn to the papers and, after breakfast, to work. Gertrud returns to her studio, our book. And I to my long, good day of patient sessions. I listen better, I hear better, as though the passionate quarrel cleared my ears and deepened my understanding.

Gertrud is recovering, stronger and stronger. Sundays she insists we go to museums. I need to write but I rejoice in her recovery. Only Gertrud is brave enough to drive with me. I love driving, being in control. I would have liked to be captain of a ship. I'm improving, though jerky.

At the Smithsonian Institute, we play a game of finding the occasional artwork scattered among the dioramas. We prefer the Freer Gallery. *A Renaissance palace*, she says, *like being in Italy*. As Italy was, not now.

I remember the frescoes in Siena, of good government and bad. Gertrud and I have escaped, the way Boccaccio's storytellers escaped the pestilence. I try to reconcile the serene beauty of Freer's collection of Japanese screens with what the Japanese have done in China. I fear for the Jews in Shanghai.

Gertrud delights in Whistler's Peacock Room, the walls and ceilings lustrous and lacquered, an extravagant dining room transplanted from England.

"Too rich to digest food in this room," I say.

"Who would need to eat in a room like this?"

One day we venture to the Phillips Memorial Gallery. I don't dare drive the crowded residential streets near Dupont Circle. Raymond drives, Sally comes. I am ashamed but no longer surprised that they choose not to enter the museum although the Phillips family has opened the door to all. They go visit a cousin in the Negro neighborhood in Georgetown.

Previously the family's home, the rooms still feel domestic with tiled fireplaces, carved chairs. The first modern art collection in America, the gallery is a memorial to the founder's brother and father. There are concerts, in a paneled room where once the brothers played billiards. The place is an oasis of culture I did not know I missed until tasting it again.

Gertrud is delighted. She says this collection is unique, and arranged according to internal rules of color, shape, and form.

She wanders ahead, and calls out. I find her transfixed, flushed.

"The iris is alive and opening right this moment! The painter is a woman!"

Pattern of Leaves. Georgia O'Keeffe, the small bronze plaque reads.

Crenellated, folded leaves, blood red petals split with a yellow bolt. I dare not say it, even to her, but it reminds me of looking into the secret folded realm, the gate of the womb. Yes, this artist is a woman.

Gertrud glows, absorbing it. She is right, to insist we make these excursions. *Art for dark times,* she says. *We must hold onto what is good and beautiful to get through.*

"Remarkable, isn't it?" A man's voice behind us. "I have others of hers, please follow me." Duncan Phillips himself! His eyes reflect pleasure at Gertrud's rapture.

"Mr. Phillips! This gallery, these paintings…" Her voice breaks.

"It means a great deal to me, to have the collection appreciated."

"Gertrud is a painter herself," I say like a proud mother.

"My wife Marjorie paints," he said. "I learn from her, about looking at a painting."

"Exactly so for me," I say.

We introduce ourselves.

"Chestnut Lodge," he says, quietly. "A friend of mine was treated there." His expression is guarded. I sense his friend did not do well.

Who might it have been? Dexter takes pride that we begin to attract Washington's best families. We do heal, but slowly, and not everyone. Success is never certain, despite my certainty that ours is the way, the best possible way. How to offer hope but not over-promise?

Mr. Phillips leads us through interlocking rooms, intimate rooms. Gertrud whispers, "I could live here."

He pauses before an incandescent blue flower. *"Blaue Petunie,"* he says, with a fine accent.

"She paints flowers the way a German expressionist paints people," says Gertrud, her voice raw. Yes, this artist renders flowers as psychological states—like Gertrud's illustrations for our book. No wonder my dearest is so struck.

He nods, smiling. "Yes, it is an experience, not just a flower, not even just color. We are the first museum to collect Miss O'Keeffe," he says with pride like Dexter's in our work. "I have just purchased another."

We pass through a telescope of rooms into a tiny one, a former sewing room, I imagine.

This painting is brutal: a skull on sand, blood red cliffs behind. The hallucinatory landscape reflects the savage state of our world. It assaults me, jarring in this close space.

Gertrud gasps. "I must study with her."

"She lives in New York, and New Mexico," he says. "Reclusive."

155

We stay for the concert, in the paneled music room, illuminated by candlelight. Paintings on the walls glow in shadows. The music is a Beethoven trio, piano, violin, cello, in A minor. Music in a minor key soothes me now. How can the disease of Nazis come from the Germany that produced this? Good and evil intertwine. Madness and sanity. I close my eyes, hear it perfectly in this resonant room, feel it through the soles of my feet, in the roots of my hair. It must have been so for Beethoven, composing and playing, already growing deaf.

Mr. Phillips invites us to sherry in their private sitting room, with Marjorie. Gertrud drinks the wine and opens like a flower in one of O'Keeffe's paintings, enthusing about our book project.

"We must see your work, Miss Jacob," says his wife.

Dr. Jacob, I want to say, but Gertrud is all artist now.

On the drive back to the Lodge, she rests her head on my shoulder, welcome weight.

We return at the couple's invitation to bring a sample of Gertrud's work. She opens the portfolio.

"Powerful," he says.

"Unique," his wife agrees.

Buy one! Exhibit her!

He does not make that offer. "My friends publish a magazine, might be interested in what you are doing."

His friends, the editors of *The Magazine of the Arts*, offer an illustrated feature story on her paintings of psychosis, request my captions for the plates.

Writing for her, on deadline, for once my words flow. She reads my caption for "Despair" over my shoulder.

Profound Sorrow such as might overwhelm any one of us at some time.

"Frieda! You capture how close we all are to each other, mad and sane."

"You are my muse."

Her glance stirs me like music.

The article appears in the August edition.

Anne and Dexter are proud. Gertrud has redeemed herself, erased the incident of the nude. He increases efforts to find a publisher for our book, offers her a patient to work with, invites her to present a paper to our Baltimore Washington Psychiatric Society. Appoints her to our training committee!

"You'll outstrip me," I say. How happy I would be if she did.

Gertrud's success is the only brightness in an ever darker time. American Nazis assemble in public. Thousands in Long Island held a "German Day" celebration, Erich told me.

***

1938

Spring comes. We see the first sharp green spears of *Schneeglöckchen*. Snowdrops, Anne says. Gertrud paints the blossoms. It snows again and freezes them.

Optimism is dangerous. Hope is false.

Hitler marches into Austria. Germany invades Czechoslovakia.

On the radio we listen to the brave American reporter Dorothy Thompson, the first to be thrown out of Germany several years ago, prescient, denouncing Hitler. Now she dares criticize FDR for not doing enough for refugees. Thank G_d someone says it.

FDR boasts of combining quotas for German and Austrian visas as though that is real progress. Disgraceful! There won't even be four hundred visas available—for a waiting list almost ten years long.

"Even if Klara would try to come, it is too late. I must give up asking."

"No," Gertrud insists. "Keep trying. You taught us not to deny patients' hope. Don't deny it to yourself."

Obstinate Klara chooses to be deaf and blind. I attempt to help my desperate former colleagues. I prepare affidavits, ask Dexter for pledges of financial support, employment. He agrees! Sadly, the odds are slim his pledges will come due, but I am grateful.

Only with my patients do I have any real hope, theirs likely the only rescue I can accomplish. *Tikkun olam.* I must do what I can to heal the world one life at a time.

In the dark of sleeplessness not even Muni's warm weight on my feet protects me. My reflection in the mirror looks even worse now than in Gertrud's hidden portrait. I snap at Gertrud, find fault with Sally. Apologize.

I am angry at Hitler, raging at evil. Without Gertrud and my patients, I might cross that tightrope between sanity and madness.

Gertrud receives a phone call.

"Frieda! Mr. Phillips has a friend who wants to give me a show the first week in November! In Georgetown at The Little Gallery!"

She becomes a painting dervish. Not manic, just creative.

Raymond drives her to the gallery on O Street the day before the opening. The owner had not permitted her to see the show before, wanting no interference with arrangement. She had fumed and worried.

Frieda, it looks so beautiful, she reports, elated. Even the stupid Halloween prank on the radio about a Martian Invasion doesn't upset her.

Dexter, Anne, Gertrud, and I go to the opening. Gertrud, radiant, floats from painting to painting. Duncan and Marjorie Phillips are there. Gertrud catches my eye as she lifts her wine glass to toast the gallery owner. "Art for dark times!"

Too excited to sleep, she chatters as she sits on the foot of my bed, brushing her hair. Thank G_d for her art for dark times.

Over breakfast, she reads the review in the *Post* aloud. Her voice quavers. "Dr. Jacob is a practicing psychiatrist and though she prefers to have this forgotten in connection with her paintings one realizes that it must be the reason that her pictures of people have a moving quality that is completely missing from her landscapes."

She pushes the paper across the table to me, unable to read the conclusion aloud. *The work is painful to see*, the critic says. *Accomplished, but depressing.*

"He is a coward! Let him enjoy pastels!" I'm shouting. Muni barks.

"I must study with O'Keeffe. Learn to express emotion in landscape."

She returns to her studio. I am proud of her resilience.

A week after the gallery opening, I come downstairs, enjoying the smell of eggs and toast and coffee. Muni leads me to the front door, eager to play fetch with the paper.

He gums it up in his soft spaniel mouth and brings it to Gertrud. She rewards him with a bite of toast.

I open the paper. Nietzsche says the man who does not lose his mind over certain things has no mind to lose.

"Gertrud!" My hands tremble. I must tell her. I cannot protect her.

A young German Jew, exiled in Paris, has killed a German official.

All through Germany and Austria they are wreaking havoc on Jewish businesses. Smashing windows. Stealing and burning merchandise. Burning synagogues and schools. A surgeon I know in Munich, arrested for the crime of being Jewish.

We hold each other.

The phone rings.

I do not answer.

Morning light glints on the silver coffee pot I purchased, filling out my life again with domestic objects—deluded into believing in the security of belongings. The thick raspberry jam Anne made last summer shines like a dark jewel, like clotted blood in the crystal dish.

Crystal. *Kristallnacht,* the paper calls it. The night of shattered glass.

The phone rings again, insisting.

It is Erich.

Tears clog my throat.

Anne and Dexter arrive. We sit like a family at shiva. I want to cover the mirrors, pin a torn black ribbon to my lapel. I want to be with my foolish, stubborn mother and I fear for her, in her parlor in Berlin.

Dexter says of course I cannot work, of course patients must be cancelled.

I must work. I will not give that villain, that monster over there, the victory of taking away my capacity to care for those who need me.

The sessions are my art for dark times. On this black day, my patients surprise me with empathy. One of the most disturbed—a true lonely one, deep in her schizophrenic's internal world—looks directly into my eyes for the first time.

"I am sorry. Do you have family there?"

How has she even known of the event? She has recognized me as a person, understood the implication of my name, my accent.

Yes, our assumptions of the line between sanity and madness are often wrong.

I weigh my response. As an analyst I must never burden a patient with my life. But I must reinforce her effort to connect. Her break-through comes out of this ugliness.

Gertrud draws the curtains against the evening darkness. We hide and listen to the radio. Thank G_d we are together. I could not bear this alone.

FDR says he cannot believe such a thing could occur in twentieth century civilization.

"How naïve he is," Gertrud says, tears streaming down her face.

Or worse, I think. Closing his eyes. Selectively blind and deaf.

He is summoning his ambassador back from Berlin, to learn what was going on.

As if FDR did not have notice. As if he did not know!

I sit at the piano and play Mendelssohn until I go to rounds. Play the laments of a Jewish composer. Gertrud and Muni go up to bed.

***

1939

Gertrude has finished the plates for our book. The plates for Anxiety, Melancholia, Hysteria, Depression, are remarkable. Dexter diligently seeks a publisher, without success.

"Are they looking for happy faces? Fairy tale stories?"

He shakes his head. "Not in a psychiatry textbook."

"Is it because we are Jewish?"

"Frieda, not at all."

I wonder.

His children have snowball fights outside, sprawl and make snow angels. Gertrud does not venture to the barn but paints in our dining room on these coldest days. She stands at the window, admiring the traces left by the children.

"I wish I could capture white. There's every color in it. Faces are easier."

She dashes off a quick impression of the children at play, gives it to Anne.

Children are being allowed into Britain, separated from their parents, but allowed in. If the parents can get the papers. Pay the bribes. Bear to separate, to save the life.

Some can only send one child. Early childhood separation and loss often precipitates later psychiatric trouble, usually we would not see this relinquishment as good. But we live in a realm of evil. This separation and loss is rescue. This is Moses hidden in the bulrushes.

A bill has been proposed in Congress to allow twenty thousand German refugee children in over and above the quota.

Would Anne and Dexter let me foster a child? Gertrud and I could share a room, the child could have hers. The Lodge carpenter made me a dollhouse for my niece, modeled after my sister's lost home. She will never come. I keep the dollhouse in the waiting room. Sometimes my patients' children visit and play with it. Sometimes when I cannot sleep, when the dream visits me of Erich's child, I go downstairs and move the furniture, the doll family, from room to room.

Eleanor Roosevelt speaks for the children, and the bill. FDR ignores her. A senator proposes barring all immigration for ten years. Blaming immigrants for the Depression!

There will be no rescue of children.

No child will find safe refuge in our cottage.

TEN

Eliza looked up dazed from the page, almost expecting Frieda to be there, sitting in the window nook of her—their—bedroom. Frieda had listened, alert for Gertrud across the hall, as Eliza listened for Nick. Love is love. Love for a friend, love for a child, love for our patients, for our work. Caring is not a neurotic need to be needed. Erich was wrong.

No, the heavy millstone burden of love and worry—for a lover, for a child, for a patient—serves as a buoy, a life preserver. The weight of Frieda's love and worry for Gertrud, love for her work and her patients, kept her afloat in the darkness of the war.

The primitive, instinctual root of anxiety is fear of death. Eliza often explained that in session—experienced it herself. But Frieda's fear for the death of her loved ones was reality. Extraordinary, horrific reality. Imagine facing peril so terrible parents send children away, perhaps in futile sacrifice.

Yes, she could almost hear Frieda say, our fear was reality based in a terrible, unnatural way. But it is not trivial, what you fear for your son. The world can be dangerous, especially for an adolescent. Love is love. Grief is grief. Fear is fear.

Yes, Eliza thought. Love is love. Fear is fear, woven through all loving.

She had been pregnant with Nick when the Holocaust Museum opened. Dee and Eliza had stood in the long line, wanting and afraid to enter. And hadn't there been lines everywhere, in the camps?

163

At the mountain of shoes, they stopped and let the crowd pass by them. Eliza could not move on, held by the smell of mold on leather, the empty shoes of every size. Eliza had always found something sad in bronzed baby shoes. This decaying mass of leather shoes was six million times sadder. Stolen shoes, stolen lives.

She felt Nick move, and stepped away, weeping, leaning on Dee.

Eliza visited the museum again with her father. Her mother had stayed home with Nick. Her dad walked slowly through every exhibit.

He almost never spoke of being a young soldier in the war. But afterward, walking to the subway, he had said, "Let's sit." They found a bench on the Mall, among the brightly clad tourists, the tour buses. He had spoken, of going into the camps with the liberating army.

He never spoke of it again, sealed it away. Now, she wondered, now that he could no longer speak, did that sorrow revisit him, over and over again?

Eliza looked out at Main, dark and empty. She stepped outside, imagining Frieda crossing the lawn at midnight, saving who she could. Saving herself.

The grass outside was cool and soft on her bare feet. Grass is meant to be walked on barefoot, Nick always said. She stood on the lawn. Come home Nick, she whispered. Come home.

Playing hide and seek in the summer evenings her mother's voice calling her home drew her like a magnet. She hurried through the dark to close the space between them. Perhaps they had been too close. Perhaps she was too close to Nick. Every separation reminds us of the final one, Frieda said.

Eliza called him. Come home. Come home. The humid dark lay heavy and close. *Air you could wear,* her mother would say. She went back inside, leaving the front door open. He'd be angry at the risk, but she left it open for him.

Eliza sat at the piano and found the music, for Frieda's song, the Mendelssohn. She began to practice. Played through the most difficult phrase and began again.

"Mom! What are you doing leaving the door wide open and playing the piano so loud you don't even hear me come in!"

He sat on the bottom step, taking off his sneakers. There had been no shoes like these in that heap of shoes at the museum, but there had been shoes for many young boys who never grew old.

Eliza sat beside him, touched his shoulder.

"I left it open for you. I'm glad you're home."

He shrugged her hand off. "I know where the key is. I told Phil I'd be over first thing. Wake me up when you go to work."

In the morning he took a long shower. Eliza had her coffee and cereal, packed her lunch for the office. She always ate at her desk, always the same: hardboiled egg, twist of salt, celery, sesame bagel. Today she added the sweet potato to bake for dinner in the office kitchenette during her five o'clock session. She'd scarf it down in the ten-minute break (if they didn't run over) before her next. Mondays she saw clients until nine.

Nick inhaled two bowls of cereal.

"It's my late night. Want me to ask Phil if you could eat with them?"

"Can I have some money and get dinner? Pay you back when Phil pays me."

"Including what you took from the lunch money drawer."

He was gone, out the door.

"Sunscreen!" she called after him. At least he was wearing long sleeves, though he'd be awfully hot.

Eliza picked up her briefcase. The photograph looked down on her, serene as always. No one would guess the heartache and heartbreak that Frieda had endured. "Thank God for Phil, Frieda.

I've got to find him a good therapist, but he's really going to be planting roses."

Driving to work, five short miles, she switched her mental gears. Home and Nick became background as she focused on what was waiting at the office. Helping Phil would help Nick, helping clients would help Eliza—which would help her help Nick. What a reciprocal process healing was. She was lucky to be in this field. Eliza ran through the roll call of the day's clients. She'd listen better, after reading Frieda. Frieda validated what Eliza believed was still most important: listening and relationship.

Her first client would be the young woman, no insurance, grieving her son's death to an overdose. She had a sliding scale fee. The clinic director warned of changes and cuts, Medicaid and sliding fees discontinued. If Eliza were promoted to department head, she could push back, maybe find a way to explain to the board what was being lost. But she'd have to give up seeing clients in that position. Well, it was a long shot. More likely she might be out of a job. The psychotherapy service wasn't breaking even. The Lodge had been a canary in the mine.

Eliza hurried past the reception desk into the department office for her files. The clinic was engaged in the costly drawn-out process of going paperless. Meanwhile, double the work, double the record keeping: paper and computer. There wasn't enough money in the budget to go totally paperless yet. Despite the extra work, Eliza wasn't sorry. Writing paper notes clarified her thinking about the client in a way no computer checklist ever would.

"She wants to see you in her office," the secretary said, with a sympathetic glance.

The clinic director's glossy helmet of short hair, her manicure, made Eliza want to hide her hands and check to be sure her own blouse was tucked in. Younger than Eliza, she had a combined counseling and business degree. She'd never practiced.

"How was your weekend, Eliza?"

"Fine. Yours?"

"Spent it here. The county grant people are coming. And the accreditors."

"Anything I can do?"

"Get your charts up to date."

"I do the case note after every session." Defensive as a kid. But the case note was vital for monitoring progress, assessing risk. "I know the quarterlies are essential, too. I'm catching up."

"We don't need you to write a book. A brief, thorough note after sessions. Hit the important parts. And get to the quarterlies. Everyone is late—but you're the worst. I don't want this to be a problem for us or you. At this point, frankly, I couldn't entrust the department to you."

She'd like to say, "You're right. I can't do what you want, what the clinic wants. It isn't what I consider best practice." She'd like to say, "I quit." But she couldn't abruptly leave her clients without a careful termination, transfers. And who could take them on here, with fewer and fewer therapists, scarcer resources, less support in every way for the work? She wouldn't leave her clients in the lurch. And she'd need the pieces in place to take care of Nick.

Walking back to the waiting room for her first client, Eliza concentrated on breathing. She must be calm, be ready to receive, to listen. Be the still, non-anxious presence each client deserved.

The woman sat very straight on the edge of her chair. Not even forty she was raising her late son's children. Her careworn face brightened as Eliza approached.

"Good morning," Eliza said. "Come on back."

They settled into their chairs, took their places. The confrontation in the director's office fell away.

"So, how can I be of help?" She'd been using Frieda's question recently. It worked well.

ELEVEN

"Want to stay for dinner?" Phil asked.

Shit, had she told him to do that? Super tempting, always good stuff to eat here. Afterward, they'd probably let him watch TV.

"That's okay." Monday nights were chill, having the house to himself till she got home. Though it felt a little weird, after maybe seeing the shrink ghost yesterday. He hadn't. He couldn't have. Though Cole said you can't rule anything out, all that ESP shit and so forth. The air felt cool once he was out of the heavy coverall and the gloves. Whew, wearing that get-up was like a portable sauna. Body armor because of the rose bush thorns. Sunblock had gooped into his eyes, it stung like crazy. Tomorrow he'd wear a hat and a bandanna and skip the glop. He left the gear in the barn and headed home.

Nick stood under the shower for a way long time. Until the water went from hot to lukewarm. She'd be spazzing out about wasting hot water if she were here. Monday nights were good.

His phone rang as he toweled off. Her usual check in call. If he just let it ring, she'd go nuts and keep calling.

"Hi, Ma."

"Hi, honey. How was your day?"

"Hot."

"You didn't stay at Phil's? Going into the square for tacos?"

"Maybe."

"If you're tired, there's yummy stuff from the party in the fridge."

Oh, good. She'd made cucumber water like Dee's at her beach house. He took the whole pitcher and a glass and sat on the glider on the porch. Definitely needed to rehydrate after today. Good thing he was getting paid.

He kept flashing on seeing that shrink lady's ghost. Couldn't get it out of his head. He lit a match from the box he'd taken from the bowl in Phil's pantry. The guys collected matches from all over and they'd been everywhere. This was a pretty one, black bird, red letters. *Uddevalla, Sweden.*

He let it burn all the way down to the pads of his fingers, blew it out when it started to hurt. But as soon as the match was out and the hurting stopped, he started thinking bad shit like seeing that shrink ghost.

He lit another. And another.

Hunger kicked in. Time to check out the leftovers.

Quiche and crab dip and yes, scallops and bacon!

He ate it all, standing in the cool air of the open refrigerator, drinking milk from the bottle.

He had that squirrely feeling, like doing something. Where were his models anyway?

He hadn't painted since moving. One of the shit things about living in a shrink museum was no place to set up the folding table. She was hyper about the wood floors and "their agreement" with the history people. *Her* agreement.

If he could find the models—big if—he'd need a place to paint. The balcony at the apartment had been okay. Couldn't use his hideout over there. Too dusty, too dark, and impossible getting the stuff over without being seen.

If he could even find the stuff.

The carport would work. With the car gone it was totally empty. He'd clean up before she came back.

He'd put up with the psycho retards on their porch smoking and maybe watching him. Lungs must be like solid tar.

First to find his stuff. At least he knew where it wasn't—upstairs in the cabinet where he'd found those freak-a-zoid paintings.

Which left the basement, which meant going down the steps with no backs. But just a short flight. And the more you do what's hard, the easier it gets, Cole said. Bullshit.

"Coming down!" he called out, in case of rats or snakes. Or shrink ghosts. Like ringing a bell to scare bears on the trail. Maybe it worked.

It smelled clammy down in the cellar. He fished in the dark air overhead until he found the string and pulled on the light. Bare bulb made it like some kind of interrogation chamber. Maybe the shrink tortured them, gave them the third degree here.

He wasn't going to think about that shrink lady. Shut up, he told his brain.

There was a stack of plastic storage tubs in the corner. The floor was slimy. The wall seriously oozed. Place needed airing. Fumigating. Ghostbusters.

He pulled the tubs down, one after another. It was the last one, all the way in the back of the pile. *Nick's Models*, she'd written on the top. Probably totally mildewed and ruined.

He lugged it up and out to the carport.

Wow! It was like a time capsule. Stuff he hadn't touched in a year. Last time he saw this was before he went to camp. Before the move, school, the mess at camp.

The plastic drop cloth smelled gross. But he spread it out. No way he was going to work on the bare floor of the carport. Filthy, cracked concrete. He wasn't getting grit in his paints. The paints were like welded shut. What if it was all totally dried out? In the kitchen he ran hot water on the tops and used her plastic grippy bottle opener thing and got them open. Some paint flecks fell in the sink. He wiped up with paper towels. Her historic sink.

The brushes at least were still soft. He'd taken good care of them, especially the camel hair ones he'd bought with the birthday money from Gran year before last. Would she send anything this year? She'd been weird over spring break. Maybe she was going senile too. Sticking Grandpa in that place. He'd never be in their house again. More stuff not to think about.

Here they were. The men he'd ordered last year right before camp.

He dipped a brush in the bronze paint. The whiff of it made him feel better. Losing yourself is called being in flow and it means you're in a good place, Cole said.

"Can I do one?"

Boomer! His hand shook.

"Don't sneak up. You made me mess up."

"Watching for like an hour. You stoned?" Boomer squatted and took a brush and a man.

Nick wanted to grab, tell him to clear out. His hand shook. He messed up again. Doused a paper towel with turpentine and wiped up. Started again, concentrating on the bronze and the silver. The shields were so small it was super hard to get them right.

"You ever go in over there?"

"No."

"Site online says it's haunted."

Just what he didn't need to think about. His hand shook again. He messed up.

"Watch this," Boomer said. He shook the silver spray paint, sprayed, and flipped a lighter.

Awesome flames exploded!

"Let me try." He held out his hand for the lighter, picked up the gold paint, shook, and flicked. He was klutzy with lighters and didn't get it going. Boomer laughed. Nick flicked again.

The ball of fire came right at him.

"Drop and roll! Drop and roll!" Boomer pushed him down.

Everything was going black. He was burning up.

TWELVE

Eliza was beat at nine o'clock after her last client left. Dinner might have helped but intent on catching up on quarterlies in the few minutes between sessions, she'd forgotten to put her sweet potato in the oven.

She could just punt, do the superficial minimum the template prompted for. Forget about how documenting should help you think clinically. Just do the damn checklist.

Eliza was so exhausted she was tempted to leave and finish her case notes tomorrow. They were allowed a twenty-four-hour window. But she couldn't. She never skipped it. Listening, assessing, writing it down was all part of the clinical process. Eliza had to think about the client right after the session. How else to spot something important you'd missed, to identify the threads to follow next time? It wasn't just about documenting for insurance and covering ass. It wasn't just protest against the assembly line mentality. The clinical note was an integral part of good treatment.

The cleaning crew hadn't come tonight, the building was empty as she left. Eliza was the only clinician who worked Monday nights. She'd told the receptionist it was okay to leave after Eliza's last client was checked in. The receptionist was a single mom, needed to get home to two little kids. Eliza was careful to only schedule clients she knew well for her last session in case she was alone in the building. Granted it was a little uncomfortable, a little risky. You can't ever completely predict violence or crisis. But if she had her own practice, even part of a small group practice, she'd be alone at least sometimes. Occupational hazard, Jeff would say. She hated that phrase.

No traffic this time of night. She changed mental gears from clients to Nick and at the first stoplight pulled out her cellphone. The battery was dead! She'd meant to charge it. Ironic, when she always nagged Nick about the phone. Really, she should get a charger for the car. Oh well, ten minutes and she'd be home.

She reached Thomas Street and headed for the carport. One of the halfway house men was wandering down the center of the street, smoking. She tapped her horn gently and he moved out of the way.

The headlights illuminated a strange mess on the carport floor. A bitter chemical smell hung in the air. She jumped out of the car. The smell was melted plastic. Nick had incinerated his models!

"NICK!" She burst into the house and charged up the stairs.

His room was empty.

Eliza checked her answering machine. The light blinked reproach.

"Everything's okay." Ben's voice was ponderous. "Nick had an accident. We're at the ER. But he's okay."

Beep. Phil left the next message. "We're home, brought him to our house."

She ran for Rose Hill.

"He's asleep upstairs." Ben's face sagged with fatigue. Eliza rushed through the kitchen, hitting her hip on the counter.

Phil sat on the floor by the bed. "He's okay," he whispered.

Nick lay in the middle of the bed. A ceiling fan clicked. He breathed and muttered.

His arm, skin blistered and raw, was propped on a pillow.

Eliza collapsed on her knees by the bed as the adrenaline of surprise drained away.

Phil knelt beside her.

"What happened?"

"Ben went for his walk. He heard screaming. Nick's friend said they'd been painting models, goofing around. Nick started a fire with a lighter. By accident, his friend said."

What friend?

Another fire.

Nick's arm looked flayed. "Oh my god, what a terrible burn."

"Second degree, Eliza. Ugly, but could have been worse."

"Shouldn't he have a bandage?"

Phil shook his head. "Air, they said."

Eliza rested her head on the mattress.

Could have been worse. Could have been worse. He's alive. He's alive.

"We hated to—just leave the messages, but…"

"My fault. My phone was dead—all the times I've been after him about that."

"Eliza—at the ER, they noticed—he's been cutting. Burning himself. Turn his arm over."

Nick moaned but didn't wake.

Horrified, she touched purple threads—scars. There were also raw, fresh scabs. He'd been slicing his wrist, the tender skin of his forearm. And his fingertips were red. There was no hair on his arm. None at all.

"Oh, the long sleeves," she groaned. How blind she'd been!

"I know. I'm kicking myself for not thinking. The ER suggested keeping him, for evaluation. Asked to reach dad, when we couldn't get you. He said he didn't have one. Before letting us take him home they got a psych consult. Not suicidal. We promised we'd watch him till you got here."

She felt ill. She should have been there. A stranger had done a suicide inventory on her son. Once when he was in daycare he'd fallen, cut his head on the sandbox. She was on a home visit to a client, unreachable in those pre-cellphone days. Dee had taken him for the stitches. He still had a tiny, almost invisible square-cornered scar on his forehead, reproaching her for not being there when he needed her. This was worse. Not just being absent in the acute moment. She hadn't seen what should have been plain all along.

"I feel so negligent."

"You're here now."

"I mean—everything."

Long sleeves in hot weather. Hiding in plain sight. Parents are often the last to know, denial is such an automatic response. She'd often said that, consoling distraught parents. Try not to blame yourself, she'd said. Though she had blamed them, a little. Had been judgmental—though she should have known better.

"I'll go get the car. Take him home."

"Don't disturb him. Stay yourself, the daybed by the window's made up."

"Thank you." Suddenly she was so tired she couldn't imagine even standing.

"The pain meds are over there, on the bureau. Almost time for the next dose. They said to stay ahead of the pain, that it would help him rest tonight."

Phil slipped out. It was a relief to be alone with Nick, just the two of them, the way it always had been, when he was ill. Keeping vigil at his bedside, with the illusion she could protect him.

She stroked his cheek. "Nickie, time for a pill."

He turned toward her, blinking, dazed.

She propped his head up. He swallowed, leaned back, closed his eyes.

Eliza felt the damp springy mat of his curls, the weight of his head. How many times had she woken him for medicine? How many gallons of pink antibiotics poured down his throat? Trying to make him well, keep him well.

"I'm so sorry." She kissed his forehead. "I'm so terribly sorry."

"Ma," he said, opening his eyes, the surprising deep brown eyes with the dark line around the iris. His eyes almost totally black tonight, all dilated pupil. "They wanted to call my dad." He closed his eyes, drifting away.

His chest rose and fell. She knelt until she was stiff and had to stand. Slipping off her shoes, she stretched out on the cool sheets of the day bed, pulled up the cotton blanket.

The fan blades clicked, stirring a soft breeze.

She lay there, mind beginning to wander. It hit her.

This was the guest room, the coat room, that night at the Christmas party.

Eliza closed her eyes. The fan clicked, steady as a metronome.

Morning filtered through the gauze curtain.

Sitting on the foot of the bed, Eliza watched Nick sleep— mouth open, head at an awkward angle. Asleep, alive. Grateful, she memorized him. How different it might have been. "Thank you," she whispered, not sure to who.

Phil was working at the computer in his office in the butler's pantry. Beside him was the deep porcelain bowl where he kept his match box collection.

"Could you put those away?" It had been a lighter last night. But he must be using matches too, to burn himself. Guess he'd mastered that fear. Why tempt fate again?

"Done," Phil said, shutting the bowl in one of the cupboards beneath the soapstone counter he used as a desk. "How is he?"

"Still asleep. I slept some too."

"Coffee? Something to eat?"

"Please." She felt jet-lagged, tired but not sleepy, empty but not hungry. Coffee might help.

Ben had left for work. Phil made her toast, with real butter and jam, and she discovered she was hungry.

How hungry she'd been the morning after he was born.

"Let's sit outside."

"Will we hear him?" She had to hear him.

"The window's open."

The koi swam to the surface, begging.

"The heron got another one last night. Have to make a cover. He can help me when he feels better."

"You'll let him work here, after this?"

"Absolutely."

"Still trying to find him a therapist." Should they have kept him at the hospital last night? Sent him to the Psych Institute?

No. Three days in a unit wouldn't do anything. And the discharge planner wouldn't have any magic to get him seen outpatient. Eliza knew that from experience. Better for him to be working with Phil while she tried to find a therapist.

She lingered, drinking the coffee, watching the fish swim circles. If she had a private practice, she'd keep fish in the waiting room.

She must call work, have the secretary cancel her clients.

"Could he stay here while I go home and call the office?"

Eliza held the last swallow of coffee a moment. There was someone else she must call. She must give him a chance to help.

"And his father."

"His dad?"

"He's never been involved."

"Take all the time you need. I'm here." Phil put his arms around her.

She appreciated his calm. Appreciated his not pressing for details.

"Could you go upstairs and sit with him? I don't want him waking up alone. I'll be back as soon as I can," she whispered, breathing in the clean line-dried scent of his denim shirt.

She walked home, praying again, if that's what it was. *Please let Jeff come through for Nick.*

The familiar light and space of the cottage folded around her. How it would feel, to come in here if Nick were never coming back?

Stop. Make your calls.

"Nick's ill," she told the secretary. "I have to be out. Could you please cancel my appointments?"

She always made those calls herself. Impossible today.

She studied Frieda's photograph. "I'm calling Jeff."

Just light reflecting off the glass, but Eliza saw a gleam of approval in Frieda's eyes.

Four rings and the recorded message began. Voices change less than faces, over sixteen years. Listening, she saw the younger man.

"Jeff, it's Eliza. I need to speak to you. As soon as possible. It's urgent. Before you go back to Boston."

She left her cell number. Hanging up, she found herself praying again. *Please. Please.* It's true what they say, about atheists in fox-holes, next she'd be down on her knees, lighting candles.

No. No more matches. No more flames.

Eliza showered.

Jeff hadn't called back yet.

She dressed fast, eager to be back by Nick's side, to make up for yesterday. She took Frieda's journal. She hoped he'd sleep. She would need company.

"Eliza!" Carter jogged up to her as she stepped outside.

He was sweating from his run. "Morning. Could I show you something? Over at the Lodge?"

She felt a warning prickle of uneasiness. "Nick's ill, over at Phil's. I'm on my way."

"Sorry. This won't take long but—you need to see it." She followed him, back toward Main, up the rotting front steps.

"Careful—especially on that one." He opened a combination lock, releasing a heavy chain holding the front door shut. "The floor's in terrible shape. I've got a flashlight. Let me carry that for you."

"It's okay," she said, tightening her arms around the box holding Frieda's journal.

The darkness smelled of rot. A cadaverous smell.

"I feel like I'm stepping into a tomb," she said.

His face looked craggy in the flashlight beam. "I still expect my mother around the next corner."

Once she'd taken Nick to the spring workday at camp. He'd begged to go. None of the kids he knew were there, only a couple of counselors. *It's no good without the people, Ma.*

Carter waited at the foot of the stairs. "Be careful. Here." He shone the flashlight. "Follow me. Don't step on that one."

Upstairs it was drier, dustier. She coughed and walked into a cobweb draping the corridor.

"Ick!" she said, frightened like a kid at an amusement park haunted house.

"Sorry," Carter said. "Should have warned you."

The door to her former office gaped open. Empty, no desk, no filing cabinet.

Carter stopped at an open door. "Take a look."

Eliza hesitated at the threshold. "This was my supervisor's office."

"Someone else is using it now," he said curtly.

She stepped into the room, clasping Frieda's journal as though for protection.

Dingy morning light filtered through the windows. A familiar sleeping bag lay wadded on the floor, next to a pile of magazines. Computer gaming magazines, Nick's she knew, even before she stooped and saw his address label. On the window seat lay her father's big, old-fashioned binoculars, the ones Nick had claimed last spring.

She put down Frieda's journal. Lifting the heavy binoculars, leather cord cracked and dry, she remembered Nick and her father birdwatching together. What had happened to Nick's life list of birds? And her dad's? What was he watching up here? How long had he been sneaking into this place? How uncanny he'd chosen—his father's office. Of all the empty rooms in Main, he'd come here. Jeff's office. Talk about a call for help, he'd been screaming silently—like that awful Munch painting he'd once had a poster of. She hadn't heard. Selective hearing, denial. Frieda would agree.

"I'm so sorry—I had no idea he was coming in here."

"He's not the first, or the only one. Just the only one who left his calling card. This is what happens, to empty buildings."

"Have you—told the developer about Nick?"

"No," Carter said. "I've warned Ed enough. This? It's his fault. Tempting kids, and vagrants. The former patients in the neighborhood. He knows what's happening. He doesn't care. Maybe wants something to happen. Take the stuff. Tell him he can't come back here." His voice was heavy.

"Thank you," she said. "Thank you so much."

"He's got to stay out. The police and their dogs will be here by the end of the week. I don't want him getting caught or hurt."

Eliza rolled up the sleeping bag, stuffed it in its sack. She slung the binoculars around her neck.

"You left this." Carter handed her the journal box. "I'll bring the magazines."

He walked her back to the cottage. "When I was a kid, I made a tree house. On our neighbor's property. They made me take it down. Didn't make a stink about it."

"Is there some kind of restitution you'd like, from Nick?"

"Just staying out. I don't want Ed knowing. I don't want a kid getting hurt," he said, with sorrowful intensity.

"He's pretty anxious. Once I tell him about the dogs, he won't go back."

"Hope you're right." His eyes were pale gray, worried.

The kindness of strangers, she thought, standing by the untidy pile of Nick's stuff on the porch. Saved by the kindness of strangers. Still no call from Jeff. Well, she'd waited sixteen years to talk to him. She'd have to wait a little longer.

Eliza splashed water on her face, combed cobweb out of her tangled hair, changed into fresh jeans and blouse.

She tried Jeff again, looking into Frieda's eyes in the photograph for strength, managing to keep her voice steady.

Please call as soon as you can. It's urgent.

She walked fast to Rose Hill. Phil had left the kitchen door open. The Siamese cat regarded her with suspicion and tagged so closely behind her Eliza almost stumbled on the steps. Phil was bedside.

"I'm sorry I took so long," she whispered.

"It's okay. How did it go with his dad?"

"Haven't reached him yet."

"I'll be downstairs if you need me."

Eliza knelt by the bed. She stroked Nick's curls a moment, praying again, to whoever. *Please, please, please.*

Please what? Please make Jeff call. Please let him help. Please let Nick be alright.

Eliza stretched out on the day bed, too tired to nap.

184

Hanging suspended in limbo. Waiting for Nick to awaken. Waiting for Jeff to call.

Thank goodness for Frieda.

She found her place in the journal and began to read.

THIRTEEN

1939

Winter mornings we wake to banging as Raymond takes care of the furnace. It must be the coal dust in the air that makes Gertrud cough. Sally soaks flannel poultices in herbs.

Evenings, we sit by the fireplace. Gertrud is discovering American poets. She terms Emily Dickinson brilliant as O'Keeffe.

I heard a fly buzz when I died, she reads. "Do you think the dead miss us, or do we just miss the dead?"

I think of my father, gone to his office on that unlikely, suspect Sabbath errand. He does not miss us. Did not (or could not) consider the wound he would inflict, killing himself, suffering so much he had to walk through Nietzsche's open door.

I think of the young men, those other German soldiers I tried and failed to repair a lifetime ago. Strange—to mourn my countrymen, German soldiers. I served that other side. My countrymen have become my enemy. All those young men on both sides of that that other war. Do they rest in peace?

I hope after death there is neither remembrance of the past nor knowledge of the present.

"I think the dead miss us. I will miss you," Gertrud says. "And Muni. This room."

"Don't," I say, though I should let her speak of it.

She gazes at the walls lined with books, hung with her paintings. As though memorizing, as though for the last time before the deep sleep.

Or the deep nothingness.

"Perhaps ghosts are absent presence. Haunting a manifestation of longing," she says.

"Homer says as long as we tell their stories, our dead live."

She gives me a long look.

Although she shouldn't drink I pour a whiskey for us each (generous tot for me, scant finger for her). I'll have another with Dexter. We must discuss a new admission, an incident with a violent patient. I'd like a cigarette but my care for her wins out. I dread the time to come when I'll be free to smoke.

After she goes up to bed, I sit at the piano, pressing keys so softly I almost play without sound. Will this be what it is like when I am completely deaf? Playing by memory, not ear? Haunted by melody?

Lying awake, I try Gertrud's trick, borrowed from Proust, she says. I've neither time nor patience to read him. I play her game. I walk through all the houses where I have lived. All my lost homes. Finally come here, come home.

I must face it. She has relapsed. Now the coughing at night, the flush—I cannot pretend or deny. No one I love is safe. Only with patients or at the keyboard can I forget the threat all around. When the session ends, or I close the keyboard, the throb of guilt and worry begins and I turn to drafting affidavits, plead with authorities to ransom colleagues, friends, friends of friends.

Walking home from Main I see the Bullard boys playing with stick guns. Just harmless practice of forbidden aggression, natural development. But there are camps in New York state sponsored by a pro-Nazi group, teaching children to hate.

"Dr. Frieda! I got my brother!" The rascal brandishes his stick.

187

I grab his weapon, break it.

Sally saw me from the kitchen window.

"Boys will be boys, Dr. Frieda."

"Lucky I'm not a mother." The anger is still hot.

"Every patient and every one of us is your child," she says. "Here's coffee."

We sit together, bend the rules. Care about each other, both caretakers of many.

"You heard," she says, "how they weren't going to let Marian Anderson sing?"

"Shame on the DAR."

She shrugs, a smile on her lips. "Mrs. Roosevelt, she quit the DAR today. And she's arranging for her to sing—at the Lincoln Memorial on Easter."

"We will go," I promise.

We go, Raymond and Sally and I—and Gertrud. She insisted, though I was afraid for her, in such a crowd, on such a cool windy day. Anne loaned Gertrud her fur coat.

We all stood together, defiantly together. I looked down the reflecting pool through my opera glasses. Miss Anderson sang from the steps, Lincoln behind her in his throne. Her voice soared and I could hear snatches.

My Country 'tis of Thee, she sang. And *Ave Maria*.

She sang a Negro song created out of bondage. *Nobody knows the trouble I've seen*. This Easter Sunday was Passover, too. She sang of enslavement, of wandering and dispossession, for my tribe, and hers. Gertrud, Sally, and I leaned together and swayed and hummed.

The doctor in me knows the outing on that cold, wind-whipped and joyous day did not cause her worsening. The psychiatrist in me knows the news of the boat full of refugee families turned away

188

from Havana, and refused in Miami, did not cause her relapse—though it sent her to bed. I know the lungs are just a bellows, and the heart just a muscle, but Gertrud's lungs and her heart are weary.

The specialist at Hopkins says she must not spend summer here. The humid climate is not good for her. He recommends the Southwest—Santa Fe, New Mexico.

"New Mexico!" she says. "Wonderful! Georgia O'Keeffe!" We can almost pretend it is an excursion, for the sake of her painting.

Dexter gives me leave to go and get her settled.

We travel west on the train, sharing a roomette.

She'll make you ill, warns Erich.

You immunized me.

I try to write as we travel, but gaze at her and the hypnotic views, hour upon hour. Trying to read her face, the Indian runes on the hillsides.

She sketches and dozes.

We find an adobe house at the foot of red hills, with thick walls, cool dry rooms, red tiles. "Our casita," she calls it. Our bedrooms adjoin and open to the patio. Evenings we lie on deck chairs and look up at the distant glitter of the most brilliant sky we've seen since we lay side by side on the *SS Berengaria*.

I hire a housekeeper. The doctor will make home visits.

I put everything she needs in place, or everything within my puny power. I must return to the Lodge.

Go, I feel better already, she says.

Every parting, every goodbye, carries the chill of the final separation. I know that lesson but must relearn it every time.

Go. I must learn to paint this land. I will have new work to show you when I come home.

When? I am a child afraid of the dark and it is all around us.

Back in Maryland, it is good to be at work. Muni mopes from room to room. He finds one of her painting rags, redolent of turpentine, brings it to me and I keep it on my desk, rubbing it between my fingers like a charm as I write.

Word comes! My mother and Grete are in England! And thank G_d, Anna and her family as well. May the channel keep them safe! May that island shelter my dear ones. Some Jews are being sent to the Isle of Man, Grete writes. Please G_d, spare my family that indignity. I am sick of the contagion of prejudice even among allies.

The first of September, Hitler invades Poland. Britain and France declare war on Germany. How can I count on the narrow channel to protect my family? No one I love is safe.

My loneliness is like physical pain, close to the madness of my patients. I understand my lonely ones better all the time. I would rather step through Nietzsche's open door and suicide than remain in this world without my family. But my patients and Gertrud need me.

Gertrud writes that she paints every day. *The light, the air, is so beautiful here, Friedl. My landscapes are not depressing here!* She has found a community of artists, has written to Miss O'Keeffe.

She plans a small practice, and to present her paper about mania and depression.

I am proud of her, relieved, must not be jealous.

Thank G_d my patients need me. The Lodge needs me—and I need the Lodge, my life as well as livelihood. No, Erich, it is not a neurotic need to be needed. It is how I can continue to live, making my small efforts to heal the broken world.

Dexter says next year I must take leave and go to New Mexico for the entire summer. He will make sure my patients are cared for. But will I survive three months without my patients?

***

190

1940

She's not well. Writes telling me not to worry, it is just a cold. She is not painting. She suspends her practice.

I will come.

No, no need. Just a temporary setback.

April and the dogwood blooms, the native American tree with star-bright scentless blossoms and rough gray bark. *Bracts, not blossoms*, Gertrud corrected me last year. She loved the beauty of the Maryland spring. She's heard there are places where flowers bloom in the desert. When she is well, she will go and paint there.

I send a post card every day, the few lines a precious connection which only costs a penny. It pleases me, to think I've touched the card and she will touch it soon.

The phone call comes, from a hospital in Santa Fe, a terrible connection. I switch the receiver to my other ear. The blood in my veins is ice.

Dr. Fromm-Reichmann, she is gone.

Gone where? I can picture it, Gertrud checking herself out against advice, saying *I'm a doctor.* Going to the casita, to lie on the chaise and count the stars.

We are so sorry. Cardiac arrest during emergency surgery, she died on the table.

What table? I sit at our table in the dining room. She should be sitting across from me.

The white dogwood gleam in that dark night. I walk the grounds by their light, Muni my shadow. I walk through the night. I cross the border of the last day she was still in this world. I cross into the morning of the first day without her.

I return home just after dawn. The newspaper waits on the doorstep. Opening it I see the date: April 16, 1940. It is just five years to the day since we arrived in New York. She has left on her final journey.

The beauty of the spring assaults me. The dissonance between my grief and soft air, the birdsong, the flowering trees, stabs me.

I remember a poem she liked, by an English poet, about April being the cruelest month. Dexter and I take extra precautions in April. The season invites some to step through Nietzsche's open door.

Nietzsche says some are saved just by the thought of suicide, the possible choice, that open door. Choose not to enter.

I understand. I resist. My patients need me.

How often have I taught that mourning is a natural process? That it resolves, with time. That in grief as in all of living, there is a natural tendency toward health.

This optimism of yours may put us out of business, Dexter once teased me. Now? What is happening in the world, and what happened in my small world with Gertrud, weighs me down with sorrow and doubt.

I am caught in a perpetual state of grief, chronic mourning. She is the precipitant, the immediate blow, but I grieve for everything and everyone lost. I can no longer pull on my wisdom like a cloak and sit across the room from my suffering patient. I am almost swallowed by sorrow, mine, and theirs.

I close the piano. I do not play records. I smoke instead of eating. I cook for Muni—who does not eat. I tempt him with chicken broth brewed until the bones melt into golden soup and schmaltz floats on the surface. Holding him on my lap, I feed him spoon by spoon.

Sally says, "Eat, Dr. Frieda." She offers me nursery foods: toast in warm milk, custard. She mothers me. We never outgrow our need, our yearning, to be mothered. To be mothers.

After my nightly talk with Dexter, I fall into bed but cannot sleep. I walk through all my past homes. I arrive here and find she is still gone.

Mourning her I mourn my father again, Erich again, and the whole lost world of the other life. I am mourning for a continent, my people. I carry sorrow inside me. It grows like a hidden tumor that cannot be excised.

She spoke to me of dying, and haunting. She was preparing me to expect her ghost—not an external spirit, but an internalized absent presence. Tried to prepare me for the internal presence and pressure of loss. No preparation is enough. This test I am failing.

You're grieving, Dexter tells me. *This is truly your most important task now. You may take leave, a break.*

NO! I would be lost without my work.

Very well, he says. *I am so sorry. But you will get through this. Grief will not kill you.*

Sometimes I wish it would. Sometimes Nietzsche's open door and the final possible choice, tempt like a siren song.

I might choose that open door, step through into the nothingness beyond, if Muni did not whine and beg. If the bell did not summon me to Main for a patient crisis.

I read her copy of Rilke. She marked the poem. We did protect each other's solitude. Shared solitude is not loneliness.

I write my mother, my sisters, sending love and prayers and money.

If only Gertrud had a grave. Impossible to have brought her shell east. I instructed them to bury her within the day. I would have liked to bring her here to the copse of trees on the corner of the Lodge property. Raymond showed me the spot, the small mounds.

Who is buried there?

Long silence. I know from what he doesn't say that the unmarked graves must be those of slaves.

I sit up all one night, writing what will be her obituary, her eulogy really, in the *Psychoanalytic Quarterly*. The words flow, as though we are collaborators again, as though she has finally painted her self-portrait and it is my task to write the interpretive notes. *A great person, a sympathetic, resolute therapist, a sensitive and gifted artist. Her brilliant and intuitive mind was passionately set for both truth and beauty.*

Not even a month after she is gone, France, Belgium, the Netherlands have fallen. Everyone trapped. The U.S. consulates are closed. Instead of helping, Congress has passed an Alien Registration Act. Foreigners must be registered and fingerprinted. There is a mania of paranoia, suspicion that German speakers are spies. I am furious when I hesitate to talk, afraid of revealing my accent.

Defiant, I take the citizenship test. Part of me not wanting to be any part of this country, not wanting to swear allegiance to this flag which seems to stand for isolation, nationalism, inaction. But I refuse to be "alien."

Her portfolio arrives from New Mexico. These last landscapes are different—fluid and vivid. Bold on her behalf, I write Duncan and Marjorie Phillips. They invite me to show them the new work.

"I am deeply sorry," he says. "You know—this gallery is my memorial, to my loved ones."

It is so easy, to be undone by kindness. I will weep if I look at him. I spread my offering across their long library table.

Such an expressive style, he says.

We sip sherry. I feel her there, imagine her nibbling a cheese straw.

He will offer a show. He will want to collect her. She will hang beside O'Keeffe.

Let me call Franz Bader, he says instead. *He has a fine gallery.*

Franz Bader declines to meet me.

Art for dark times. I will have an art show—at the cottage. This will be her gallery, her memorial service.

I hire the carpenter to install picture rails in every room, to construct frames.

Invitations go out to staff at the Lodge, the Institute, patients and their families. The proceeds will go to the Red Cross.

I supervise the placement of every work—except for the two canvases I've hidden: my hideous portrait, the troublesome nude.

The house is full. People want to buy! I find I cannot part with any. I promise instead, after I am gone.

Sally washes the glasses we've borrowed from Dexter and Anne. I dry. Before she and Raymond leave that night, I give them their portrait, the only one I relinquish.

I sleep soundly, Muni at my feet, the first good sleep since she died.

When I awake, the dog is cold. Raymond buries him in the secret cemetery on the edge of the grounds, where I would have buried her.

Anne, without consulting me, sends Raymond to Virginia.

He returns with a new puppy.

Dexter would have told her not to, to give me time. You cannot replace a lost beloved, should not even try.

The puppy stares at me with liquid brown eyes, and yawns and shows his rough pink tongue.

"What will you call him?" asks one of the children.

"Muni," I say.

The puppy cries in the night. I confuse him for a sleepy moment with my Muni. The puppy needs me. I answer. The two dogs blend into one. The new Muni becomes my Muni. I go downstairs to my desk, carrying Muni. He sleeps in her armchair as I work.

Insomnia is good for my writing. I am writing on the role of the mother in the family group. I read it aloud to Gertrud, sitting in my own chair across from her empty one.

I reluctantly give FDR my first vote here. May Eleanor exert her influence on him! Dexter says I am too harsh, do not understand that FDR is preparing for war—but cannot alienate the isolationists. *Think of FDR as an analyst, listening to a patient, moving slowly, so the patient himself decides on change.*

But FDR promises these people their boys will never go to war. Defending Europe is necessity, I say.

He will, he will, Dexter says. *Look how he's supporting Britain and being called a warmonger for it.*

Have some spine, I would tell FDR. Cruel expression for a man in a wheelchair. That demagogue Lindbergh calls Jews war agitators. Gertrud is spared this. Cold comfort, but comfort nonetheless.

***

1941

Gertrud would have loved the bright March day when Anne, Dexter and I attend the opening for the new National Gallery of Art. The building is enormous, a city block of pale rose-colored marble. Galleries with thick glass skylights stretch from a grand rotunda. A real art gallery! I glimpse her in the crowd, the trick of grief. I take in the sculpture, the Italian paintings, through her eyes. I must enjoy it all for her as well as myself.

Erich's book comes out. *Escape from Freedom* he calls it here in the States, though it will be *Fear of Freedom* in England, a telling difference. He sends a copy. I've declined the invitation to his talk in New

196

York. I read it in one night, sitting in the leather chair he gave me, reading passages aloud to her empty chair.

It is brilliant, and timely. Yes, fear of the risk and responsibility of being free, fear of defending freedom, leads to authoritarian disaster as we see now.

I have been at my desk all through the dark December morning, working on a new paper about how the seemingly rote gestures of schizophrenics communicate so much. My patient strokes his head gently when I understand him, violently when I misinterpret.

I barely hear Dexter ring the doorbell, lost in my writing.

"Turn on the radio!"

He brushes past me and snaps it on. "I was listening to the football game," he says. "The Japanese have attacked our ships in Hawaii."

He invites me back to Rose Hill and I come, with Muni.

Dexter, Anne, the children, and I cluster before the fire. The children enjoy the excitement and the maid's sandwich dinner on trays. I cannot eat, I cannot swallow. I go to the bathroom and vomit in primitive response to the emotion. Bells peal from all the churches.

Evening rounds cure my nausea. Main is the same as always, comforting to be in the changeless zone of the ward. There is madness abroad, but it is always mad here on the ward. Dexter and I walk back together to Rose Hill for our nightcap. Anne joins us by the fire. It is not a night to be alone.

"We are in!" He raises his glass. "To joining forces against evil."

Anne's eyes fill. "What can we do, for the war effort?"

"Our work here," I say. I know from the other war when we will be most needed—afterward. Now, I will continue to do what I can do, help patients battle internal enemies. We learn lessons now we can apply afterward—if there is an afterward.

I talk to Gertrud, walking home. A stranger might mistake me for a muttering patient. We are all more alike than not, and times like these reduce us to what matters. "Young soldiers' ruined minds led me to this work. Here we are, again. I am relieved we are in, but I wish I felt more hopeful," I tell her.

Wrapped in my worn yellow robe, I pray like my father did, rocking back and forth in his *tallit*. He is gone and not gone. I have no belief in afterlife. But love lasts.

FDR asks Congress to declare war. Orders blackouts. The National Gallery, the Capitol, the monuments fall dark; the Lodge, my cottage, all of Rockville follow suit. We hold my Monday night seminar behind thick drapes, and people attend, creeping through the darkness, hungry to be together. Study for dark times.

I like this darkness, in tune with my mood. The blackouts link me to my family in England. I write to them of the news, walk to the new post office, study the mural a government-sponsored artist painted. FDR at least understands the necessity of art for dark times. The painting is of a local scene, fields and the rolling hill they call Sugarloaf Mountain. I lift up my eyes to study the mountain and the green valley and hear my father recite the psalm. May the mail I've dropped through the polished brass slot reach my mother and sisters. May my love protect them.

We continue our routines, quiet daily defiance. Anne's dairy cows and chickens thrive. Chicken is not rationed; we eat it almost every day. How fortunate we are to have enough. We cannot make our own sugar or gasoline at the Lodge and feel those shortages. And cigarettes will be scarce! I hide them in one of my storage cabinets. I am learning to re-ink my typewriter ribbons. Every shortage reminds me what is really at stake, these are such easy sacrifices.

I've accepted the presidency of the Washington Psychoanalytic Society. Dexter encouraged me. "Good for you, good for the

Lodge." Anne is volunteering with the Mental Health Association and the TB Association, testament to Gertrud.

Erich's book is doing well. I am pleased, and it also sparks our old competition. I am publishing in journals.

I've filed for divorce.

The divorce decree, the finality of the piece of paper, hurts more than I anticipated. I would hide it away with our Ketubah, but that is left behind. Still, divorced, Erich and I draw closer professionally. We are good colleagues. We should never have crossed that other line. He's asked me to read his next manuscript. The working title is *Man for Himself,* which I tease is perfect for him. He pushes me to complete the paper I've promised to deliver to the New York Institute.

I confide in him that I resist finishing out of fear that I will no longer be able to hear and respond to the questions in a large hall, before a crowd.

Come to New York. Get fitted for an aid.

He's so confident there is a mechanical solution. I've tried before. The device buzzed and made me feel more distant not closer. Gadgets cannot save me. I must save myself, sharpen my wits and my talent with non-verbal communication, unspoken language.

Didn't Beethoven manage? I have returned to my piano, silent since she died. I play the Mendelssohn songs. I put "Lost Happiness" on the record player and discover it scratched from many repetitions. I hum the missing bars.

Young doctors have asked me to join their string trio. They want to play quartets, need a pianist. I suspect Anne and Dexter have suggested the invitation, worried I work so much, rest so little.

I refuse, claim my piano is out of tune. (Afraid my deafness will be found out.) Anne sends a tuner. The trio comes. We play. It requires full attention and is difficult, but I must make music while I still can. Art for dark times.

Over weekly practice sessions, over cigarettes and beer afterward, I even laugh. I am losing Gertrud as grief begins to heal. I understand why some patients fight to hold onto grief. It is not pathological, but part of loving, part of resisting the final separation.

We give our first performance at the doctors' talent show at Rose Hill, not a great success. My fault, I chose the difficult piece by the young Czech Martinů, a Jewish refugee in the States. Martinů's dissonance echoes my ache, the times. But the audience doesn't know what to make of it. "Not a crowd pleaser," as the cellist says, cheerfully.

Next time we'll do something more approachable. I don't regret my choice. Art for dark times should include discord, and wake everyone up a bit.

I invite a dance therapist from St. Elizabeth's to the Lodge. She is tall, graceful, and fearless. She leads patients in a dance across the lawn. One strips and runs nude in and out of the trees. Anne is furious with me. *We lived down that naked portrait! Now this!* I almost laugh. Gertrud could have painted the scene. I do see the world through her eyes. She does inhabit me. I welcome the haunting.

I read the news to Muni. The army has started sending condolence telegrams instead of delivering letters since there are too many dead to make personal visits. Japanese American families are taken from their homes and businesses and sent to prison camps! The Gestapo have come to the States. Italian Americans, and German Americans are also suspect—but not treated so harshly. *Because they're white,* Sally says. *Our boys are good enough to fight and die. But in training camp? They're digging latrines for the white boys.*

Even our weather is apocalyptic: a flood so deep a tow truck driver died. Sally says it may be the end of the world.

She is right, I think, reading the headline in the paper Thanksgiving morning. It confirms what well-named Rabbi Stephen Wise has been saying all along, what we've known. The Nazis are not just locking us in work camps. They are murdering us, two million gone.

I vomit. I pull the shades down and go to bed. Telephone and tell Anne I cannot come to Thanksgiving dinner.

Please, Frieda, she entreats.

What is there to be thankful for?

The more we learn, the more I despair. The mentally ill, the physically handicapped, homosexuals, are targets of the Nazi campaign for so-called purity.

Over there, our lonely ones, our patients, would be exterminated. For the sin of being who they are, I tell Dexter as we sip our bourbon and smoke. I fear for this country, too, I tell him, consider the lynchings.

Dexter says, "But Marian Anderson finally sang at DAR hall last month. Don't you always say there is a tendency toward health?"

"The army is segregated, black and white—blood donations are segregated."

He sighs and finishes his drink and pours another.

***

1944

I tell Muni it is easier to be a dog. He knows nothing of having your ex-husband say he is marrying again. Henny. What a silly name. Henny.

Lucky to be a dog who knows nothing of the world outside his life here. Muni is the only one I love who can be content, and kept safe. But now? A rabies epidemic. The police will shoot any dog acting odd. For the first time I wish we were a typical psychiatric asylum, walled and gated and locked.

Muni strains against the unaccustomed leash. A patient leaves the door ajar. Muni escapes outside. I run like the maddest woman on the ward and catch him.

Violence is contagious. We evaluate a young man who shot a classmate at a school in a nice neighborhood nearby. We deem him dangerous. Yet how ironic. He's almost old enough to go to war and be trained to kill, authorized to kill, ordered to kill.

I ask Dexter, "What is dangerousness? What is evil? What does any of this mean?"

"Oh, Frieda. At least we are approaching the end of the war," he says. "There are preparations for occupation. You must present your paper on your therapy with veterans of the last war, to the Psychiatric Society. The lessons will be timely."

I can't believe this war will end. And what if it does? What will be left to occupy of my old world? Who to occupy it? None of my people.

A new word has been coined, by a Polish Jew, a refugee, a lawyer. Genocide: extinction of a race.

But I do present my paper, trying to believe the time will come to attempt healing war-damaged minds.

One soft June morning, I sit with my patient. Someone pounds on the double doors.

Her nurse bursts in, shouting. "We've landed in France!"

Bells are ringing. The lawn is thronged with staff and patients.

I stand aside from the jubilant crowd.

***

1945

Five years since Gertrud's death. Her yahrzeit candle burns on the day the double news breaks. The U.S. Army has crossed the Elbe. FDR has died. I do not join Sally and Raymond who go to watch the train with his body. I think of other trains, boxcars full of Jews. Of ships with living refugees turned away. Children denied entrance.

I carry Muni up to bed. Does their dog comfort Eleanor tonight?

Pictures appear in the papers, obscene photographs from the death camps of a few skeletal survivors. I do not make it to the toilet before I vomit.

I have sworn an oath to heal. I would kill Hitler if I could.

Hitler suicides. He escapes through Nietzsche's door.

Raymond drives us into Washington the night the Capitol is reilluminated. I insist on sitting with them on the front seat. The traffic is thick and the drive takes forever. The blare of horns makes the ringing in my ears worse.

The Capitol gleams, the dome is whole and beautiful.

Sally cries for joy. I cry, too. Thinking of ruined cities, ruined lives.

Anne, Dexter, the children go to the victory parade in Rockville. I stay home. The walls listen to me, hold me now, protect my sorrowful solitude as Gertrud would have.

FOURTEEN

The cat was lying on his arm. It hurt like hell.

He shook his arm. No cat. Moving hurt worse.

Opened his eyes.

She was there, sitting by the bed, reading like she used to do when he was sick. Where was he?

"Ma."

"Honey." She kissed his forehead, real light, a butterfly kiss, crying. She held out a pill and a glass of water.

He cricked his head up to swallow.

"Nickie, I'm sorry about not being there last night."

Last night. The fire ball coming at him. The freezing cold hospital.

"I was scared, Ma. I thought I was going to die."

She patted his hair, softly, but even his hair hurt. Now he was crying.

"Where were you? You didn't answer."

"My phone was dead, sweetie. I'm so sorry."

He was the one whose phone was always dead.

Tears kind of oozed down her face. "About your dad, about them asking about your dad…" Her voice was so soft it was hard to hear. If she stopped crying maybe he could stop crying.

"Forget about it, Ma."

She kind of smiled. "I love you."

"Me too."

"I'm sorry you've been hurting."

"The pills help."

"I'm mean—all of it. What you've been doing."

His eyes felt heavy. No way to keep them open any more. No way to talk.

Her phone was ringing.

"Sleep," she whispered, kissed his forehead. "Sleep tight."

He tried to say *till the bed bugs bite* but his mouth was too heavy to open. Wanted to say *don't leave.* No way his jaw would even move.

When he woke up, she wasn't there. His heart kind of skipped around.

Phil was there. But she wasn't.

"How you doing, kiddo?"

"Okay. My arm hurts."

"Yeah, it's going to, for a while. Here, you're due."

He swallowed. Lay back.

"Where's my mom?"

"Over at the house. She'll be back. How about something to eat?"

"Not hungry."

"A smoothie?"

That sounded okay. Phil helped him stand up, walked beside him down the stairs.

Nick was a slow-motion video, floating the David Bowie astronaut way.

The Siamese kept watching with those intense blue eyes.

Phil fixed an awesome smoothie, strawberries in it, and mint from the garden. He drank it real slow. One sip at a time. His teeth ached but it was good. His arm looked gross with puss and blisters and was throbbing. Nick put his head down on the smooth counter and wished he was home with her but didn't have to move to get there. He felt super exhausted like falling asleep in the car and needing her to carry him to bed.

"When is she coming back?"

"Pretty soon. Had some calls to make."

He didn't want the Siamese staring at him. He wanted to be home with his normal cat purring on his belly and her across the hall reading or even on the phone with Dee, telling Dee how he'd screwed up again last night.

"Help me feed the fish?"

He sat by the pond, watching them swish and blow bubbles. Nice being a fish, cool water, nothing to do but swim and eat.

"Heron ate the calico."

Maybe it wasn't so great being a fish.

"We're going to have to build a cover."

"You still going to the quarry for the stones for the pool deck today?"

"It can wait till you feel better."

What would make him feel better was to be home with her. He was getting flash backs of the fireball. His heart was doing that skipping thing. He was getting a really bad feeling.

"I need to go home."

Like a jerk, he started crying.

"It's okay, kiddo. I'll run you over."

"I can walk. It's my arm that's fucked up." He didn't mean to sound so grouchy.

"Let me just give her a call and tell her we're on the way."

"I'd rather walk." He didn't wait. Phil caught up with him.

It seemed very far to the house. The grass smelled good from being cut but made him sneeze and that made his arm worse.

There was a white car by the house. Great. He felt like crap and someone was there. If it weren't broad daylight, if Phil weren't here, he'd go to his hideout. If his arm didn't hurt and if he didn't need to lie down so bad.

And if he didn't need to be home with her.

They made it to the porch. He felt kind of dizzy and might have keeled over but Phil caught him.

"Whoa, buddy. Sit here." He helped him onto the glider. "Eliza! We're here."

What was all his stuff doing here? The sleeping bag, the magazines. Grandpa's binoculars. His hideout stuff dumped here on the porch.

Was he like busted?

She thanked Phil. Practically pushed him off the porch. Rude. He'd never seen her rude.

"What's my stuff doing here?"

"The architect found it. You can't go in there anymore. The police are going to have guard dogs."

The police!

Just then a man came out of the house. Who was he? What had he been doing in there?

He was short, kind of old. Plain clothes cop? But wearing cowboy boots?

Nick's heart was pounding so hard it could break through his chest.

The guy stepped toward Nick. Staring at him. Too late to make a break for it and he'd probably just get tasered. He was looking at Nick like he'd seen a ghost.

Looking out of dark brown eyes with a really dark line around the colored part. Nick's eyes. His own eyes. It was like he'd died and his eyes been donated and stuck in someone else's face.

The hair was curly. Gray, but curly. Lots of people have curly hair. Like her.

But he'd never seen anyone else with his exact eyes.

208

She put her arm around Nick's shoulders, super-light and care-ful. It felt good. He wanted to hide behind her like a little kid.

"Nick," she said. "This is your dad. Jeff Wilson."

The guy kept staring like the game of chicken he and Ma used to play. Who would break first?

"Kind of a bombshell," the guy said. At least he didn't try and hug him.

"Donors are anonymous. How did you find out about us?"

She butted in.

"Jeff and I worked here. We got together once, just an accident really. I told everyone—even him—it was a donor."

"I'm an accident you lied about?" He didn't realize he was yell-ing till his throat hurt after.

"That's not what your mother means," the man said.

Like he knew what his mother would mean.

"You a mind reader or what?"

The guy kind of smirked. "I'm a psychiatrist. Been accused of reading minds. But I don't."

Great. A social worker and a shrink hook up and have a nut-case kid. Like some pathetic joke and he was the punch line.

The cat came out and rubbed against Nick's ankles. He squat-ted down and would have picked her up except for his arm.

"I owe you an apology," she said.

"For what? Letting me be born instead of having an abortion?"

"Nick!" She burst out crying. Well, tough.

"There's plenty of blame to go round here," the guy said.

"How's it your fault? You didn't know."

"What do you think about that?" Fake question. Fake smile. Oh, yeah. Definitely a shrink.

"That if you're not a complete idiot you had to know."

The guy nodded. "Yeah. Ever been in a spot where you knew something and you pretended you didn't? Knew you should check something out, knew you should like step forward for something you'd done and chickened out?"

The dude had a slick answer for everything. Nick kept patting the cat. He wasn't going to look at him. Definitely wasn't going to look at her. He couldn't bear it when she cried. He wasn't going to say another word. At least the asshole had the balls to admit he knew and copped out. Admitted he knew and didn't want him. Well, it's mutual, buddy. I don't want to know about you either. Better not to know than have a chicken-shit father. A short father on the chunky side with gray hair. An old full of it shrink. Wrinkled. Much older than her. Geriatric.

"If I were you, I wouldn't want anything to do with me."

You got that right, bozo.

"It was a mistake," the guy continued.

"Yeah, me!" Shouting again. The cat skittered away.

"Not you," she said. "Not being honest with each other and people who should know."

"Like me."

"Right," she said.

"Like Grandma and Grandpa."

He was kind of glad his grandfather was too far gone to get it. Well he wasn't changing his name. He was still going to be a Kline, like his grandfather.

The guy was old. He had that pathetic dried up look like someone who wanted to still be a rock star and was way, way past it. "Your parents are dead, right?"

He nodded.

"You married?"

"Yes," the guy said.

"Were you married then?"

"I was," he said. His eyes were sort of darting around. Gottcha, asshole!

"Going to tell her?"

The guy looked at his mom like he needed help. Her lips clamped shut in a straight line.

"Going to tell her?" Nick repeated.

"Yes," the guy said.

"She going to be mad?"

"Not at you," he said.

"You going to get a divorce?"

He shrugged. "Don't expect to."

"You have kids?"

The guy didn't answer.

"Maybe another kid, another accident you accidentally on purpose don't know about?"

The guy didn't say anything, which was as good as admitting it. He was taking the fifth, like they learned in Government. Copping out so as not to incriminate himself.

Nick peeked at his mom. She had this blank expression on her face.

His arm really kicked up. He was done here.

"I need to go lie down."

That snapped her out of it. "You can have some medicine," she said.

"What do they have him on?" Know it all doctor.

"Oxy," said Nick, just to pull his chain.

"No, it's not," she said, going inside to get the stuff.

"She told me you've been having a rough time. Hurting yourself."

"I'm not hurting myself. It's just a thing I do."

"And that you've been breaking in over there. Say, your hideout was my old office."

What the fuck? His office?

211

She was back. Took his hand, put the pill on his palm, touched the scars on his wrist. "Seriously, Nickie. Too many accidents."

"I'm the accident. Should have had an abortion."

"Shut up!"

She never used language like that.

"I wanted you from the moment I knew. And you know why I didn't tell Jeff—didn't tell your father?"

She was whispering, super hoarse.

"Because I wanted you so much. Because I loved you so much. And I was afraid—I was afraid he'd want you too, and we'd fight over you, and you'd have to live with him and his wife part of the time, and I couldn't bear it. I couldn't bear to share you with people who might not love you the way I did."

She was like getting hysterical now. Maybe super doc had a tranquilizer.

Neither he nor the guy said anything.

She sat crying and pushing the glider back and forth like crazy. Nick couldn't bear it and went and sat by her. Her crying jag began to stop.

The guy said, "Eliza, that must have been hard to acknowledge."

Like he had any right to say anything. Like he was the boss of the whole situation. She kind of laughed then, not like she really found it funny. A sarcastic laugh, not her usual.

The guy didn't say anything more.

Nothing about wanting Nick or not wanting Nick. Then or now. Nada.

After a while sitting there in this lame silence, the guy pipes up. He'd like Nick to see someone. He'd make some calls.

Nothing about wanting to spend any time with Nick. Just wanting to find someone to fix him. Nick wasn't talking to anyone this guy knew, that was for sure.

"I saw that was coming."

The guy fake laughed at that. "Just a thought," the guy said. "Just a completely original thought. Not that you didn't just dis what we do, or anything."

Hilarious. Yeah, quite the card. Everything one big joke, including knocking up his mom.

The guy said he'd have to go. Giving grand rounds at some hospital.

"What's that?" Nick asked.

Turned out it meant the guy going around showing off how much he knew.

He was in a hurry to leave. Scribbled what he said was his private cell number on the back of his card like it was a big deal top secret. He'd be going back to Boston, but Nick should call anytime. "Anytime at all, anytime."

He didn't say anything about getting together before he went back to Beantown. Whenever that was going to be. Fine.

His mom walked this Jeff dude out to the car. Spent a long time leaning on the car, talking. Talking about Nick behind his back.

Which pissed Nick off so much that even though his arm hurt like crazy he grabbed his skateboard and bombed past them, slamming over the speed bumps, pretending not to hear her shouting.

FIFTEEN

Nick sped down the driveway.

"No helmet?" said Jeff.

"I tell him, all the time."

"Likes the edge. Risky stuff."

He was talking about Nick with clinical remove, as though evaluating him for his psychotherapy group. He hadn't touched him once. Not that he touched his patients, as far as she knew, just his interns.

What a fool she was. Why was she surprised? Why was she so disappointed? This was that scene with the wizard of Oz, when you realize how small the man is, behind the curtain.

He hadn't even responded to him with the warmth he showed patients. With kids in trouble he had given off calm and kindness.

Easy, when you can leave the kid's problems at the office. What was that expression? *Those who can do, those who can't teach.*

"When he pulls these stunts, what do you do?" he asked. "Chase him down?"

"Sometimes. Confiscate his board, sometimes. He'll skate it off. Come back. I hate the risk, the waiting, but it's better than ramping the conflict up."

"Well he clearly doesn't want anything to do with me."

"Don't you get it?" she snapped, and paused. Okay. Benefit of the doubt. Maybe she was being unfair. Give him a chance. How slow she'd been to get it, even living with Nick, knowing Nick.

"What he's doing—some of it is about you. About needing to know who he is. Who you are."

"This is about me? Sorry, Eliza, you can't pin this on me."

"I don't mean it's anything you've done. It's the negative space, what he doesn't know."

"And so now you decide to send an SOS. When you're in really deep water." He spit the words at her. They'd never argued. You have to be equals to argue.

"I'm not looking to dump him on you. I'm not coming after you with a paternity suit if that's what you're afraid of, if you've made a habit of this. Just find some way to be there for him." Eliza caught her breath. She was so angry she verged on tears again. Hold it together, for Nick.

"Like what?"

His voice was flat, but at least he was asking. He was afraid.

Be careful, don't push him away. Nick needs him. Give him a chance.

Start small, Jeff had taught, when you're working with someone who's scared.

"Before you go back to Boston, just ask him out to dinner. He might not go, but ask." He should know how to approach a kid in trouble. His kid in trouble, theirs. "And try to find a therapist."

"Don't really have that many connections down here anymore."

How small the man behind the curtain is.

He got into the car, leaned back against the seat. Jeff spoke straight into the windshield, not turning his head toward her. "I'm sorry."

About everything, or today? Oh well, an apology is an apology, and she owed him one as well.

"Me too." *You've got to tell Xandy,* she wanted to add. *No more big secrets.*

Not good to push. Jeff was limited, imperfect.

216

So? Eliza certainly was too.

She must keep her expectations down. Start small.

Maybe Jeff couldn't be a good father, given who he was, so late in the game. But she had to give him a chance to come through in some small way. If he couldn't be good, or even good enough, at least maybe be a little good enough, for Nick.

"Just ask him to dinner. Please."

"I hope he's back soon. In one piece," he said, turning the key in the ignition.

He'd taught her that patients always say the most important thing as the session ends. Hand on doorknob remarks. She had a choice. Take his remark as criticism of her parenting, or an admission that he cared, he was worried.

Give him the benefit of the doubt, for Nick's sake.

"Me too. If you still pray, now's a good time."

"I'll be in touch," he said.

"Please."

He held a hand up in salute as he drove away down the long driveway.

What a mess, the way it had gone. But she'd done it. She'd tapped the ball and started it rolling. No, she'd thrown it at him. He hadn't caught it yet, but it was in the air.

Eliza walked toward the cottage, praying again, or whatever it was she did at these moments. Please let Nick skate out some anger. Please let him come home okay. Please let Jeff come through.

The cottage made her feel safer. She and Nick had gotten this far together, without Jeff. Worst case scenario, they'd carry on without him. Whatever happened, she could make it good enough. For starters, she was teen-proofing this house.

Eliza began in the kitchen. She dumped the boxes of matches from the drawer into a plastic garbage sack. Upstairs she emptied the medicine closet of her razors. Action helped, doing what she could to take control of the situation. She'd been a world class baby-proofer, another illusion of maternal power.

The cat sat guard on Nick's bed.

"Scat," she said, grabbing the pillow. She flinched at his stash: sharp-edge razor blade in a paper jacket, several matchboxes, her Bic lighter. Added all of it to the bag and carried it to the trash.

The phone was ringing when she came in.

Hearing Dee's voice, Eliza began to cry again but she could always talk through tears with Dee.

"You're kidding! Jerk! I'm coming right now!" Dee said.

"No, I'm okay. Really." She was. She would be. Nick needed her to cope. "It has to just be me, when Nick gets home."

"I'd disappear right away. I don't like you being alone."

"I'm okay. I know you're there."

She couldn't even tell Dee. Frieda was with her.

SIXTEEN

1946

Mother is settled for good in England. Grete must stay with her. Anna and her family are going to Palestine. It is only geographic distance. I did not *lose* them. I try to count one hundred daily blessings as my childhood rabbi taught.

But the distance is deep as oceans and time.

I have lost them.

My dream recurs of the child I will never have.

I put on my analyst's mantle and take on more patients, seek out difficult patients.

We are seeing acute need here among some new patients, veterans struggling with returning to civilian life after committing and witnessing horrors. It triggers psychosis for some, exacerbates distress for others.

Anne's mental health association finds families to be in grave distress. She's lobbying for funds for a full-time community educator. Shell shock, soldier's heart as we called it, affects the family, too.

Erich sent me a subscription to the *New Yorker*. On the anniversary of Hiroshima, the entire issue is a piece on the bombing. Civilians incinerated—differently than my people in the camps, but incinerated. So much new evil perpetrated in this war.

We have a drought. The lawn is crisped brown. Even this corner of the world is burnt.

It will rain again. I know that, as surely as I still believe in healing.But not all wounds and damage heal. Sally knows a Negro soldier attacked and blinded on the bus home after discharge. To survive war and be blinded by countrymen! Will the evil ever stop spreading?

My childhood rabbi said there has always been evil and always will be evil. He taught that presence of wrong does not absolve us from doing right. I hold to that truth but feel so weighed down.

Erich and I have dinner in his neighborhood restaurant after the Institute meeting. Speaking of the trials in Nuremberg, I break down.

Friedl, have you considered—going back into analysis yourself?

No! I thought I could talk freely to you.

His pale eyes glint with tears. *I am honored to listen. I only suggest it out of concern for your melancholy. Keep writing, Friedl. Keep working. It is the way out.*

Finally, he has learned to listen. Perhaps his wife Henny has taught him that, as she struggles with her own depression. I am proud of my student and proud we have found our way to friendship. But deeply ashamed he thinks I, the helper, need help. I have no need of analysis. I know myself, my strengths, my weaknesses, my conflicts. Erich is wrong again.

I am writing, trying to document our treatment model, to capture the essence of what we do. It's hard to put the process of healing relationship down on paper. I feel as inadequate for the task as Dexter's son struggling with a class assignment—to write directions for folding a paper airplane.

I do have hope. At weekly conference I look around the table and witness young colleagues maturing. In session, I see a patient respond to being heard, being respected, being accompanied in suffering. My heart lifts, for the moment.

***

1947

Now there is gasoline again, I am practicing my driving. Muni by my side, I drive out to the ferry or we motor to the new neighborhood nearby built for veterans using the GI Bill. Every young woman seems to be pregnant. Everyone making babies to refill the ransacked world. I follow the looping lanes, mindful of children at play. The streets are named for the battlefields where the new homeowners fought. I follow Ardennes Avenue as though it might lead me into the forests of my childhood.

On the seventh anniversary of Gertrud's death, a spring day of white dogwood and violets, I light her yahrzeit candle and leave it to burn out in the sink after my last session.

"Come, Muni!" We drive out to the canal and walk the tow path. I tell Gertrud what has happened this year.

Anna lives in Palestine, I tell her. There is a resolution pending, to split it. Yes, our wandering, persecuted people may have our own land, our own nation.

Dexter has succeeded in having the local hospital admit alcoholics in crisis. He says he hopes to never do another postmortem in the jail, to have alcoholism considered a disease not a mental condition.

Anne is president of the board for the county mental hygiene clinic. I'm so proud of her.

My presentations have been successful, in Baltimore, New York, and our research seminar on manic depression with the Washington School of Psychiatry is well subscribed.

Erich has given me a television. I play the volume loud for the broadcast of Arturo Toscanini. Imagine, Gertrud! A performance of Beethoven's Ninth right in our living room.

Erich does love his Henny. I truly wish him joy with her. Loving you, Gertrud, has released me.

The war is over, we are at peace, my dear, but I fear this new "cold war." It reminds me too much of how hot wars begin.

Muni chases a squirrel, and almost falls in the canal, cutting my recitation short.

I hear her laughing. Gertrud had the purest laughter I have ever known. Music of the spheres I will hear even when I am stone cold deaf. Stone cold dead.

***

1948

We cannot admit all the patients who need us, and it is the most desperate who apply. We are known as the place of last resort. *Lourdes on the Potomac*, Erich teases, *but you cannot do miracles.*

I hate to turn any away. Young impatient doctors at our case presentation meetings say we should develop more efficient, shorter treatment. Use more chemicals. Use more electroshock.

Not treat so thoroughly, you mean, I respond. Yes, our method is long and costly. But what is the price for saving a life?

The youngsters imagine a quick cure for the mind and spirit must be found.

There is no quick fix, I tell them. I remind them that for all my differences with Freud it is to his great credit that he called attention to the importance of the mutual interpersonal relationship between psychiatrist and patient. We must remain true to that bedrock principle.

The mind is not simple as the heart and lungs. We are the Chestnut Lodge. Trees and healing relationships grow here. We do not try to make square pegs round. We help square pegs be strong and find a unique place.

Should we be efficient and inadequate? Should families and patients be afraid to enter and want to leave? Should our atmosphere be punitive, pushing for "results"?

NO!

Dexter backs me. We will adapt, we will assimilate changes, but the core remains.

Some resent my relationship with Dexter. I know they call me the Queen behind my back. Well, we are king and queen of this realm.

People underestimate him, and he uses that. Prefers I catch the limelight. Sends me out as the Lodge ambassador and recruiter, with the gleam of my pedigree, my assumed association with Freud (though I detest his reductionist theory of urges—especially with women!). I dramatize our Lodge theory with vignettes showing how we cure psychosis with relationship; reach the loneliest with listening. I paint pictures with words. I'd like to work up an accompanying slide show with Gertrud's plates for our stillborn textbook.

I am working on a book for therapists, drawing my thoughts together. *Principles of Intensive Psychotherapy*, I will call it though Erich suggests something less prosaic. Dexter cheers me on. *It will put us on the map!* he says. As though we weren't already.

Dexter consolidates our position behind the scenes, drawing on his deep ties to the medical community, family roots, Anne's good works. Anne may be the essential one, keeping us on solid ground, her eye on the books, not letting us expand too fast nor dream too big. She conserves the practical assets that carry us through, too— and provides food for our table.

The Lodge is like a human body. The grounds and buildings are the skeleton. The trees? Our green lungs. I am the mind, and Dexter the skin (all important, all containing organ). Anne is our heart. Nurses, aides, psychologists, social workers, cooks, gardeners? The venous system. The stream of patients is our life blood.

Dexter and I consider the applicant files weekly. He deals out the manila folders as though we're playing cards. We read and exchange. We assess need and priority, our resources and the patient's.

He closes one file, lays it aside. "Too young."

We make the decisions together. I reach for it.

He is right. Sixteen is too young for us, even younger than that boy sent only for evaluation after the shooting.

I have never treated anyone so young. And she has been through so much failed treatment.

Lourdes on the Potomac. I read her file again, remembering the doomed children sent away, sent back on the boats to Europe and death.

I can no more refuse to take her than pass by the scene of an accident. I am a physician and have sworn an oath.

"Frieda?" He's abrupt, sensing mutiny—we know each other.

"She needs us."

"She needs a secure adolescent unit. Tutoring. Peers for social development. The whole person approach, as you say."

"She can't handle peers yet, look at the history. Academics? That could be arranged, but hardly a priority until she's stabilized."

He shakes his heavy head (he and his Great Dane resemble each other, as do Muni and I with our long noses and deep-set eyes). "You mean she needs you." His tone is angry. "Don't overreach, Frieda."

We are friendly antagonists, battle things through together in service to the patients and The Lodge. It has become part of our method, over the thirteen years at this table.

"We could help this girl, Dexter."

"Out of the question. She is simply too young and too damaged. You are too busy, can't take another challenging case, have never treated anyone this young." He's glaring, the shed of brows pulled down. The temper he keeps in check is brewing.

"Exactly. We must take her. Must stretch and prove our techniques generalize."

"You may fail."

"Or find we succeed. A younger person has less scar-tissue." I must be strategic. Let him want this as a new way to put the Lodge on the map.

He paces, stands at the window, stiff back to me. "The stakes are higher with a young person. The cost and heartbreak would be worse, disappointing parents of a child. The damage to our reputation."

We have indeed failed before, even lost patients. I could not bear to lose a child.

He turns back to me, eyes and voice downcast. "Frieda, forgive me, you have never been a parent. I know as a parent how it would be, if someone failed my child trying to prove her method generalized."

"Every patient is my child."

"Trust me on this, Frieda."

"Trust me!"

"She's seen the best."

"Not us. Not me."

"You know our expression? Fools rush in," he says.

"Where angels fear to tread. I don't believe in angels. But I'm no fool."

The taut line of his lips relaxes.

"Your stubborn courage!" That's Dexter's way, to praise strength rather than criticize weakness. Calculated to disarm me.

"I was a major in the Prussian army. My theologian friend calls mine the courage to be. You have it too," I say, playing his game of disarming with true praise.

I interrupt our deadlock. "Look!" The dance therapist is leading patients across the lawn. A patient is swaying and almost skipping. "Remember her? Frozen catatonic when she came."

"If we fail this child…"

"I won't. We cannot turn her away. It would be cruel cowardice." I emphasize my point with hand gestures usually reserved for big audiences. My gesturing warns me (and likely Dexter, too) that I am afraid. Would it be wiser, more ethical, to turn her away?

"She is very ill, Frieda," he sighs.

"Human nature tends to health like plants to sunlight."

"We may not have the soil she needs."

"We push doubt aside every day to believe in ourselves as well as the patient." I'm gesturing, overemphatic again.

"Anne will be furious with me."

I listen. Listen, as with a resistant patient. Listen.

"Very well. Take her," he says.

"Thank you." I am jubilant and terrified.

The first day I pull the double doors closed in my office. Her pale face is expressionless. Burns on her arms speak of pain.

She may be too scarred in every way.

We sit in my quiet room. The air hums and buzzes with the current only the most distressed emit.

Her skin lesions remind me of my young self in the mikvah on my wedding eve, trying to scrub myself clean. I would have scrubbed off my skin if I could.

I must not fail her. We must succeed.

The proverb says when the student is ready the teacher appears. Between this girl and me, who is the teacher, who is the student?

We sit in silence. I listen to the silence. Wait.

A fortnight in she gestures with her fists, poised as though to strike.

I wait.

She inhabits her own world, trapped.

Her index finger moves back and forth, the movement of a child's game.

I study my own hands, my short fingers, my nails cut for the piano. I raise my index finger and bow to hers.

We've saluted each other.

She walks with her nurse back to Main—stiff as a mechanical toy wound too tight.

I will wait and listen for the moment the spring uncoils. Ours is a very long game of patience, with very high stakes.

She speaks her own language, her own dialect of psychosis. I understand somewhat since I rely more on hearing with my intuition than my ears. She lets me sit beside her.

But I must hear her voice clearly! I cannot miss any nuance.

Erich accompanies me to the audiologist in New York. He tells me his news as we wait for the doctor.

He and Henny are moving to Mexico City. He has an appointment at the University there, he hopes the climate will be better for her health. My brilliant student must know there is no climate in the world that cures depression like Henny's. But I do not deprive him of hope. He who has always said I have a neurotic need to be needed, is consumed by worry over Henny.

"You will fly down. Visit us. It is wonderful."

We know I will not.

I am losing him, again.

Every loss stirs every prior loss. But I do not grieve now. The girl needs me.

I sit in the audiologist's waiting room and think of my mother and father, the isolation of deafness.

227

"Dr. Fromm-Reichmann?"

The nurse invites me to the consulting room. I panic, almost reach out to Erich. I recover, hold myself straight and tall as my scant height allows, cross the room with my Prussian major stride.

"Better like this, or like this?" asks the doctor. He is plump, kindly, dressed in street clothes. His cuffs are frayed, which immediately makes me trust him. He works too hard to worry about his clothes. His hands and eyes are expressive. He understands patients who need cues. "Like this? Or this?"

"Neither." I weep, disgraceful tears.

He listens. I drink in the luxury of someone listening to me. Could Erich be right? Do I need to return to analysis? I tell the doctor about being my parents' ears. And that for my patients I must be able to *listen*.

I accept the ugly device. Vanity is not important. The priority is to hear my girl.

But the static distracts me. And vanity aside, I cannot look handicapped to the young staff. I put the device away. I must watch harder for the silent language of non-verbal cues, the language my lonely ones have taught me.

***

1949

Her baffled, sad parents visit.

I reassure. They have done their best all these years.

I do not say it, but their best was inadequate. They know.

How much is nature, how much is nurture, how much is fate? I do not know, but there are questions of fit between mothers and children, and this was a bad one.

Dexter cautions me I am too absorbed in this case. No, I tell him, just deep into the challenge. I am aware of the dangers of countertransference. And haven't I just published an essay on the personal and professional requirements of our work?

But privately I wonder. Am I stepping over the line? It has even crossed my mind that had I been her mother…hubris perhaps, but I do believe I would have been a better mother to her. I cannot admit my strong countertransference to Dexter, nor my doubts about my work. All analysts make mistakes. The important thing is to be self-aware, identify the mistakes, forgive our imperfection, learn, and move on. This is no moment for me to exhibit weakness. Think what happens to old dogs in a pack. I am sixty. The young ones are on my heels. No queen reigns forever.

***

1950

Last night on the television there was an incredible show! A human birth! My hands trembled, remembering the thrill of the pull. There will be outrage from prudish American viewers. The sessions with my girl are a long labor, but she is giving birth to herself. I am helping this child into the world.

But what a world it is. There is a contagion of evil in Washington. A rabid junior senator from Wisconsin promotes suspicion and accuses leaders in the arts, in public service, of being communists. He should be forced to listen to the song from "South Pacific," a profound musical I saw in New York. *You've got to be taught to hate and fear,* the refrain goes.

Mother fell down the stairs, on Friday evening. She should have been safe at her Sabbath table. Father "fell" to his death on the Sabbath. I am so far away. Grete assures me she will recover.

Grete calls to tell me she is gone.

229

Another has left this world and once again, I was not there to say goodbye.

Every loss opens every other loss.

Mother has been Grete's life. Come to me!

No, she will go to Anna in Israel.

I am alone. I am a motherless child however imperfect our fit was.

Thank G_d for the girl, my girl. She is making such progress. Winning against her demons. Recovering, slow but sure.

***

1953

She's recovered. She is leaving for college.

She will see me as an outpatient.

Dexter is proud. I have achieved the goal he, everyone, thought impossible.

Healthy development means separation. This is the success every parent wants for a child; every analyst wants for a patient. She can have an independent future. It is an accomplishment, not a failure. I have proved myself and the Lodge.

Why do I not feel victorious? Why so sad? Every goodbye to every patient has loss mixed in. But there's never been a termination like this. Is this how parents feel? With every baby garment outgrown there is loss as well as joy.

There is no one I can admit this to. Dexter would disapprove. Erich would insist on analysis.

Erich in Mexico is self-involved more than ever. Wrapped up in happiness as he prepares to marry again, incredible, with his Henny's suicide only a year ago. Indestructible man. Annis is the love of his life, he says. I've heard that before, I want to say.

Gertrud was the love of my life. But dare say it only to Muni.

Every loss opens the old ones. Losing my girl to health, I am preoccupied, careless. I traveled to New York to speak at the Institute. I left my train case underneath a restaurant table. My jewelry was lost, none of it valuable, all of it precious.

Trivial material loss but those pieces travelled with me from Germany. I weep for my semi-precious stones as though I've just lost everyone dear to me all over again.

And I weep over the news of Ethel and Julius Rosenberg put to death, leaving children behind. I dream of my phantom child again.

I am frightened. A dozen staff have fallen ill—student nurses, a psychiatrist. Polio is suspected! I boil Muni's water, knowing I am ridiculous. I cannot risk losing him.

***

1955

I present my preliminary draft of my paper on loneliness to our very first Chestnut Lodge symposium. I must finish it, polish it, publish. It is hard to separate from work I care so much about, almost like saying goodbye to a dear patient, to my girl.

And then, unexpected, the honor came. An honor which felt like a threat.

I can't go, I told Dexter, when the invitation came from the Ford Foundation Center for Advanced Study in California.

You must. Frieda, you are the first woman they've ever selected for Fellowship.

But my patients.

It will help them to learn about separation and attaching to another, Frieda. This time will free you to write.

He is not obviously impatient, but often asks. How is the paper on loneliness progressing? How is my work on writing up the work with my girl going? More and more we must publish, to validate our method, keep us on that map of his.

Perhaps Dexter wants to separate from the inconvenient deaf woman at the seminar table. I have critics, rivals, around that table. Have there been complaints?

Remember you told me I could not refuse, Frieda? Now you must accept your due.

Yes, I pushed him to accept the presidency of the Psychiatric Association. Strange, how hard it is to accept praise and take in validation. How quickly my paranoia stirs! We are all a little mad.

I agree to go, for sabbatical, for a long sabbath rest and re-creation, after twenty years here at the Lodge. I will go to this Palo Alto mountaintop and rest and think—and write. If only rest might cure deafness! Am I being put out to pasture? Will I manage without the structure, the exoskeleton of sessions?

We travel by train, Muni in his basket; my typewriter, my trunk of books shipped ahead. Muni is the only one who needs me now. I travelled this route before with Gertrud. I see the passing scenes with her eyes, too.

We break our journey in Colorado for my girl's wedding. Coincidence of timing that I can attend, though Dexter disapproves and reminds me there are no coincidences.

The bride looks so happy. Her mother and father thank me for giving them their daughter back. Her father gives her away. Gives her away…

She was never mine. I am at best the fairy godmother whose hard magic helped her.

She gives *me* a wedding gift. She has written of our work together, as I asked. I must do my part on this sabbatical. I will bring the completed paper home to Dexter.

Palo Alto proves to be my magic mountain. The air, the vista is invigorating. And among the fellows are several German speakers! The mixture of disciplines is stimulating. We study films a British cultural anthropologist made of the interactions in families of schizophrenics. He slows the film, goes frame by frame. I catch every nuance, seeing it over and over. Released from worry and competition I enjoy theorizing. Rest does not cure deafness, but I hear more easily in this mountain air, this convivial atmosphere. We sit together on the terrace on evenings, drink cool white California wine, dark beer. I have not felt this connected in a long time. How much like my lonely ones I have become.

In the cozy bungalow I've been assigned, I pick up Muni, and sing. *For you're a jolly good fellow! For you're a jolly good fellow!*

***

1956

The golden months have flown by. On the last evening, we sit on the terrace and watch the sun set over cedars. My comrades toast me. Ridiculous how I feel the ache of separation and loss with even this goodbye.

Time to return to chestnut trees, and shade. This last evening feels like the ultimate sunset night after a very long Sabbath. I have rested too well. I haven't finished the paper on loneliness. I haven't written up my work with the girl.

On my way east I stop at the casita in New Mexico. I welcome the fresh sense of Gertrud's presence and even welcome the renewed pain of missing her. My father's voice is lost. I never want to lose the echo of Gertrud's laugh.

Dexter raises the shed of brows. "You've not finished writing up your work with her?" He is disappointed. "When do you think you will have it done?"

"I will have to fit it in. Around the patients." I will be better, once I am with patients again. I will lose this delinquency.

"We have been talking of adjusting your workload, reducing your caseload, giving you more time to write." Who is this we? Who has been his collaborator in my absence?

"Not necessary," I say, Prussian major ready for battle.

I claim my place at my end of the seminar table, opposite Dexter: king and queen, mother and father. I strain to hear the discussion, and strain to hide my effort. I feel an imposter. Patients have described this, now I understand. I sit in my usual place, but I feel like an empress unclothed. I have interrupted a game of musical chairs begun while I was away. I must be agile, recover my place.

They tape record patient sessions now and play the tapes at meetings. Following the recording is hopeless for me: distorted sound divorced of visual cues.

Afraid of revealing what I've mis-heard I am reticent in discussion.

But in sessions, one on one with my patients, behind the double doors, I listen, deeply listen. I live for those hours.

After rounds, over our bourbon, Dexter and I discuss our new grant for a five-year study of the efficacy of psychotherapy in treating schizophrenia. We must document our results, our outcomes.

"We must not lose the art to science, Dexter."

"We must move with the times. This will prove what we do, keep us on the map."

"If you split the lark to find the music, you may lose it," I warn him, twisting a line from Emily Dickinson, a poem Gertrud loved.

He sighs. "I miss you taking me on, your insights at meetings."

Pure Dexter, a compliment to disarm me.

"Have you considered—looking into a new hearing device?" He knows my secret. Everyone knows. "There's a new one, Miracle Ear. All transistor."

"I will," I lie. I'm done with gadgets. There is no miracle ear for me.

***

1957

Muni dies. Déjà vu. Warm at my feet as I fall asleep, cold weight when I awake. Sleeping the false drug-sleep (the dose to quiet my mind and tinnitus) I failed him. I should have awakened. I would have held him one last time. I have not been there at the end for anyone—Papa, Mama, Gertrud. Not even awake for my dear dogs' deaths.

Raymond digs the grave beside the first Muni, in the copse of trees. I sprinkle earth on the new grave, whisper Kaddish.

"We'll take a ride, one day soon," Raymond says. "Go get the new Muni."

I do not have another dog in me. I do not have it in me to love another living being. I do not have it in me to lose anyone or anything more. I walk home. I expect his scamper when I open the door.

Make coffee, smoke a cigarette, prepare myself for the patients.

Thank G_d for the patients. Behind the double doors, in the almost quiet enough room, I can attend to every gesture and glance. It is easier to accurately read one face, observe one body, than filter group cacophony. I study my patients the way we studied film strips in California. Break each sign and signal down to read face and gesture. Could I film my sessions and play them back? No, practice observed, reaction observed, is altered by the very fact of observation.

I rise alone to face the bright morning, take the morning dose calculated to cancel out the nighttime dose. I try to regulate myself with medicine, seek the quick fix of chemicals. I preserve my facade.

They never summon me at night from Main for urgent consults. Instead of taking care of others, I am becoming an object of care.

This is loneliness, not solitude.

Only the patients save me from myself, hour by hour, hour after hour.

My loneliest one's husband and son have come today. He loves her, moved here from out of state, so that he and the boy could be near when I suggested it would advance her treatment.

I've brought the dollhouse into my office for the child Carter. I hope to entice her to engage with him. Doubt it is possible but cannot deny myself hope any more than deny it to a patient, a family. We must believe in the possibility of health to succeed. The forces of nature are in our favor. The child is perplexed. And the husband? Chronic sorrow.

She is getting worse not better. Those young doctors doubtless say I have failed her. She has every reason to live in the world—but cannot.

What if I had been younger when she came to me? Or if she had been younger, like my girl?

The boy plays with the dollhouse intended so long ago for my niece. His face is sharp enough to cut your heart.

He's put the mother doll in the bed, pulled the handkerchief sheet over her head.

I kneel beside him. Modeling for his mother. She can't see. His father cannot take his eyes away from her and tend his suffering child.

"She's in bed," I say.

He squeezes the child doll under the mother's bed.

"Is he hiding?"

He doesn't answer.

She weeps, the father buries his face in his hands.

I reverberate with the family's pain, once again too acute a tuning fork for emotional frequencies, as in my own childhood. I must beware, be wary, of countertransference. But I must hold that poor child.

I shelter the child on my lap, another child who is not mine.

They are all mine.

April the cruel, beautiful month is here again. The dogwood gleams—as it did that night seventeen years ago when the call came from New Mexico.

My girl, my far away Colorado girl, is about to have a baby of her own. I wish I could deliver her.

I have been ill for weeks with flu, cannot shake the bone aches. A friendly young doctor invites me to dinner. I almost refuse. But I need allies.

It does lift me, watching his children at play. In my next life, perhaps I would work with children. Did I shy away from it out of fear that yearning would compromise my work? Stir my longing like delivering babies?

I did my finest work with my girl.

Walking home, I pause at my graves, sit on the stone wall and smoke. The cardiologist I see in secret in Washington (ears, heart, what will fail me next?) says I must stop smoking.

Well, what if this addiction hastens the failure of my pumping heart? Worse things have happened.

Nietzsche's door appears, torn into the sky beyond the branches. The open door that invites me to leave and helps me stay. Thank G_d for the possibility of exit.

My heart aches. The pump is weary.

Would it be so bad, to die here?

Worse things have happened.

Tonight, I will double the dose of my sleeping potion, just to ease the angina, quiet the arrythmia, achieve the heavy drowsiness that will weigh my limbs down, pin me to the bed with sleep. I crave dropping deep into sleep like a child after too long a day.

I must put this self-indulgent diary aside. The unfinished paper on loneliness, and the lecture for the conference in Geneva wait on my desk. The long promised, long overdue paper on the girl, waits.

I must make the changes to my will. Erich is too far away to remain my executor. Dexter too busy. My capable secretary will handle everything, dear Virginia.

But tonight, I cannot write over the roar of this tinnitus.

Playing the piano used to quiet the noise in my head, but no longer.

I should burn this journal, but I am too tired. Burning is so close to forbidden cremation. There has been enough incineration.

Virginia will know what to do, she must decide. I will hide my journal deep in the cabinet and then—a hot bath. I will bathe; I will sleep.

The cardiologist cautions me against hot baths. I have told him that hot springs are curative. He is against every sweetness—smoke, whiskey, the benison of hot bath water. Why should one live without sweetness?

Why should one live?

I will sink into the deep, hot water.

And if the doctor is right?

Why should I live? Why shouldn't I die?

Behind the fear is the wish, perhaps.

Worse things have happened.

I would like to know, when my girl's baby comes, if it is a girl or a boy.

But if I do not know?

Only one more loss.

The trill of birds outside my window—gone.

The piano tuner's random notes and then the perfect scale—gone.

The tinkle of ice in a glass—gone.

The low hum of Gertrud's voice—gone.

Father, Klara—gone.

Six million—gone.

I will run the bath and sink down into the water and lean back and close my eyes.

If the heat shocks this troublesome muscle in my chest and stops its beating?

Silences the ringing in my ears?

Would that be such a tragedy?

Who would see to Muni?

But Muni is gone, too.

There are worse things. I will bathe and close my eyes and rest.

SEVENTEEN

Being loopy from the medicine he hit the speed bump too hard. He barely held on to the landing. He hoped that guy Jeff noticed his style. Probably too busy talking to her about what a loser nutcase Nick was. Probably telling her she should get a DNA test. Probably saying he's not mine.

Except for those eyes Nick would say the guy couldn't be his father.

So what if the guy thought Nick was a loser? Nick wasn't impressed with him, either.

No one was hanging by the fountain. The bike cop rode by which pretty much explained no one being there.

His arm was killing him. He hadn't noticed while he was skating. And he was starving! No money. He'd have to settle for ice cream samples. The bakery used to give out bread but the skaters and the cross-country team from school ate too much.

The girl at the counter in the ice cream store was Jenn from the row in front of him in chorus. A memory flash hit of the super nice shampoo smell to her hair.

She was squatting to wipe down the glass front of the case. The belt of her jeans and the bottom of her T-shirt gapped.

She turned around and caught him peeking like some pervert.

Her skin was super pale and a little zitty but she was so pretty it didn't matter.

"What would you like?"

"Actually—just realized—forgot my wallet." Lame moron excuse.

"Sample?"

"Coffee?"

She scooped him a full-size. Her wrists were skinny. There was a little tattoo of a flower on one.

Jenn smiled, handing him the cone. Her teeth had a big space in front, but it made a great smile. "What happened to your arm?"

"Had this accident." What to say? "With a blow torch where I'm working."

"Wow. It must really hurt."

"Oh, a bit."

She looked kind of impressed.

An older boy came out of the back room. College, at least.

Nick left.

He sat on the edge of the fountain, finishing the ice cream.

Finding out about his father, he was supposed to feel what? Some kind of Ah-Hah moment like Cole talked about? But he didn't. He felt kind of like erased. He'd imagined a way different father. Scratch that. And she lied. She lied about this humongous fact.

The girl was walking straight toward Nick, carrying a white paper bag.

Her hair really was white. She looked almost like a ghost. Even that ghost shrink lady wasn't this pale.

"Hi," Jenn said.

"Did I get you in trouble with your boss?"

"He's not my boss. It's okay. Anyway, I paid for this for my mom." She swung the bag.

Up so close her eyelashes and eyebrows were there but almost invisible. She was practically albino.

They sat on the edge of the fountain. The bike cop went by again, pedaling real slow.

"His job is to harass skaters," Nick said.

"That's discrimination."

"Yeah."

Jenn stood up. "I should get home."

"I should get out of here, too. He'll be back." Lame. She could tell he just wanted to walk with her. He was turning red.

"So how do you like your job?" he asked. Lame.

"It's pretty boring, but I'm going to start driver ed soon. At that place here in the square."

"The one with the yellow cars?"

"That's it. How's your summer?" she asked.

"I'm doing some work for our neighbors. Odd jobs."

"At that new house?"

She knew where he lived! She must have looked him up in the school directory. Sweet.

"No, the old house over in Rose Hill."

"Oh, it's so pretty."

They were passing the funeral home.

"Creepy place," she said.

"Yeah." It didn't seem so bad when you weren't alone. He kept getting whiffs of her shampoo smell. Better than petrichor. Way better than dirt smells after rain.

They reached the stoplight by the Lodge driveway. She pushed the button to cross the road.

"Is it spooky living next door to that place? They say it's haunted."

"It's okay."

He'd like to tell her about seeing the shrink's ghost. He'd like to take her to the hideout and make out.

But the hideout was history. Remembering that made his heart hurt. Not skip around but ache. He wondered what the guy would say about his heart stuff. He wasn't a real doctor, just a psychiatrist, but he should know, right? Not that he'd be talking to him anytime soon.

The walk signal turned on. This was where they'd split up. There weren't any lights on at home. She'd either gone to bed super early or gone over to Ben and Phil's.

"Nice talking," Jenn said. "See you."

He didn't feel like going into an empty house.

"I'll walk you."

"It's not far. Over by the elementary school."

"I know."

She sort of smiled.

At the playground they sat on the swings. Their legs were too long but it was a nice place to sit. She took the ice cream and a plastic spoon out of the sack. "She's probably asleep. It's melting." She stuck the spoon in, held it out to him. "Coffee."

Just about the most delicious ice cream he'd ever tasted. She used the same spoon after him. Well, there was only one.

They went on eating the ice cream, passing the spoon back and forth.

"I met my father today."

"Like a—custody visit or something?"

"No. First time ever."

"Are you like adopted or what?"

"No. My mom and this guy hooked up. Once. She told everyone, him and me included, she used a sperm bank."

"Wow! That's like something you'd read in a magazine. If they were famous. All this time he didn't know about you?"

"He just about admitted he figured it out. Didn't want a kid."

"That sucks. But how could he know he didn't want you when he didn't even know you?"

He must have been clenching every muscle all day. Now, sitting with Jenn, talking like this, everything felt kind of looser. Maybe this was what his mother meant, why she was always pushing talking to someone. Cole at camp said you meet the person you need when you need them. Which Nick personally thought was more new age shit. But maybe Jenn was like that person.

"Yeah, it's kind of lame. She said she didn't really want him to know. Told this like huge dishonest lie because she wanted to keep me all to herself."

"That's sort of sweet, when you think about it."

"I don't know. I feel like a mistake. That's what they called me." He scraped up the last of the ice cream. "I hope your mom won't be mad we ate this."

"Don't worry about it. Like I said, she's asleep." Jenn was twisting her swing around and around. "What's he like? Does he look like you?"

"He's old, gray hair. I'm taller than he is. Nothing like me at all really. Except for we have the same eyes."

"You have very unique eyes."

Good thing it was dark. He was red for sure.

"Are you going to like split your time or what now?"

"He doesn't live around here."

"You going to visit?"

"Nah. He's married. Doesn't want to have anything to do with me. And vice versa, believe me."

"My dad left in third grade. If he showed up—well, it's not going to happen. He knew me for eight years and left. I used to call him. He lives with someone else now out in Nebraska. He has kids. He doesn't even answer now. Got caller ID."

"That's shitty."

245

She shrugged. "You get used to it. I never think about him."

They just kept twisting around in the swings.

"I can't get over her lying to me all these years."

"But—she kept you. She didn't like give you up for adoption or—you know. She must of really wanted you."

It felt good, hearing Jenn say it. "He didn't want me." His arm was throbbing.

"He might of changed his mind if he knew you. Not like mine."

"He just left?"

"Yup. They fought all the time. They never got married, so it was easy. Grownups." She had this way of kind of blowing air out her nose when she laughed.

"So called," he said.

She laughed again.

"I should be going, if she wakes up and I'm not home she goes ballistic."

"Tell me about it, her too," he said.

Jenn's house was one of the small brick ones that all looked alike. When she opened the door he could smell cats and cigarettes. No wonder she washed her hair with such good stuff.

There was television noise.

She stepped inside, looked back out at him through the screen door.

Jenn put her hand up against the mesh of the screen. He put his hand on hers. A high five through the screen. How warm her hand was.

His mother's bedroom light was on. He went in super-quietly.

She heard him, naturally. ESP.

Popped out like a cuckoo clock.

"How are you doing, honey?"

"My arm hurts. I could use some medicine."

"Come up here. Let me see."

It looked gross in the bathroom light. All weepy with ooze.

"Yuck," he said.

"It's healing. Can't put anything on it or it might get infected. Here." She gave him the pill and the tooth glass with water. "Starting tomorrow, regular Tylenol. But you're going to feel better."

"How do you know?"

She made like she was going to hug him. He backed out of the bathroom.

"I'm going to eat, go to bed."

"I'll fix something," she said. "It's been—quite a day."

Great, she wanted to talk. "Ma, I just want to have a bowl of cereal. Don't follow me around, okay? I'm alright."

He fixed a bowl of cereal and took it out on the porch.

It was pitch black over at the Lodge. His father had his office in his hideout. Cole would say it was like fate. More like coincidence. But if he'd known, Nick could have looked for signs.

The cat was on his pillow. He pushed her off. Slipped a hand under.

His arm was killing him. His heart was jumping around.

Shit. She'd taken his stuff. No blades. No matches. No lighter.

He felt like banging on her door and telling her to keep her hands to herself. She had no right to touch his stuff. He wouldn't even need it if it wasn't for her.

And for Deadbeat Dad. Smart ass doctor who pretends not to even put two and two together when he sees he knocked her up.

Call any time.

Well he would. Tell him where to go.

The card was in his pocket. He added the number to contacts. Deadbeat Dad.

Punched in the numbers.

Got a message, the typical shrink message like hers even though this was supposed to be his personal cell, all the usual stuff blah-blah-blah about emergencies and 911. With hers at work he could just hit 5 and skip over it.

He had a voice like a radio voice. All fake warm and fuzzy.

"No emergency, Doc. Just your long-lost son calling."

He hung up. He felt worse. This shit about this being his private line, call me. And he doesn't even answer the frigging phone when Nick calls.

He still had matches and a lighter and blades, over in his hide-out, in the window seat.

The dogs weren't there yet. This would be like his last chance.

A strip of light showed under her door. Quiet. Not talking to Dee for once. Must have fallen asleep with the light on.

He sneaked out. Sprinted across the lawn.

The window under the forsythia bush was nailed shut! That architect dude, making things difficult.

He tried the other basement windows, testing the plywood covers. He found one a little bit loose and pried the plywood off.

He squirmed inside and dropped onto the floor, awkward on account of trying not to bump his arm which hurt like blazes. Used his cell phone for light till he reached the stairs. He was good from there.

Nick scanned all around the room. Empty.

What if the architect or his mom had taken his stuff out of the window seat? That would be just like her. Sneaky. Take his blades, take his matches, not tell him.

He opened the window seat. Matches, lighter, blades—all still there.

He went for the matches. He wanted to smell that sharp wood and fire smell. They were better than the lighter. He was lousy at the dragging and rolling and clicking action. What an uncoordinated spaz.

He wanted to light a match and let it burn right down to his fingers and blow it out.

He did. Over and over and over. Lighting, burning, blowing out at the last possible moment. Like always it worked. Made him stop thinking.

His arm ratchetted up the throb, like it was complaining, like it was remembering being burnt. He even sort of liked that extra pain. He blew the matches out a little sooner than usual though. Just before it would really hurt the maximum.

It wasn't that he couldn't do it. It wasn't that he was scared. It was just that he didn't want to. And as far as this shit went, he was the boss.

He lit another match and walked around holding it like a candle, blew it out and opened his phone for light. No sign on the walls the guy had ever been here. But what had he expected? Some graffiti?

There was no sign Nick had ever been here either, now his stuff was gone.

A can of spray paint would have been handy.

He pretended. Let his hand swoop across the wall. *Jeff fucked Eliza.*

Cole used to say the thing about anger is anger fuels anger. The angrier you let yourself get the worse you feel, he said. Yeah, well, so what? Maybe that was the point.

Nick emptied the match box, shook the matches out and piled them in the fireplace like a miniature bonfire for mice.

He lit it with the lighter. Got it to light first time, perfecto. Watched the matches spark and burn.

What was that sound?

Someone was in here. Someone was walking around.

Witch lady, or one of the psychos.

Or the police! The dogs!

He almost fell down the stairs.

Didn't see anyone at all. Didn't hear anything either.

All of a sudden he was freezing cold.

It was the shrink ghost.

He ran to the old stone wall on the edge of the property, sat there to catch his breath.

Were the matches still burning? Couldn't be.

No way he was going back in to check.

EIGHTEEN

Eliza read Frieda's final entry again. She stacked the pages, tapped the edges straight, placing the manuscript in the box. She didn't want to close it. She didn't want Frieda's voice to fade away.

Frieda had never been able to finish writing about working with the girl. That would really mean separating. The girl had been ready, not Frieda.

So hard to let go. Look at her, holding on to Nick so tight, from the beginning.

He'd needed her, to be all and everything. It had worked, up to a point. But now? Wasn't she part of his pain, part of the trouble?

Eliza didn't like what Frieda had said, about the girl's parents being inadequate. Presuming she could have done better than her mother. Maybe, but she would have made mistakes. Brilliance and wisdom can only take you so far. Being a parent would have softened Frieda's edges. She cut analysts slack to make mistakes. How about mothers? Eliza would like to talk to her about that. Tell her to read Winnicott about good enough mothers.

She smiled, remembering Nick's pediatrician saying a little dust around the house helped keep a child from being too sensitive. Well, Eliza had aced that.

She couldn't forgive herself for excluding Jeff, letting him excuse himself. Maybe she'd made a new mistake today, inviting him in. Was he going to come through at all? Was he even able to? Not much chance of being a good enough father this late in the game. That was her fault as much as his. At least she could be Nick's safety net.

Eliza sat on the edge of the bathtub, staring into the blank porcelain. A college friend drowned in a deep New England pond. No one knew whether it was an accident. After his memorial service she and Dee had walked around the pond. The opaque surface of the water didn't give up any answers.

And neither did this glossy tub. Frieda had been tired, and alone. By accident or on purpose, her life had ended here.

Worse things have happened. She almost heard her say it.

Dying that night, however it happened, wasn't really defeat. Her life, her work, had been victory. She'd left a legacy. Frieda hadn't been right about everything, hadn't saved everyone, but she had certainly been a more than good enough mother to lots of therapists, Eliza among them.

Downstairs, Eliza studied the portrait over the mantel. Not beautiful, but Gertrud had painted the weary young woman with love and concern. How different this Frieda looked than the happy, confident woman in the photograph with Muni. Frieda had thrived here. Done good work, loved and worked, for as long as she could. She hadn't lingered. Lots worse things than dying.

Eliza stood on the front steps. There was no whir of skateboard wheels. Main was dark. She must wait. Learn to separate. He was teaching her. When the student is ready, the teacher appears.

She left the light on and the door unlocked. Let him be angry, about that risky unlocked door.

Eliza sat at the piano and played a few bars of Frieda's song. Maybe she'd take lessons again.

She lay down on the sofa to wait.

Let him be safe. Keep him safe.

Let him come home.

A dog was barking.

Someone was screaming.

No, the smoke alarm was going off.

The air smelled scorched and burned her throat. The windows glowed red.

The Lodge was burning!

"NICK!" She raced upstairs, threw open his door. His bed was empty. The cat jumped past her down the stairs. Eliza followed and burst outside, the cat darting ahead.

Eyes streaming, coughing, she ran straight toward the inferno. Someone tackled her.

"Ma! Get out of here!"

Nick pulled her to the edge of the lawn, stopping near the carport. A cluster of neighbors stood on the street, fuzzy shapes in the haze of smoke. Trembling, she wrapped her arms around him. The air split with percussive thunder.

"The windows!" yelled someone. Sirens blaring, fire trucks roared up the drive. The roof groaned and collapsed in a geyser of sparks. The tower wavered for a long moment, illuminated by flame, and imploded.

A man from the halfway house paced up and down rubbing his head. The little boy from the new house rode his father's shoulders, yelling.

A television van arrived. Lights on a long metal stalk illuminated Ruth in her bathrobe and Ben, talking to a young woman with a microphone. Across the lawn headlights silhouetted Carter with a policeman.

Jets of water arched into the blaze. Would the fire reach the cottage?

"I have to get the cat!" Nick said.

Eliza restrained him. "She got out."

"Get back!" A fireman, a giant in orange yelled.

Eliza pulled Nick into the shadows by the forsythia.

The cat appeared from under the bushes, rubbing Nick's ankles. He squatted and gathered her up just as Carter arrived.

His face was streaked with soot, eyes bloodshot, the gray crewcut ragged spikes. "I was looking for you two. Don't go home." He left, vanishing in the smoke.

Phil ran up. "Oh, good, you're okay. Bring the cat, come back to our place."

"Good idea," she said, eager to disappear, to hide Nick.

"I'm staying," said Nick.

When he was a toddler, she'd been unloading groceries and stepped away for a moment. Returning, she found he'd smashed a dozen eggs and was watching the goo run over the floor. She'd tried to pull him away from the mess. "No," he'd said, insisting on sitting by the sticky puddle he'd created. "No."

Where had he been when the fire started?

Hours later, the hoses were rolled up and the firetrucks pulled away. Gray dawn broke over a damp ruin. The air smelled dirty. Ashes covered the lawn between the cottage and the ruined Lodge. The cottage had survived. Eliza rubbed her stinging eyes; her hand came away black.

Nick showered. She ran a load of wash right away, putting everything he'd been wearing into the machine. Erasing evidence. But there was no getting rid of the smell in the house.

Her phone rang. *Jeff!* He'd heard. He was frightened for Nick, he was parent material after all.

"I just heard on the radio. You're okay, you're both okay?" Dee asked.

"Yes."

Dee didn't ask about the night before, didn't ask if Nick had been home. Times friends know not to talk about something. Times you know to protect each other's solitude.

Maybe Jeff still hadn't heard. A hotel room can be such a bubble.

He should know. She must give him a chance. Eliza dialed.

There was the noise of television in the background.

"Have you heard about the Lodge?"

"Watching right now. What a disaster."

"We're okay," she said. "Both of us."

"That's good."

"Can you come out?"

"Oh, Eliza, no, sorry. Something's come up, with a patient. I have to go back today."

She hung up without saying goodbye.

Frieda's double doors were shut. Nick couldn't hear her swearing.

Nick banged on the door. "Ma? The architect. Says he wants to talk to us." His voice cracked.

Carter sat on the glider. "The police are posting these," he said, holding out a flyer.

Nick took it. She looked over his shoulder at the grainy black and white photo of the Lodge, a report of the fire. A request for anyone with information to call the police tip line.

Nick took a shallow breath. She touched his back.

Carter leaned back heavily. The glider creaked as it rocked back and forth. "Police spoke with me. I'm a person of interest, naturally, for the investigation."

"But you're the one who's been predicting this, saying Ed had to get security," she said.

He nodded, a rueful expression in his bloodshot gray eyes. "Mostly formality, customary in a situation like this. Knowing my routine, that I check on the building. They don't suspect me so much as want to know if I saw anything. Anyone."

"Did you?" she asked.

"I saw signs someone—maybe more than one—had been in. Not unusual. I went in again, around midnight. Didn't see anyone. The building was empty, when I left, as far as I know. And thank god, they didn't find any human remains."

Nick's shoulders tensed.

"The developer must be of interest too. What about the insurance?" she said.

Carter shrugged, shaking his head. "People always assume that. There's no insurance."

"Really?"

"Prohibitively expensive on a project like this—precisely because things like this happen."

"So, no reason for Ed to burn it down."

"No monetary incentive. No reason unless he was giving up on the project, wanted it gone."

"How about wiring?"

Carter shook his head. "The utilities have been off."

"Do they think it's arson?"

"Building is totaled. Unlikely to be any definitive evidence. Rare to pin the blame on someone without eyewitnesses."

"What happens next?" Nick asked, his voice cracking.

"They'll start taking it down later today."

"Already?" asked Eliza.

"Dangerous, to leave it as is. Someone might go in. Get hurt."

After Carter left, Eliza drew Nick over to the glider. They rocked. The way they used to in the rocking chair when he was small. How many thousand miles had they traveled in that chair?

"Ma?" The dark line around his iris had disappeared the way it did when he was frightened. "I was there last night. Lit some matches—in the fireplace. I didn't mean to start anything. I'm pretty sure they just burned out."

Don't tell me. Don't tell anyone, she wanted to say. Made herself listen.

"I heard someone. I didn't see anyone—just like Carter didn't. I think it was the ghost. Your shrink lady. She was here after the party. I saw her."

"That was an actress, an impersonator."

"No. Honest. She disappeared. Left this cold force field. It must have been her I heard in there last night. Maybe she didn't like the idea of condos in her hospital."

When he was little, she had crawled under his bed to confirm there were no monsters. Now, he needed to believe, needed her to believe, in a ghost.

"You never know," said Eliza.

"Maybe she wanted to scare me out of there. Before she did it."

"Maybe," said Eliza.

He let out a big sigh and leaned closer. "Is it going to be okay, Ma?"

Eliza closed her eyes for a moment before answering. "Yes. I'm not sure exactly how it's going to turn out, but it's going to be okay."

"I'm starving."

After two bowls of cereal and two English muffins, he said he had to go to work. Help Phil.

Eliza wanted to keep him home, glued to her side, safe and quiet.

Every separation is practice. Eliza needed to get good at this.

"Okay," she said. "Keep that arm covered. Long sleeves."

Her phone was ringing and buzzing in her pocket. It was the therapist Cole had suggested. He sounded young. Which could be a good thing.

He asked the right questions. He took insurance. She scheduled the intake appointment. She'd get Nick there if she had to carry him in. "He may be hard to engage."

He laughed. "We'll give it a try."

Eliza hung up with a sense of relief. Did clients feel this way? As though immediately the problem was just a little lighter, shared?

Across the way, a bulldozer and a dump truck kicked up clouds of dust. Carter stood beside the yellow disaster tape, like a solitary mourner at a grave.

She walked over. The jagged walls and the charred timbers around the site were hideous. "How long will it take?"

"A lot longer than it took to burn. A lot shorter than it took to build."

"I'm sorry about the building. Your project. The condos."

"They would have been crap."

They watched for a time and then walked away from the noise, through the trees, toward the cottage.

"At least the trees didn't burn," she said. "I don't think I could bear that."

His expression was bleak and angry. Saying goodbye to the Lodge. His mother.

Before she could think, before she could talk herself out of it, she stepped closer to him, and put one hand on either side of his face, just a gesture of comfort.

The kiss was a very different kind of comfort.

His lips were dry and warm, tasted of smoke and sweat. She hadn't intended to kiss him, when she stepped so close, though Frieda would say there are no accidents.

"What's that for?" he whispered.

"I wanted to. And for not mentioning him."

His smile was lop-sided, tentative. "A kid is way more important than a building."

Later, home in the study, she sprayed Windex on the smoke-smudged glass on Frieda's photograph, polished it.

"I'm glad that efficient secretary didn't find your journal," she said. "Thank you for leaving it. Forgive me for reading. I won't burn it, there's been enough of that. I'll put it back. Someone else may need it."

She almost heard a soft voice with a German accent. *When the student is ready, the teacher appears.*

NINETEEN

Phil took him out to I-Hop for lunch, even though Nick knew he thought the pancakes there were crap. His heart started fluttering and he couldn't finish. Everything just stuck in his throat and he felt like he might choke or throw up.

"What's the matter?" Phil asked.

"My heart does this thing."

Phil asked a whole lot of questions about when and how long and what it felt like. "We'll tell your mom. Get it checked out," he said, not super upset or worried. "Might be anxiety."

Nick finished his stack of pancakes.

"Feel up to that trip to pick out the stones, over at the quarry?"

"We should tell her if we go."

"Of course. Give her a call," Phil said.

She was okay with them going for a drive. Nick didn't want her feeling left out, asked if she wanted to come. She had calls to make for work.

"Have fun," she said. As if. Here he was, maybe wanted for arson. His arm hurt and he'd barely had any sleep.

He told Phil while they were driving, about camp. What had happened. And about meeting his dad. Not about last night though.

Phil was cool. Said he thought the fires and the cutting were like bad strategies for dealing with bad feelings. Put in a plug for therapy.

Of course.

261

When they got back, she was on the phone. Phil and Nick walked over to the Lodge with a wheelbarrow. He flashed on a day he'd been mad for some reason or other and trashed this Lego castle he'd spent like weeks building. It had been a surprising amount of work taking apart all the bricks.

Phil said Ruth was going to sell the old bricks they collected as souvenirs at the historical society.

"Think I could buy a brick?" Nick asked.

"You can have one," said Phil. "Pick one for your mom, too."

He went for one that was kind of twisted and had a shiny black patch on it for her, and for himself one that had almost like a bubble in it.

His dad didn't call him back. Big surprise. He told her.

She said he'd had that patient emergency, back in Boston.

She was lying. Covering up for the asshole to make Nick feel better. "Don't lie, Ma. We're the emergency. He's chicken."

She didn't argue. Looked like she could use some cheering up. Not worry so damn much about things outside of her control, like Cole would say. Assholes outside of their control.

"You know what I say, Ma? Good riddance. We did okay so far."

She looked better. She hugged him hard.

Took him out to dinner, the place with the giant popovers. She said the waitresses used to dress up in French costumes, big puffy hats like the popovers.

He told her about his heart doing the jiggling thing again. She didn't freak, just said they'd get it checked out. She said it might be anxiety or it might be something else but either way they'd get it checked out.

She told him about her friends at work leaving the clinic. And how she'd started talking to them, about going in with them.

"Eventually. If I can work things out. Would take a while."

And she asked him, about moving. Last year she just sprung it on him.

"Our lease is up in August. Should we think about a fresh start?"

After all this time hating this crappy little house, he didn't really want to leave. And the shrink ghost had been kind of looking out for him. "Phil says I can work some, after school starts. And I'm not changing schools again." He'd signed up for chorus. Maybe Jenn had, too.

She looked surprised, but happy. "Maybe I'll have a home office. See patients where Frieda did."

When they got back, he got his Theremin and she played piano. Frieda's Song, she called it. He jammed along with her. Didn't sound too lame.

TWENTY

Nick asked if he could have money for ice cream, go into the Square.

"I might stay and see a movie with this friend who works at the ice cream place. She gets off at nine."

Eliza wanted to keep him right on the piano bench beside her, to play music together all evening.

Let him go, Frieda would tell her.

"Okay," she said. "But it's on your tab. Phil better give you lots of overtime."

"Jenn—my friend—she's going to start driver's ed. At the school right in the square. You know? The little yellow cars?"

"I've seen them."

"Can I take it?"

"Don't you need your learners?"

"Not to take the class."

She wished they lived in the middle of Manhattan and there would be no question of driving ever.

"I'd help pay," he said.

He had a friend. He'd have a goal. Structure. Learn a life skill.

He was playing her, the rascal.

She could play, too.

"Find out how much it costs. And if there's room."

"Thanks, Ma."

"And Nick—if I'm going to let you do this—you have to see someone."

The grin melted. "How's one thing connected to the other?"

"Driving's a super serious responsibility. Requires really good judgement. Rental car companies don't even let you rent a car till you're what? Twenty-five?"

"Ma, don't be ridiculous."

"You've done some scary things. You're dealing with a lot. Including—this disappointment with your dad."

"You're the one who's disappointed. I've written him off already."

She wished it was easy as he thought. Wished it was like the flattened Road Runner in the cartoons plumping up and running on. Nick would be dealing with Jeff's absence for a long time. Forever. Dealing with her presence, too.

"Well, you have to go to therapy. If I'm going to trust you to learn to drive."

"You're log rolling, right? Like politics."

"Right."

"How long do I have to go for?"

"How long's the course?"

"Eight weeks, I think."

"Okay. You go to therapy for eight weeks and then we'll talk." By then the relationship would have clicked, or not.

"So—who is it? Not someone the asshole recommended!"

"No. Someone Cole knew, actually."

He skated away down the driveway.

She glanced up at Frieda.

The unchanging faint smile. The inviting, receptive analyst silence.

"Maybe like you say, the heart is just a muscle, but this is giving mine a workout. I might even need some therapy."

She'd have to clean up the study to see clients. Maybe she'd invite her friends to meet here sometimes for peer supervision—in Frieda's office.

Eliza started with the bookshelves. The family pictures had to go upstairs. She could still use the pottery pencil holder he'd made her. One photograph was staying, though. You could certainly have a non-family member on your wall, an eminent psychoanalyst.

Frieda's eyes gleamed.

EPILOGUE

You are free to leave. Ashes to ashes.
Beloved and place are gone.
What holds you?
Your song will remain.

Acknowledgements

I grew up in the 1960s in a new Rockville suburb. My husband and I raised our own family in Rockville, living just blocks from the Lodge. I practiced psychotherapy in a nearby clinic.

Smoke and sirens awakened me on the June night in 2009 when the deserted hospital burned. Frieda Fromm-Reichmann's Cottage survived. The Lodge and Dr. Fromm-Reichmann intrigued me. I researched, imagined, and wrote this novel over the next decade. Many have helped me along the way.

Much gratitude is due to Peerless Rockville for restoring Frieda's Cottage and preserving and documenting Rockville's history. Peerless Director Emeritus Eileen S. McGuckian's history of the town and its residents, *Rockville: Portrait of a City*, was an invaluable resource. Gina Sullivan graciously let me visit her home, Frieda's Cottage.

I am deeply indebted to Gail A. Hornstein for her biography *To Redeem One Person Is to Redeem the World: The Life of Frieda Fromm-Reichmann*. Dr. Ann-Louise S. Silver's paper "Chestnut Lodge, Then and Now" (*Contemporary Psychoanalysis, Vol. 33, No. 2, 1997*) provided an eloquent glimpse of practice at the Lodge. The late Dexter M. Bullard selected and edited the significant posthumous collection of Dr. Fromm-Reichmann's papers, *Psychoanalysis and Psychotherapy*.

Susan Gillotti, psychotherapist, author, and friend, enriched my understanding of the interrelationship of the neighborhood, Lodge patients, and their families, through her memoir, *Women of*

Privilege. Susan and I, many years apart, lived in the same house in Rockville and know something of ghosts and walls that talk.

David Brinkley's *Washington Goes to War* provided rich detail about day-to-day experience. Jerry A. McCoy, Special Collections Librarian and Archivist at the District of Columbia Public Library, guided me well. The Virginia Center for the Creative Arts once again granted me time and space.

Susan Scarf Merrell read the first draft of this novel, and many versions that followed. Gerald Marconi, Brad Chesivoir, and Vicki Blier read drafts. A book cannot develop without discerning readers. I am grateful.

My son Tim Pskowski provides expert technical support and has often saved a day, and a manuscript. He and wordsmith daughters Martha and Rebecca Pskowski have borne with my obsession with old buildings and connecting imagined ghostly dots. They bring me cheer and cheer me on.

Special thanks and much love to my husband Harold Pskowski, boon companion in our endeavors, reader and editor, local and family historian, the love, and co-author, of my life.

Finally, my profound gratitude goes to Frieda Fromm-Reichmann. I studied her *Principles of Intensive Psychotherapy* first as a young social worker and beginning psychotherapist, returning to her book many times over more than thirty years in practice. Her life, her work, and her voice inspired me both as psychotherapist and author.

Frieda died at the Lodge on April 28, 1957, the same day my parents John and Nelle, brother Don, and I moved into our new house in a Rockville suburb rising out of farmland. April 28 was also my mother's birthday. She recalled being kept awake by the beauty of the white dogwood outside the bedroom window. Our first night in our Rockville home was Frieda's last night on earth. If indeed there are no coincidences, if teachers appear when students are ready, and if books choose authors, I hope Frieda's spirit infuses these pages.

About the Author

Ellen Prentiss Campbell's collection of stories *Contents Under Pressure* was nominated for the National Book Award. Her debut novel *The Bowl with Gold Seams* received the Indy Excellence Award for Historical Fiction. A second collection of stories *Known By Heart* was published in 2020. Her short fiction has been recognized by the Pushcart Press. Essays and reviews appear in journals including *The Fiction Writers Review,* where she is a contributing editor, and *The Washington Independent Review of Books.* Campbell has been a Fellow at The Virginia Center for the Creative Arts several times. A graduate of The Bennington Writing Seminars and the Simmons School of Social Work, she practiced psychotherapy for many years. Campbell and her husband live in Washington, D.C. and Manns Choice, Pennsylvania. She is at work on another novel.

Connect online at ellencampbell.net.

Apprentice
House Press
Loyola University Maryland

Apprentice House is the country's only campus-based, student-staffed book publishing company. Directed by professors and industry professionals, it is a nonprofit activity of the Communication Department at Loyola University Maryland.

Using state-of-the-art technology and an experiential learning model of education, Apprentice House publishes books in untraditional ways. This dual responsibility as publishers and educators creates an unprecedented collaborative environment among faculty and students, while teaching tomorrow's editors, designers, and marketers.

Outside of class, progress on book projects is carried forth by the AH Book Publishing Club, a co-curricular campus organization supported by Loyola University Maryland's Office of Student Activities.

Eclectic and provocative, Apprentice House titles intend to entertain as well as spark dialogue on a variety of topics. Financial contributions to sustain the press's work are welcomed. Contributions are tax deductible to the fullest extent allowed by the IRS.

To learn more about Apprentice House books or to obtain submission guidelines, please visit www.apprenticehouse.com.

Apprentice House
Communication Department
Loyola University Maryland
4501 N. Charles Street
Baltimore, MD 21210
Ph: 410-617-5265
info@apprenticehouse.com • www.apprenticehouse.com